GURDON MARION

Phil Yocom

Permissions
Stephen F. Austin State University Press
P.O. Box 13007, SFA Station
Nacogdoches, TX 75962
sfapress@sfasu.edu
936.468.1078

ISBN: 978-1-62288-271-7

First Edition
Production Manager: Kimberly Verhines
Designer: Karina Chacon

Contents

Acknowledgments

This book is based on a 1901 trial transcript from the District Court in Jasper Texas. Most of the names in this book are people who actually testified at the trial. With some of the testimony, glimmers of what seemed to me to be individual personality could be discerned. However, with over one hundred and twenty years passing since the trial, the true personalities, wants, desires, peculiarities, passions and past-times of these folks are lost to history. The personalities portrayed in the book are based on what I gleaned from the transcript. I believe that I have not intentionally disparaged or intentionally misrepresented any of the real characters in the transcript. The characters that were not in the trial transcript were made up out of whole cloth and any likeness to anyone living or dead is completely incidental. Those fictional characters were necessary in the telling of the story as much to relate the way of life and dialect as any other reason. I have tried to capture the way of life and the dialect of East Texas in 1901. Having been born, raised and lived in East Texas all my life, most of these things had not changed significantly as I grew into adulthood. Until the 1980's, all it took was a trip down any dirt road and the 1901 way of life could still be found.

I have spent the last thirty years of my life living in Sabine County Texas and some of the descriptions of different things are taken from various locations in Sabine, Jasper and San Augustine Counties. In particular the courtroom is a combination of the actual Jasper County District Courtroom and the same space in the San Augustine County courthouse.

Jasper is a thriving small town that is being led by some very talented citizens with an eye to the future. The town has become a central retail center for the surrounding area and explodes on weekends when bass fishermen head to Lake Sam Rayburn and Toledo Bend Reservoir, both consistently in the top ten largemouth bass lakes in America. The local citizens and the economy have recovered and healed from the black eye given to them by three racist idiots in 1998. Brookeland is still a place on the map, but is now more of a wide place in the road that provides access to Lake Sam Rayburn than the thriving community it once was. Remlig was an actual place and was a sawmill town that is now covered by the waters of Lake Sam Rayburn. It was founded by Alexander Gilmer who owned the sawmill. When he went to register the town's name in Austin, he discovered that a Gilmer, Texas, located in Upshur County, already existed. On the spot he reversed the spelling of his name and the town was named Remlig. The cedar tree is a locally famous landmark in Hemphill Texas and is also located on the southeast corner of the courthouse there. For decades, old men could be found under the cedar tree playing dominoes on one of two handmade, rickety tables. That tradition has unfortunately faded into history. The old tables were replaced with newer, sturdier ones several years ago, but that couldn't revive the tradition.

My greatest appreciation goes to my good friend Robert "Bob" Mayhar who retired as the Postmaster in Jasper, Texas in 2012. He and I were peers. I retired as Hemphill, Texas Postmaster in 2007. He provided the copy of the transcript to me in 2019 and it took me three years to develop more to the book than just what was reflected in the transcript. Bob also provided insightful guidance on writing, storyline subplots and publishing. He was always very patient with me when I bounced storyline ideas off of him and without fail, had great advice. Without his involvement, this volume would never have happened. I will be forever indebted to him. Postmaster Bob Haymar in the book is loosely based on my good friend.

If you find this book easy to read, then the credit goes to Bob's wife, Becki Mayhar. Becki is a retired English and Spanish teacher who has spent most of her life in Jasper County. I can never state how much Becki's command of the language and punctuation helped this book, and most of all, kept me from embarrassing myself with simple grammatical and punctuation errors. I can never thank her enough. It is too bad my old high school English teacher can't read this as she passed away several years ago. But I would think she would believe, based on my performance in class, that I had absolutely nothing to do with the writing of this book. Well, Mrs. Moughon, credit a fellow English teacher.

Chuck Russell, local artist, carpenter and true Renaissance man also provided me with wonderful ideas and insight whenever I would get stuck and not know where to go next. He and Bob are the two most well-read people I have met in my seventy trips around the sun. Chuck is patient, a great listener and mostly allowed me to bore him when discussing the book. Just listening was a tremendous help as verbalizing a conundrum or a storyline would seemingly always provide me with more energy, thought and direction for the book.

I cannot leave out John and Judy Johnson with the Jasper Historical Society that is located in the historic old jail. They provided me historical documents, papers and insight into the incident that gave rise to the trial. They also provided me information about the incident written by Nelda A. Marshall in her book, *The Jasper Journal* which chronicled dozens of historical happenings in early Jasper. I will admit to taking some literary license regarding the jail and the southside of the square in the description of the book. The jail is an amalgamation of the old Jasper jail and the historic Sabine County jail in Hemphill. However, the Jasper County jail still stands on the southeast corner of the courthouse square, much as it was when first constructed. This "jail house" actually did not exist in 1901 but was built several years later. The courthouse on the cover of this book is a photograph of the Jasper County courthouse as it appeared in 1901. Much appreciation to the Jasper Historical Society for providing this wonderful photo.

Preamble

It was the end of May 1901 and life was typical in the small East Texas town of Jasper. People were beginning to pick their crops or truck patch, cows had finished weaning their calves that were born over the winter, and the logging crews had been back in the woods for a couple of months.

Although summer wouldn't officially begin for another three weeks or so, the typical east Texas summer had begun to settle in with the humidity always being the thing folks complained about the most. It was a wet heat similar to that all through the south as opposed to the dry heat out in the Chihuahuan Desert of West Texas.

Following the spring storms and rains, the winds tended to become light, if the air moved at all. With the tall native longleaf pine trees growing thick around that part of the state, the breeze had a hard time penetrating them.

The summer weather could be stifling during the day. Most people, regardless of how they made their living, had sweat through their clothes by the time the sun was at high noon; The only relief from the heat being a dip in the creek or waiting for the sun to go down and the cool of night to arrive.

Nearly everyone agreed the spring rains were just about right this year. Some years they are a curse for the deluge's they can leave. They brought exactly the amount needed for gardens and crops, but not so much as to turn the roads into muddy obstacle courses.

The gardens and crops were how these folks survived. If they had a bad crop, they either didn't have enough food to keep them fed over the winter or they didn't have enough to sell so they could buy staples like flour, salt, coffee and pay off the loan at the bank. Many folks would take a loan at the bank to buy seeds for their planting each year. This is where the term "seed money" came from. Most, when they borrowed their seed money in the late winter, harvested enough food to last them through the coming year and then sold enough to pay back the bank, the merchants and the years property taxes. May was a typical time of year when folks began selling part of their crops. This cycle was repeated, never having enough to ever get ahead and just barely surviving year to year.

Heifers were good livestock, but hogs were coveted. The cow would give milk year-round but the hogs would eat nearly anything, were easy enough to care for, were prolific at reproducing, and would provide enough meat during the fall hog killing season to last through winter.

Hog killing was a large social event attended by family and neighbors with the men helping with the hog killing, the women fixing a huge meal and the kids playing.

A large cast iron pot would be set over a large fire where, after being killed and gutted, the hog was scalded.

Nothing on the hog was left to waste. Everything had been used from the hog but the squeal. The hams, chops and roasts were the prime parts. Particular attention was paid to the belly and sliced as evenly as possible for the bacon. Even the intestines were removed, cleaned and either fried for chitlin's or the casing was stuffed for sausage. When the hog had been completely butchered, the meat was salted and hung in the smoke house for weeks to cure with a small oak or hickory fire providing both flavor and preservative.

It wasn't living a life, it was just trying to live.

Most farmers and their families that owned their land lived hand to mouth, if they were lucky. The back breaking work, day in and day out, was never ending; plowing the fields, repairing the plows, harnesses and wagons, feeding the chickens and hogs, hoeing the rows, feeding the family, chopping wood for warmth and cooking, hauling water from the well, cleaning out the stove of ashes, emptying the slop jars and digging out the outhouse of shit and corncobs.

The sharecroppers had it worse, and were at the mercy of the landowner. They had to do the same work to survive as the landowners, but had no equity in their efforts. They were seen as a lower class than the dirt poor land owner, but still not as low as the Negro. Often the sharecropper and the landowner would make a deal in the spring, then when the crops came in, the land owner would change the deal to get a bigger percentage of the crop. There was not much the sharecropper could do. The landowner had rights and privileges the sharecropper only wished they had.

Life was hard.

But these folks had it good compared to the Negro's.

There was a fairly large Negro population in or around every town in East Texas and Jasper was no different. Most of the adult Negro population were either born a slave or were the children or grandchildren of former slaves.

Of course, they were segregated to their own part of town. In Jasper, it was known as Vinegar Hill or The Quarters to the Negros. To the whites, it was called the Dixie Community, a nod to the whites continued sense of superiority following the Civil War.

Like every other town in the south, the Negros were treated as second class citizens and had rules they had to follow according to the whites Jim Crow rules: Off the streets after dark; stay in your own part of town; no fraternizing with whites; allowed in the back door of stores only if the owner allowed them to buy there; step off the sidewalk for white folks; denied an education; always respectful of whites, even the ones poorer than they were. They were barely one step above the slavery that, although legally abolished after the Civil war, was still being effectively practiced in every town in the south.

Human nature dictates that everyone is stronger in larger numbers. That, along with culture and race, moved the races to segregate from one another. The whites quickly swindled many of the Negros out of their "forty acres and a mule" following the civil war, but many joined together and formed small freedom communities. One such community was Freedman's Community, located about two miles south of Jasper.

The differences in culture, language, education and skin color easily let each race move in their own common circles of familiarity with few of one interacting with the other, much less attempting to find common ground.

It would take centuries before either culture began learning in earnest about the other, but in 1901, regardless of economic or racial status, a change was about to come that would improve the lots of some and find a few trying to claw their way out of the mess they made for themselves.

.

Part One

1

The Sheriff

Sheriff J.M. Brown rose from behind his desk in the new jail house, walked into the hallway and picked up the receiver from the phone hanging on the wall. He turned the crank three times and waited.

"Switchboard. Oh, hey, Sheriff. Been a busy mornin'. How you doin'?"

"Good, Maybelle. You?"

"I'm fine. Hey, listen. Ain't none of my business, but you may want to check on Oleta Goates. She called Sarah Lancaster and Maudine Caruthers last night. Was beside herself. Said Lowell was at it again. You know how he gets when he's been drinkin'. Said he had a snoot full last night."

"You know, I'm just about to get tired of Lowell and all his shenanigans. I'm beginnin' to think a night or two as a guest at Jasper's newest hotel might do him some good."

"Where's that," asked Mabelle, not believing something that new had escaped her attention.

"The Jasper County Hotel," deadpanned the Sheriff. "Right here at the jail house."

"Oh, you're funny this mornin', J.M. But like I said, I just hate to see Oleta havin' to keep puttin' up with his crap. Excuse my language."

"I know. Me too. I'll check on her. Anyway, do I have any messages?"

"Nope. Not right now."

"Ok. And thanks for the information on Oleta," he said and hung up.

There was only one Deputy Sheriff, and that was Andrew Wayne. There hadn't been a jailer since Pop Juniper died winter before last. Normally there wasn't anybody in the jail. Such was the population of Jasper that there really wasn't much need for a jailer. Pop had got the job after he broke his leg when his horse threw him. He couldn't do too much after that. Pop was the father-in-law of the Mayor at the time and needed a job, so Pop was appointed.

Andrew Wayne was County Judge Lester Bartlett's nephew and had a personality you couldn't help but like. He was a little goofy which was enhanced by his awkward walk. His intentions were always good and he was liked by everyone. Regardless of how hard he tried, his style of dress was always "disheveled". In his early twenties with a shock of blond hair and clean shaven, he was extremely thin, and as the old saying goes, 'you could use him for a whip.' And next to Mrs. Georgette Philpott, he was the biggest gossip in town.

"Fixin' to take the prisoners down to the wagon yard to get ready for day after tomorrow. First Saturday of the month, weather is supposed to be good and I s'pect a whole bunch of folks'll be in town. Especially what with the dance Saturday night," said the Deputy.

The wagon yard was at the bottom of the hill on Main Street that ran along the west side of Nix's store down to the banks of Sandy Creek. The country folks, when they came to town on Saturday, would hitch their wagon around the square if there was a place. If there wasn't, they'd take them to the wagon yard while they did their shopping. The merchants in town pitched in together and bought hay for horses, and being along the creek, there was always plenty of water.

The yard wasn't too bad during the cooler months, but during the warmer months, when the heat would work on the horse apples that accumulated in the yard, the odor could be stout enough that a hog would turn up its nose. The town folks said they liked to see the country folks leave because they took most of the flies that had gathered in the yard home with them.

"I figure you're right. Wagon yard'll be full. So will the whole square. Anyway, hopefully this dance'll be peaceful and not like the last one. Probably gonna need you available Saturday night just in case. You goin'?"

"Thinkin' about it. Thinkin' 'bout askin' Ruth Svenson. You know, Harold and Hattie's daughter."

"Yeah, she's kinda cute. If she takes after her daddy, she's probably a good cook. Hey. By the way, you hear anythin' bout Lowell lately?"

"Heard he ain't been treatin' Mrs. Oleta too good lately. No particulars though."

"If you hear anythin', let me know. Okay?"

"Sure thing, Sheriff."

As Andrew went up the stairs, Brown returned to his desk, looked at all the papers, shook his head, stood back up, retrieved his hat from the peg beside the private outside door of his office and waited for Andrew to come back down.

As the Deputy and his prisoners got to the bottom of the stairs, Brown said, "Awright. I'm fixin' to go make my rounds."

"You goin' by Nix's?"

"Can. You need somethin'?"

"Yep. If you don't mind, would you pick me up a plug of Levi-Garrett?"

"Sure. Headin' over to the Post Office anyway."

"Awright. Thanks," and turning to the prisoners said, "Let's go fellas."

The Sheriff used the private entrance to his office and stepped out onto the west landing of the jail house. The 'hanging jail' was a white stucco two story structure with two doors at the top of two sets of steps, with both sets of steps beginning on Houston Street, one each on the east and west sides of the front of the building. It was brand new in 1901 and boasted two stories and a working gallows. Once you stepped inside the east door, there was a reception area where the jailer, when there was a need for one, and deputy would sit. A large pot-bellied stove sat in the center of the room. Immediately to the right of the east door was the stairs that went to the three jail cells upstairs and the trap door for the hanging gallows. All three cells faced the gallows so that the incarcerated could think about their fate; either what they had avoided or what awaited them. Because it was still new, the gallows had yet to be used. But there were more than a few in the community that felt that since taxpayers paid $2,100.00 to build the new jail house, they ought to be getting their money's worth out of it.

J.M. Brown began his stroll around the courthouse in his normal leisurely manner. But even at this unhurried pace, he exuded authority. He moved with authority, spoke with authority and carried authority on his chest in the form of the Sheriff's badge. He had the build of a formidable man and was a few inches taller than average. His size was deceptive and most knew not to challenge his strength. Several had tried and learned too late they shouldn't have. A peaceful man, he only occasionally carried a gun, and when he did, it was his father's single action .36 Colt Navy revolver.

While not what anyone would call handsome, he was a good-looking man whom the ladies had fawned over back when he was single, but those days were long behind him. He felt lucky that he had met Midge and even luckier that she agreed to marry him. She took good care of their two daughters, kept a clean house, was an excellent cook and managed to keep herself attractive enough that she still turned a few heads when she shopped around the square. Midge was frugal, but not a penny pincher. She would spend little on herself, but would occasionally splurge on the girls so they had the latest fashion from back east in Atlanta and New Orleans.

They had a good life. Their neat three-bedroom home was a few blocks off the square on Hodges Street, sitting on nearly an acre. It gave them enough room for a chicken coop, a garden to provide all the produce they needed and a small orchard with apple, pear and peach trees. He had built a two-holer in the back corner of the lot next to the small barn where he kept Molly. With three women in the house and only one man, he figured a two-holer would be prudent. The well in the front yard was handy and was also frequently used by the neighbors.

He walked most places in the small, tight knit community, but when he did have to travel, he hitched Molly, the sorrel Tennessee walker, to his surrey. The surrey was small and nimble enough, but also had enough room if he had to arrest somebody and haul them to the jail house.

Brown went down the steps of the jail house, turned left and walked across Austin Street. It was one of those pleasant mornings when everything is in full bloom. The weather was still pleasant ahead of what would likely be another sweltering day. Come August, everyone would wish they could have a day just like today. The sun was bright in the clear sky, a red-tailed hawk circled over the courthouse and the squirrels barked to each other in the oak trees around the big building.

This was his normal routine when he went to the Post Office. He took the long way, counterclockwise, around the square so he could see what was going on and so that everyone could see him.

As usual, his first stop was for coffee at the White Swan. It was one of two cafés on the square, the other being McReynolds, and sat on the corner of Houston and Austin Streets. The White Swan had a better breakfast and the coffee that Brown liked. McReynolds had the better blue plate special at lunch.

"Mornin' Sheriff. Coffee?" asked Hattie, the waitress and wife of the owner Harold Svenson.

"Yep. Thanks, Hattie," replied the Sheriff.

Brown made his way to the back corner where the men's gossip table gathered each morning. While they were in the White Swan, it was the gossip table. After breakfast most would move to the benches under the large cedar tree on the southwest corner of the courthouse lawn. When occupied it became what the locals called the Spit and Whittle Club or the Hook Worm Bench. Others would sit at the handmade table on the other side of the tree and play dominoes. They had been playing dominoes under that tree for as long as anyone could remember. The domino table and cedar tree were a few steps away from the city well where townsfolk would come and draw their water if they didn't have a well of their own.

While playing, discussion of politics or religion was strictly forbidden. Gossip, however, was a different matter. The Club would pick up tidbits of seemingly trivial information from folks visiting the well and before lunch, it would become so twisted and added with information, it was unrecognizable from the initial innocent utterance.

"Mornin' fellas," Brown said as he sat down.

"Mornin' Sheriff," they replied in unison.

"Well, what's the latest?" asked Brown.

"You hear anythin' about Lowell last night?" asked Jimbo Caruthers.

"Heard a little bit. Whadda you know?" asked Brown.

Jimbo replied, "Well, Oleta called Maudine last night late. I'm figurin' it was about nine. Said Lowell was drunk again and was a cussin' her somthin' fierce. Said he went to grab the rifle over the fireplace and was goin' to kill Harvey Nickerson. Accused Oleta of foolin' around with Harvey. Said he was watchin' the house Tuesday when Harvey came to deliver the ice and that he stayed a little too long and went out the back door. Oleta told Maudine that she was havin' trouble with the well pump in the back yard the last few days and Lowell wouldn't do nothin' 'bout it. She thought it had lost its prime and asked Harvey if he could help. Said he went out there by hisself and looked at it. Fooled with it for a bit, then come back to the back door and told Oleta he didn't know what to do and couldn't help and she might want to holler at Frank down at the blacksmith shop. Told Maudine she told Harvey thank you and he left around the side of the house. Whadda you think Sheriff?"

"Well, puts me in a kinda predicament. Him bein' the Mayor and all. He's a really good fella when he ain't drinkin'. I done talked to him once. I guess I can talk to him again."

"It's kinda gettin' embarrassin' the way he acts bein' Mayor and all," said Hector. "Not sure how much longer I can keep from reportn' on him."

Hector Henry was the editor, publisher and writer for the *Jasper News-Boy* which came out once a week. It had the usual fare of articles; church notices, Lodge news, information about the school, goings on at the courthouse and city hall, birth announcements, engagements and weddings, arrests, and of course, the gossip column. The gossip column was titled, "Out and About" and had news about who came to visit whom, local's trips out of town, distinguished visitors, who was sick at Doc Davis' dispensary and, frequently, a little juicy gossip.

Some said that you could sit down and read the *Jasper News-Boy* while eating a bowl of Post Toasties and when you got through, you didn't have nothing on either your mind or your stomach either.

"Aw, come on Hector. Stay away from this, please. Let me talk to him. Again. Don't publish anythin' without askin' me first. Would you at least do me that favor?" pleaded the Sheriff.

"Well, ya' know, it's really gettin' embarrassin'," said Hector with the other heads at the table nodding their agreement.

"Hey fellers, just let me see if I can take care of it first. I'll talk to him again and see what he's got to say. Maybe I'll talk to Winfred over at the

Texas Rose and see if he can maybe cut him off earlier than he has been. I don't know. I'll listen to any ideas that anybody's got," said the Sheriff. As he looked around the table, there was nothing but blank stares and no ideas.

"Awright, then. Let me think on it and I'll try to come up with somthin'."

The talk then turned to normal discussion of the weather, crops, cows and the latest rumors.

Brown finished his coffee, stood up, laid a tip on the table for Hattie and made his goodbyes to the table. He made his way over to Harold who was walking out of the kitchen, wiping his hands on his apron.

"What's the damages?" asked the Sheriff.

"You know we don't charge you for coffee," said Harold, "But I was a wonderin' if you'd heard anythin' about Lowell."

"Yep. Just did. Not sure how much of it is right, seein' as how the source is the gossip table," replied Brown with a grin. He would always protect the information he got from Maybelle. She heard everything that went on over the telephone and he had used her information a time or two without her knowledge. There was no way he would ever divulge her to anyone as one of his most valuable resources. And he would never tell her, either.

"Well, Oleta called Hattie last night after Lowell had pulled his stunt. Gave her an earful. Town's startin' to talk about how embarrassin' it is, him bein' the Mayor and all."

"I know, I know. I got a couple ideas. I'm about at wits end with him. I'll see what I can do. Lowell can be a handful, ya' know."

"Ya' know, that just don't sound like somthin' Harvey would do. Been knowin' him for years, ever since he come to town. Just ain't him I don't think," said Harold.

"I know, I agree. Just don't sound like Harvey. Then again, you never can tell. Think ya' know somebody and sometimes they'll fool the socks right off'n ya'. I'll look into it. I seriously doubt it involves somthin' goin' on between Oleta and Harvey. Anyway, gotta make my rounds. See ya'," said Brown. He turned, twisted the knob on the door and walked back out onto the wooden sidewalk.

The Sheriff continued his counterclockwise walk around the square. Passing the news stand where Marylee sorted the days and weeks old newspapers and the countless weekly and monthly magazines; Montangue's hardware store; Farmers feed and seed; Landis' mercantile; McReynolds café; Buford Baxter's barbershop and his wife's beauty shop next door; Lindeman's dry goods and then he stopped in Nix's Dry Goods.

2

The Storekeep

Brown ambled into W.P. (Billy) Nix's General Store. It was seldom busy on a Thursday morning, particularly at eight o'clock. Nix was behind the counter, as always, dressed in his normal flannel shirt, dungarees, galluses and, apron. He was middle aged with the looks that came with middle age. The once curly, thick black hair was beginning to show a little salt around the edges and his middle was beginning to get just a little wider. While he said he was 'still as strong as a bull' he did admit that he didn't move as quickly as he used to.

"Morning, Billy," said Brown.

"Morning, Sheriff. How ya' doin?"

"I'm doin' good, how about you? Hey, Dave," said Brown acknowledging Billy's helper.

"Mornin, Sheriff," replied Dave.

Dave Depotti was by all accounts a dependable, trustworthy and steady worker. He never got in a big rush, but he always finished whatever job he was doing in a timely fashion. He would never be the fastest person around, but steady usually wins the race.

Nix let him sleep in the feed room so he could keep the mice and rat population under control. Dave didn't mind as he had no other place to stay and he had worn out his welcome with a few friends.

"You know, I'm a blessed man," said Nix replying to the Sheriff. "Got my health and now that Alma is recoverin things are lookin better."

"How's Alma doin?" asked the Sheriff.

"She's doin' much better, thanks for askin'. Doc Davis says she ought to be back to normal first part of next week. This whole thing has been kinda scary, you know."

"I can't imagine. I don't know if I could have handled it as well as you. Walkin' in and findin' your wife thrashin' round on the floor. Doc say what caused it?"

"Distemper," grinned Nix mischievously. "Just kiddin'. He said it was likely kinda like an epileptical fit, but he weren't sure. Said it may happen again, but then it may not again for the rest of her life. It's just strange.

Scared me half to death, I'll tell ya'. Hell, I was already thinkin' bout funeral plans by the time Doc Davis got there."

"Well, I sure have missed her the last few weeks. Midge don't like to do the laundry, much less the ironin'. Alma does such a good job. I bet she does half the town."

"Nah, not really. Mostly the business folks and some elected people."

"Well, I'm still glad she's doin better. You got a plug of Levi-Garrett?"

"Does a rooster eat with his pecker? Sure, but I thought you was a Beechnut guy."

"I am. It ain't for me, it's for Andrew. He's watchin' the jail. Got a couple of loggers in there since Saturday night. Judge Davidson weren't none too happy with 'em neither."

"I didn't realize Andrew was deputin'. Isn't he the County Judge's nephew?"

"Yep. I owed Judge Bartlett a favor the way he settled my daddy's affairs. Judge Bartlett is a good man and honest as the day is long. Glad to help him out, but dang that Andrew. That boy ain't the sharpest hook on the trot line, if you know what I mean."

"Aw, I think Andrew's okay. Like you say, the boy is definitely lackin' something upstairs, but he's a good kid. Anyway, what'd the loggers do?"

"Aw, they was over at the Texas Rose and was already way into their cups when Tiny Woods come in. They started arguin' with each other about somthin' and kept getting' louder and louder. One thing led to another and, well, Tiny walked over and asked 'em to hold it down. Winfred, the bartender, said he asked 'em kindly but they bowed up and told Tiny to do something to himself that is physically impossible to do. Evidently Tiny didn't like their attitude, grabbed each one by the collar and told Winfred to go get me. By the time I got there, they was both laid out and Tiny was drinking a beer that I'm sure he'd helped himself to while Winfred was gone. Anyway, Judge Davidson weren't none too happy to be woke up that late on a Saturday. Gave 'em seven days in jail and they have to clean the wagon yard everday."

"You know it's a shame can't be somebody clean that thing everday all the time. Hey Dave. Put this down on Andrew's ticket," said Nix as he handed the plug of tobacco to Brown.

"Yes, sir," replied Depotti.

"Well, thanks," said Brown, sticking the plug of tobacco in his pocket. "Tell Alma me and Midge said hello and hope she gets better real soon."

"I will. Come back now."

"Will do," replied Brown as he turned to leave.

Nix ran one of the two dry goods stores on the square where he carried whole cloth, shoes, boots, women's ready-made dresses, tack, groceries, guns, ammunition, tobacco, fine confectionaries, malt and other goods. He kept up with the latest catalogs and had a keen eye for what would sell in his community. Most of the folks in the surrounding area shopped at his store.

He was getting up in years, being in his mid-forties, and had begun to slow down just a bit. Billy had hired Dave Depotti a few months back to help out around the store and do most of the heavy lifting, including loading and unloading the flour, sugar and feed sacks. Billy always arrived at the store around seven and normally left with enough daylight left to walk home. A kind and affable man, he made the church meetings ever Sunday and on Wednesday nights without fail. He was raised in the Methodist church, but moved his membership to the Baptist church when he met his future wife. He met Alma at a Fourth of July celebration on the square and was immediately smitten. A good Christian woman, Alma was a good wife that doted on him.

Both were severely disappointed when they tried repeatedly to have children, but finally gave up after six years of trying. The following year during a typhoid outbreak in the Remlig community north of town, a two-year-old boy and a six month old girl were orphaned when both parents succumbed to the disease. The parents were from Murfreesboro, Tennessee and had no relatives around East Texas. They attended the Baptist church that Billy and Alma went to and when word spread of the death of the parents, church members, led by Billy and Alma, flocked to the home.

They found the children in a desperate state; soiled diapers, dehydrated with a vacant look in their eyes. They'd probably had nothing to eat or drink for days. The children were cleaned, put in the wagon and given milk on the way to Doc Davis' where they were pronounced healthy but hungry.

Alma insisted on taking the children home with them until relatives could be found. Everyone judged this was an agreeable solution and a magnificent one for the childless couple. They had tried so hard for children and been so very disappointed, their church family, as well as the rest of the community, were excited and happy for them.

Since they knew none of the kid's relatives in Murfreesboro, the couple approached Judge Davidson for advice. He advised that they advertise in the local Murfreesboro newspaper stating the parent's names, the children's names, the circumstances and add the Nix's address if anyone wanted to contact them. He said if they had not heard anything in six months, he would be open to approving an adoption by them if they wanted. They left the Judge's office with smiles so big they hurt.

They wrote a want ad addressed to 'The Newspaper' in Murfreesboro with the information suggested by Judge Davidson and asked how much it would cost. Two weeks later, they received a reply from the *Murfreesboro News Messenger* there would be a charge of eight cents a week. The Nix's immediately responded with forty cents to run the ad for five weeks.

Billy and Alma talked everyday about the children and what might happen. They were both on edge that some long lost relative might come and take little Zachery and Claudia away from them. They fell in love with the children more and more each day. Alma doted over them even more than she doted over Billy. She reveled in the daily chores of feeding, bathing, changing diapers, putting them down for naps and making sure they were happy and taken care of.

After four months, they began to get their hopes up. After five months, they didn't even want to think of what would happen if a relative suddenly showed up; they went to talk to Judge Davison again.

"Judge, it's been five months now," said Billy, "Can you set a date for us to start the adoption?"

"Still haven't heard nothin'?" asked Judge Davidson.

"Nope, nary a word," said Billy while Alma nodded her head.

"How the kids doin'?"

"Oh, they're fine," both said in unison.

"Good. I knew they'd be well taken care of. Let's see here; let me look at my calendar. How long has it been?"

"Five months today, Judge," said Billy.

"Come on, it's just us. I'm just Matt when we're in here. Okay, that would make the fourteenth of next month six months since you got the kids?"

"Yep. Matt, we really want these kids. We've really taken to 'em. Alma and I couldn't love 'em any more than if they was our own. We want to do what's right, but it would nigh kill Alma and me if those kids got took away."

"Well, I'm gonna set a court date for nine o'clock on the fifteenth of June. You ought to go over and see Cecil Farmer to represent you. He can draw up all the legal papers. I like Cecil. He's a good lawyer and a fair man. Tell him to be in court at nine on the fifteenth with adoption papers ready for me to sign."

"We'll go over there right now. Thank you, Matt," said Billy with a grave look of concern on his face. "I have a question though. What happens if one of the kid's relatives show up after the adoption?"

"Well, worst case is they file a lawsuit to get custody," said Davidson as he could see the couple exchange looks of worried disapproval.

"Can they do that?" asked a visibly shaken Alma.

"Yep. They can do it. Won't do 'em any good though. You two folks are upstanding, long time and very respected members of this community. You know how folks around here feel about outsiders. First of all, they probably won't be able to find a lawyer to take their case and second of all, they would have to file the suit in my court," Davidson trailed off, not elaborating, but being very clear that any suit for custody of the children in his court would be a fool's errand.

They were able to raise Zachery and Claudia without interference. They were good kids that only got into the usual mischief, but never anything serious. They were always polite and well behaved and adored by friends and neighbors.

Zachery, after graduating from school, attended Texas Agricultural & Mechanical College, joined the Corps of Cadets, did his four-year stint in the Army, loved it and made a career of it.

Claudia began courting the new preacher at the Methodist church, much to the chagrin of her parents. Lonnie Furth was six years older than Claudia and it caused some concern for Billy and Alma. But love normally has its way, and it did with Lonnie and Claudia. They married when Claudia was eighteen and had their first child when she was nineteen. Lonnie continued to preach at the church and Claudia would bare two more children shortly. Billy and Alma's initial concern about the age difference soon was replaced with the love and admiration of the first, second and third grandchildren.

3

The Postmaster

Brown walked out of Nix's store and turned east and went in the Post Office next door. His first stop in the Post Office, as always, was to look to see if any new wanted posters had been tacked to the wall. Satisfied there weren't any new ones, he sauntered over to the stamp window.

"Mornin Bob," said Brown.

"Mornin. How ya' doin'," asked Robert Haymar the Postmaster.

"Doin' good," replied the Sheriff.

"You hear about Lowell and Oleta?" asked Haymar as he walked to the Dutch door off the lobby to let in the Sheriff. "Coffee?"

"Believe I will. Yep. Just heard it at the gossip table."

"It's just a shame. Lowell's smart and a nice enough fella. He comes in here some days for a visit and we talk. It's funny how a man can be so smart and be so dumb."

"I know."

Haymar was physically larger than most and was educated. Standing just over six feet with a solid frame, the now thirty-two-year-old Postmaster was still quick with a smile and even quicker with his wit. He was likely the most well read, if not the best educated man in town. Haymar always had a studious air, but never a superior one. He was easy going and well respected by the folks in Jasper. And it didn't hurt that he was well connected with the most influential politicians in East Texas and in Austin.

Many of the locals sought his advice, particularly when it was too embarrassing to talk to the preacher. Everyone knew he would never violate a confidence and that anything shared with him ended with him and went no further.

He was appointed Postmaster the year before. Moses Broocks was the congressman that represented Jasper, but lost re-election in 1900; the same election in which Theodore Roosevelt rose to the Presidency. Broocks had lobbied Roosevelt to appoint another man, but Roosevelt waited on the winner of the election, Samuel Cooper, to recommend who to appoint.

Haymar had backed Cooper in the election. He had invited Cooper to Jasper during the election and thrown a sizable BBQ for him. Doing so was very common when you were trying to land a government job. Because of the respect that Haymar had in the community, many believed if he supported Cooper, they should too. The large event likely influenced enough voters so that Cooper carried not only Jasper, but Jasper County by sixty four percent of the vote.

Following the election, Haymar had sent a letter to his old friend Theodore and to Cooper seeking the appointment. In his letter to Roosevelt, Haymar reminded his friend of their encounter at the Menger Hotel in San Antonio several years before when he helped Roosevelt form the Rough Riders. The outfit would later gain fame during the Spanish War in Cuba. Haymar had to leave San Antonio before the final formation when he received a telegram that his pregnant wife was sickly and that he should rush home. Before he could get back to Jasper, she and the baby both died in childbirth.

Devastated, the twenty-six-year-old threw himself into his business of buying and selling land and homesteads. He did little else for the first few years following her death. Many in the town mourned with him. Such a young, fine looking and friendly couple should not have to suffer such a heart wrenching and tragic loss. Without family nearby, his numerous friends were his nearly constant company.

Four years after the death of his wife, the new schoolteacher, Rebecca Schonfield, had come to town. She was looking for a house, and after seeking recommendations, sought the assistance of Haymar. They struck up a conversation and found each other's intellect entertaining and stimulating. Soon they were seen together at most of the community events and talk of impending nuptials had tongues wagging.

They married a year and a half later and settled into Haymar's house on Peachtree Street a few blocks north of the square.

"And I can tell you something else," said Haymar, "Harvey didn't do anything. I can practically guarantee it."

With the serious, straight expression on the Postmaster's face, Brown had no reason to doubt him, but still couldn't imagine how he could be so certain. "Just how are you so cock sure?"

"Promised I wouldn't tell. Harvey can tell you if he wants. But, I'm not."

"Well, can you at least give me a hint?"

"Nope. May have said too much already. But have you ever heard of anyone complaining about Harvey? Nobody complains about Harvey. He's a good, decent, nice fella. Never heard a scintilla even of any kind of rumor that Harvey has acted inappropriately around anyone. If you are going to do anything with Lowell, I highly recommend that you talk very privately with Harvey first."

"Well, now you done got my curiosity up. What can Harvey tell me that's so important? I can't believe there is anythin' that earth shatterin'. Anyway, I plan on at least talkin' to Lowell. I'll talk to Harvey first if you think it's that important. Don't know much else I can do. You know I'm in a tight place on this."

"I know. I don't envy you a bit. But I think if you will talk privately with Harvey, things may get clearer."

"Ok, then. I will. Not sure it'll help much, but I'll talk to him. You goin' to the dance Saturday?"

"Not hardly. I'm getting too old for that young foolishness."

"Yep. Me neither. Same as you. Don't hold the same liken as it used to," said the Sheriff.

Over coffee, they began their usual conversation about city pride, how to stoke progress for the community, family news and politics. Always politics. Local, state and national. Both finished their coffee, said their goodbyes and Brown left the Post Office. He turned right and headed back toward the jail. He passed the Texas Rose, Galvin's Grocery, T.M. Stone's Drug Store and down to the end of the block past Hinson's Domino Parlor. He crossed Houston Street to the southeast corner of the courthouse grounds to the jail house.

4

The Ice Man

Harvey Nickerson had come to town at the age of nineteen with nothing more than the bundle on his back and a strong work ethic. When asked where he had come from or where he grew up, Harvey was circumspect and had the same attitude about why he settled in Jasper. Tall at six feet-three, he wasn't quite lanky, but he wasn't what anyone would call stout either. He was always clean shaven, fresh faced and properly dressed with shirttail tucked and matching braces.

Billy Nix was the first person that gave Harvey a job. Mostly it was part-time; stocking shelves, gathering orders for the ladies that came in the store, sweeping and dusting the goods and keeping the feed room in order. Mr. Billy let him sleep in the feed room at no charge as long as he kept the rat population down and provided him with a .22 pistol and rat shot.

The town ladies liked Harvey's manners and nice looks, mostly because he never said anything or did anything out of the way. He never made any of the ladies think less of him or that he was wanting more than to take care of their order. Always respectful, he worked hard and earned his money.

When the ice house came up for sale, Nix sent Harvey over to the bank to see S. Joshua Tidwell about a loan to buy the business. Billy agreed to provide the down payment to be repaid at three percent interest over three years and co-signed the note. As one of Tidwell's best customers, he readily agreed to the loan as much because of Billy Nix as Harvey's work ethic.

Harvey had owned the ice house for fourteen years now and was in his mid-thirties, having never married or dated anyone in town. He would go out of town to Nacogdoches or Beaumont every month or two for a weekend but never told anyone where he was going or what he did. He was a very private and quiet person, keeping his personal business to himself.

He was just turning the wagon onto Main Street when he rounded the corner and spied the Sheriff. Pulling the one-horse wagon to a stop, Nickerson said, "Howdy, Sheriff."

"Mornin', Harvey. How you doin'?"

"Well, sir. And yourself?"

"I'm doin' good," replied the Sheriff. "Harvey, you get a minute this afternoon, can you stop by the office?"

"Sure, but what's it about?"

"It's kinda delicate and probably not a good idea to talk about here."

"Oh, it's about Lowell isn't it?"

"Well, yeah. It is."

"I didn't do nothin' Sheriff, I swear!"

"Aw, hell. I know that. But I'm in a delicate situation here. Him bein' Mayor and all. I just want to make sure that Lowell knows nothin' happened."

"Well, I'm not sure how I can prove nothin' happened. It was just me and Mrs. Oleta. But I swear, Sheriff, nothin' happened," he said adamantly.

"Haymar told me the same thing. Said he'd guarantee it. Said I should ask you why it was that he could guarantee it."

"What did he tell you?" asked a now nervous Nickerson.

"Nothin'. Wouldn't tell me nothin'. Said I had to ask you myself."

"Sheriff, what do you say I meet you at the Cedar Tree after the spit and whittle club leaves this afternoon. We can talk about it then if that's okay. Not sure I want to be seen goin' into the Sheriff's office what with the Lowell situation bein' what it is."

"That's fine. Again, you ain't in no trouble. I just got to figure out a way to deal with Lowell and I need your help."

"I'll be glad to, but...", he trailed off. "There's got to be a condition. We'll talk about it this afternoon,"

"Okay. See you then," he turned and continued toward home for lunch.

5

The Blacksmith

Frank Marion's father, Otto, had first settled in Jasper in 1836 as a result of the Runaway Scrape.

His grandparents, Otto and Gretchen Marion, had just begun to settle on their land grant in Austin County outside of Burleigh when the Alamo fell, then Goliad. General Sam Houston told everyone to burn everything and kill all the livestock they wouldn't take with them as the Mexican general was burning and killing everything anyway. They should evacuate to the Sabine River as quickly as they could and get across to Louisiana to the protection of U.S. troops.

So, they burned the small log house they had yet to finish, took the plow mule and milk cow and left the dead chickens and the hog behind and began walking the two-hundred-mile trek to Sabinetown, just east of Hemphill on the Sabine River in the Sabine municipios.

When they reached Jasper the latter part of April, the town had just received word that General Houston had routed Santa Ana at San Jacinto and that Texas had won its independence from Mexico.

With literally nothing to go back to, they decided to settle in Jasper after learning that two days before they arrived the town's blacksmith had died, leaving the community without a figurative critical spoke in their wheel. The Marion's were welcomed into the Jasper community and soon found others of the Lutheran faith. Several began gathering on Sundays at their home to worship.

Otto Marion had been the village blacksmith back in Bessenbach, Germany where he also blew glass. He and wife Gretchen were part of a large contingent of German immigrants to Texas seeking free land on which to make their fortune and signed on with the empresario Sterling Clack Robertson. Robertson was in competition with another well-known empresario, Stephen F. Austin.

Frank, the son, grew up in the blacksmith shop and took to the skill instinctively. He began swinging a hammer and using tongs by the time he was eight. As a result, he had massive arms and a broad chest which made him look larger than his five-foot-eight-inch frame and with his shock of blond hair, he was the subject of gossip at most quilting's.

Exceedingly polite, he was respected by everyone in the area as being an excellent craftsman and a fair businessman. He was dedicated to his Lutheran church, which now had its own building on North Peachtree Street. He was known for his exceedingly good manners and fair treatment of everyone he came into contact with, even the negros.

He saved enough money to buy a small home on North Bowie Street, three blocks north of the square and directly behind Mayor Goates house. There, along with his wife Inez, he raised his family including son Gurdon, and daughters Valley and Minnie.

As Frank walked home, there was something in the air that had the harbinger of being a nice, soft, cool night. His wife Inez had gone to visit her sister in Nacogdoches for a week. As he strolled through the house, that he helped Inez keep neat and clean as a pin, he admired what he had accomplished. He had a good life at this point, consisting of good health, a good family, and a good business. The only issue he had was his personal life. And that could go either way at any time.

He took the dishpan full of water from the kitchen counter, opened the screen door and stepped out onto the back veranda where a piece of paper fell to the wooden porch. He threw out the water and stooped to pick up the paper. Unfolding it, he read, "We can't see each other for a while. Sorry." It was unsigned, but Frank knew who had written it and considered himself lucky that Inez wasn't home.

6

The Meeting

Thursday was beginning to wind down. Merchants were getting ready for the country folks that would be coming into town Saturday. The locals that weren't getting ready for the country folks were getting ready for the dance at the Armory Saturday night. From all the talk, there would be a larger than normal turnout.

The sun was well past mid-afternoon and the dropping temperature was beginning to feel good on this late spring day. Some of the old timers said that rain was on the way. They could feel it in their bones, but one couldn't tell it from the bright blue sky and the warmth of the sun. It seemed like a perfect day in East Texas.

There were still a few folks in and out of the stores and offices around the courthouse. The courthouse folks would be closing the windows and locking the doors shortly. The stores would close soon enough after that so the proprietors could walk home before it got dark. The domino players had played their last game and the spit and whittle club had swapped the last rumor of the day and gone back home.

Brown sat on one of the benches under the cedar tree enjoying the afternoon and thinking all was right with the world. He started with his wife counting his blessings, including the girls, his job, his community, and his health. Then his thoughts turned to Lowell and Harvey.

He saw Harvey turn the corner at Zavalla onto Lamar and walk west toward the cedar tree and domino tables. Brown noticed he had a worried look on his face and he was confused by the look. If it were true what Harvey and Oleta had both said, there was nothing to worry about. Brown thought he better be slow and careful with this little talk.

"Afternoon, Harvey," Brown said as he stood up and extended a hand.

"Afternoon, Sheriff," replied Nickerson, taking his hand as they both sat on the bench.

"So, tell me what happened with Oleta," said Brown, not wasting time with pleasantries.

"Well, nothin'. I made the normal delivery yesterday afternoon, just like I always do. Knocked on the front screen door and Oleta hollered from the back to come on in, so I did, just like always. She was in the kitchen peelin' potatoes. I said afternoon to her and she said afternoon back. I said somethin' about it bein' a nice day and she agreed. So, I put the block of ice in the top of the icebox, the usual twenty-five-pound block, and that's when she asked me if I'd take a look at the pump out back because Lowell wouldn't. I told her I didn't know much about pumps but that I'd take a look at it. She said she thought it had lost its prime. I went out back and looked at it; I pumped the handle a half dozen times and it did nothin'. I went back to the back screen door and she came to the screen and I told her I didn't know how to prime it. That it may be broken and she should see Frank over at the blacksmith shop. She said thanks for lookin'. I told her I didn't mind and to have a good evenin' and I went around the side of the house and left. That's all, Sheriff. That's the God's honest truth! I never touched her or even bumped into her. Never even looked at her wrong. I never said nothin' out of the way. I swear it J.M."

"You sayin' you ain't attracted to her? She's not a bad lookin woman."

"No!," exclaimed Harvey. "You ask any of the folks I deal with. That'd be a really fast way to kill my business if folks started thinkin' I was that kind of fella. I've never done anythin' out of the way to nobody. Never said anythin' out of the way. I just don't get why Lowell is accusin' me. Oleta has always been nothin' but nice to me."

"I believe you. My problem though is convincin' Lowell. You have anything for me to help me convince him?"

"First, tell me what Haymar told you."

"Nothin'. Just said he could guarantee you wouldn't do nothin' like that. Didn't say why. I've got my speculatin' goin on, but I don't know."

"How long I been in Jasper, Sheriff?"

"I don't know, fourteen, fifteen years I reckon."

"How many rumors you heard on me with any of the women in town?"

"Well, now that you mention it, none I can think of."

"Think about that for a minute, Sheriff. I live alone. I don't date. I go out of town every month or so for a long weekend. What do you think?"

"That you ain't attracted to nobody around here, I guess. Either that or you been injured some way that your equipment don't work."

"I need to know what all Haymar told you," demanded Harvey.

"Nothin'. I swear," said Brown holding up his right hand in surrender.

"Can I trust you, Sheriff? It has got to stay a secret or I'll get run out of town. You understand? Now, I want you to think hard on it, Sheriff; think real hard. Put it all together."

If anyone had been witnessing the conversation, they would likely have found it was interesting how it had reversed itself from Brown interrogating Harvey to Harvey being the interrogator.

"I don't know what you're getting'…" Brown trailed off and Harvey could see the epiphany come over the Sheriff's face.

"You figure it out, Sheriff?" asked Harvey somewhat amused.

With a look of bewilderment and astonishment, Brown looked completely lost and unsure of himself. The authority that normally exuded from him was gone. It was almost as if he was a small child and suddenly found himself lost in the woods and an instant later, saw the path home.

"I think I understand," muttered Brown. "I'm not sure what to say. I kinda understand what Haymar was sayin' now, I think."

"You're right Sheriff. Again, if this ever gets out, I'll have to leave town. I've never caused any problems here, have I? And I won't."

"Your trips out of town, that's for…" again Brown trailed off.

"Aw, hell, Sheriff, I'm queer. Now you're only the second person in this county that knows that other than Haymar. You've got to keep this a secret. I didn't want to tell you because I didn't want to put the burden on you. But now you have it and have to bear it. You now have my reputation in your hands. You have my business and my future in this town in your hands. All in all, Sheriff, you control my future. Can you handle it? Can I count on you, Sheriff?"

Brown was pensive and didn't immediately respond. He was still confused about what to say. He certainly couldn't use the information with Lowell; that wouldn't be fair to Harvey.

"Sheriff?" said Harvey with a raised voice and a questioning look.

"Yes. Yes. You can count on me. Your secret is safe with me. I don't understand it and I don't agree with it. Goes against what the church teaches. It'll take me a while to study on it and figure out what I really think about it. I just don't know how to deal with it right now."

"If word of this ever gets out, I'm done for in this town. I'd have to move to Arkansas to get far enough away where people wouldn't know. This secret is my life, Sheriff. I understand you may not like it, but I have told you a deep dark secret in strict confidence and I expect you to hold up your end of the bargain."

"You know, if you hadn't told me, I'd have never known. I've always liked you." He quickly realized what he had said and quickly followed up with, "No! Not in that way!"

Harvey smiled at the quick rejoinder and when Brown thought about what he'd just said, he smiled too.

"Okay. It's settled. Your secret is safe with me. I won't use any of it in talkin' with Lowell. But, do you mind if Haymar and I discuss it a little. I think he can help me understand it better than me tryin' to figure it out on my own."

"Sure. Bob is a good friend and I respect him. He's open minded.

I think he believes every person creates their own destiny and it's not ordained by some supreme bein'. Not to question what you believe the church teaches Sheriff, but there are other ways of thinkin' out there."

"Maybe I'll get there at some point. It's been an eye-openin' talk."

"It has." Harvey stood with a look that the Sheriff couldn't quite figure out. It wasn't pride nor shame, but something in between. Then he asked, "Shake a queer's hand?"

Brown stood, didn't hesitate, and extended his hand. "I promise not to tell anyone. Everyone deserves to be happy. You've got an uphill pull, and I hope you find what you're lookin' for."

"Thanks, Sheriff," said Harvey slightly shaking his head. After taking a deep breath, he said, "I think I'm kinda wore out."

"It was a hard conversation. For both of us. Mostly you. But I'm kinda wore out too," said Brown with a smile. "Have a good evenin', Harvey."

"You too, Sheriff."

They both stood there, facing each other for a moment trying to analyze what had just happened. Then, they both turned and headed toward their respective homes.

Dang, Brown thought to himself as he slowly strolled toward home. He wasn't in any real hurry to get there and was trying to digest what had just happened. So that's what they're like, Brown thought. The bible and the church teach it's wrong, but how can the bible and the church condemn somebody to hell like Harvey, he questioned. Harvey is an upstanding member of the community. He's respected by everbody. He's liked by everbody. He's never done nothin out of the way or actin like a queer. Dang if this ain't a pickle. Church says it's wrong, but dang; it's Harvey. Harvey's different. He ain't like what you hear about how queers act. He's like ever other merchant in town. He's honest, hard workin, fair, he don't drink or carouse, and he goes to the Methodist church ever Sunday. I just don't get it, though. How can somebody like Harvey that has everthin' else goin' for him be a queer? Why would anybody want that? How can any man want to do that, he questioned? It just don't make no sense. A man and a woman, Brown understood. A man and a man? Why?

He stopped and looked up at the late afternoon sky then turned around and headed straight for the Texas Rose. If anybody needed a drink, it was the Sheriff.

7

The Conversation

The next day was Friday. Brown left his home and walked to the jail house to check on things then went to the White Swan to get his usual cup of coffee. But today, like most days, it was mostly to hear the latest at the gossip table.

The sun had been up for about a half hour and the morning air was still on the cool side as he ambled down the street toward the square. He still couldn't get his mind off of his conversation with Harvey Nickerson. Nothing about Harvey squared up with what he had been told and taught about queers. Harvey wasn't anything like that. Hell, he was just Harvey.

When he walked in the door, Hattie greeted him with a singsong 'good mornin'. He smiled, replied mornin' back, and strode to the gossip table and took a seat next to Jimbo Caruthers.

"Mornin', gentlemen," said the Sheriff.

"Mornin' Sheriff," came the reply in unison.

"Here ya' go," said Hattie as she sat his coffee down on the table.

"Thanks," said Brown. "So, what's the latest gentlemen?"

"Nothin' much," replied Jimbo Caruthers.

"I got nothin' either," said Hector Henry. "Feels like rain though. My knee says we're gonna get a late cool front with it."

"Thunder in March; storms in May I've always heard," said Harold as he placed the eggs, sausage and biscuits in front of Hector.

"Well, it's May," replied Hector, "but it certainly feels like a cool front." As Hector began eating his breakfast, the conversation trailed off.

"What are you up to, Sheriff?" asked Jimbo.

"Just gonna make the usual rounds. Prisoners get out this afternoon after they finish cleanin' the wagon yard. Andrew's been wantin to go fishin' over on the Angelina so he's headin' over there this morning. Things been nice and quiet."

"I'm glad Judge Davidson has folks clean the wagon yard," said Jimbo. "Be nice to have somebody do it all the time."

Nods of approval all around the table.

"Anything new on Lowell's situation?" asked Hector.

"Dang it Hector, I ain't tellin' you nothin' if you're gonna put it in the paper," the Sheriff retorted with a scowl on his face.

"Won't say a word, but have you talked to Lowell yet?"

"In due time," said Brown as he drained his coffee and rose to leave, having had enough of this conversation.

As he walked by the front counter, Brown said, "Thanks Hattie. Have a good'un now," as he tipped his hat and walked out the door.

"You too, Sheriff."

Brown stepped outside onto the wooden sidewalk that ran all the way around the square. It had been put in two years before when jail labor was provided by the seven prisoners he had at the time. They all were very willing to provide labor to so they could get out of the jail during the day. The city and county chipped in, along with all the merchants around the square, to buy the lumber from the Gilmer sawmill up at Remlig. It was a modern addition to the town that many towns in East Texas didn't have. There was some talk about laying bricks in the streets around the square, but that hardly seemed practical. It would be too expensive and take too long to finish. But there were a couple of city council members that had it on their to-do-list.

"Mornin', Marylee," said Brown as he stepped into the news stand.

"Mornin', Sheriff," replied Marylee. "Just got day-before-yesterday's Houston Post in this mornin' if you're interested. They had a hangin' there last weekend. Article said there was a couple of thousand folks there to see that nigger get hanged."

"It say what he did?"

"Said, he was caught with a white woman. Didn't have no trial. The woman he got caught with, pleaded with the lynch mob not to do it. Said she had been livin' with him for the last three months and if she was okay with it, why couldn't they be. They hung him anyway."

"Not sure what I'd do if a lynch mob tried anything here. I swore to uphold the law. Lynch mobs ain't the law," said the Sheriff as he shook his head in disgust.

"Well, you know how it is Sheriff."

"Yep. Don't make it right, though. You hear any good rumors lately?"

"Nothin worth repeatin'. But everbodys talkin' bout Lowell and his antics. Can't believe Oleta puts up with his crap."

"Yeah, I know. And the hard thang for me is that everbody 'spects me to do somethin' bout it. Boy, I sure could use some advice on this thang. Everbody says somethin's gotta be done, but aint' nobody sayin' what that somethin' is." He picked up several papers and a couple of magazines, read the headlines and laid them back down.

"I wish I could help you, but just like everbody else, I don't know what to do neither."

"Yeah, I know. Awright. I'll see you later. Thanks Marilee. Have a goodun," said Brown as he turned and strolled out of the News Stand into the morning sun.

Brown continued his walk counterclockwise around the square and decided to stop in at City Hall to see if Lowell was in. He was reluctant, but realized that the longer he put off talking to the Mayor, the problem would get bigger in his head.

He opened the door and walked into City Hall. "Good morning, Walter." Walter Hinsen was the City Clerk.

"Mornin Sheriff. How are ya'?" replied Hinsen.

"I'm pert near awright. Is Lowell in?"

"Yes, sir. He's back there in his office. Go on back."

"Thanks." Brown very reluctantly ambled toward the mayor's office with dread and trepidation.

Even though the office door was already open, Brown still knocked and said, "Mornin', Lowell."

"Well. Mornin', Sheriff. Good to see ya. Have a seat. Sit down. Coffee?"

"No thanks," said Brown as he began to sit down, "Had my cup over at the White Swan already."

"Well, what can I do for ya?" asked Lowell.

"You mind if we close the door? It's kinda personal."

Lowell, looking confused and curious at the same time, rose from his chair, walked around the desk, closed the door and returned to his seat.

"What's this about?" asked Lowell.

"Well, it's hard for me to talk about and I ain't real comfortable talkin' to you about this. But I've had too many folks come to me about you and how you been treatin' Oleta lately."

An astonished look came over the mayor. "What are you talkin' bout?"

"Got a lot of people tellin' me that you been spendin' a lot of time at the Texas Rose lately."

"So, what. It's a public place. I'm free, white and over 21. I've got my own money. Nothin' illegal bout it. Ain't nobody else's business. And, just what business is it of yours? I ain't broke no laws," said Goates defensively with his voice rising along with the color in his face.

"You're right. You ain't broke no laws…yet. But you're headed in that direction if you keep on drinkin'. You're gettin' meaner and meaner to Oleta. She's a good woman. Been a good wife to you, hasn't she?"

"Yes. But that's personal between me and her. I still don't know what gives you the right to come in here like this and talk to me like I'm some kind of juvenile delinquent," said Goates with the color in his cheeks maintaining their reddish hue.

"Well, I've been asked by several people to talk to you about how you been actin'. Mostly it's your friends that are worried about you. Some of them are Oleta's friends, too. I think the final straw was when you accused her of bein' inappropriate with Harvey."

"So. That's what this is about. Her and Harvey. Well, it ain't none of your damned business, J.M.! But I'll tell you this much, she's been actin' kinda funny lately. Kinda different. Can't put my finger on it exactly. Don't know exactly what it is, but she ain't her normal self. Foolin' around's the only thing that makes sense given how she's actin'. She's keepin' herself a little better. Keepin' her hair just so. Bought a new dress at Nix's a few weeks ago. Ain't never seen her wear it. Just saw it hangin' in the chifforobe. Last week she started wearin' toilet water. What would you think if Midge started actin' like that?"

"Well, I can't speak to Oleta's goin's on, and you may be right. But I spoke with Harvey yesterday about the incident and he swears he never did anythin' inappropriate toward Oleta. The story he told me about the well pump matched up with Oleta's. I believe Harvey and I believe Oleta. I just think you need to get that out of your head."

"So, what are you goin' to do, Sheriff?" asked Goates sarcastically. "You goin' to arrest me for questionin' my wife and havin' a drink ever once in a while. Huh? That what you gonna do?"

"No. I'm not gonna arrest you," he said somewhat exasperated. "Look. You and I've known each other for a lot of years. Again, this ain't easy for me. I'm riskin' a friendship here that I don't wanna risk. All I'm sayin' is, that if you and Oleta don't get things straightened out, Jasper will probably have a new Mayor come election time next year."

"I don't want Harvey at my house no more unless I'm there. I ain't convinced yet. If there was another ice house in town, I'd use it. But I don't have no choice. I want you to tell Harvey bout this. That I want to be there when ever he delivers."

"You not thinkin' of doin somethin' stupid are you, Lowell?"

"What are you talkin' about?"

"Bodily harm," replied Brown with eyebrows raised.

"Aw, hell. I'm as peaceable a man as there is. I just want to protect what's mine is all," said Lowell defensively.

"Ok. You didn't ask for my advice, but I'm gonna give it to you anyway. My advice is to stay away from the Texas Rose for a while. Maybe that's what Oleta is doin' with changin' her hair and the new dress and usin' the toilet water. Tryin' to get your attention so you'll stay home and not spend all that time at the saloon. Think on it and see if it don't make some sense."

"I don't like it you comin in here like this, accusin' me of stuff that's rightfully between and man and his wife," said Lowell, anger rising in his voice. "But if it might affect my re-election chances, I'll at least think on it. Probably not for long, because I don't think enough people in this town care. Anythin' else, Sheriff?"

"Nope. Knew I wasn't gonna like havin this conversation as much as you wasn't gonna like hearin' it. But people are talkin'. A lot. You might want to think about walkin' the chalk line, at least until after the election."

"Again, I'll think on it," replied the Mayor with sarcasm, "You got anythin' else you wanna say? Otherwise, it's time for you to leave."

"Nope. Don't guess so. I was just tryin' to help. Aw, to hell with it. You don't wanna listen, that's up to you. I just think you need to take your mind in a different direction, that's all. Oleta may be actin' the way you say she is cause of all the time you're spendin' at the Texas Rose. It could be all your fault and you're too blind to see it. Take it or leave it. I don't care. I'll still consider you my friend no matter how it turns out," said Brown as he stood and began walking toward the door.

"Goodbye, Sheriff," said the mayor as he swiveled in his seat turning his back as the Sheriff opened the door to leave.

As Brown walked through the front of city hall, Walter said, "Weren't pretty, were it Sheriff?"

"Nope. Not at all," as he kept walking out the front door.

Out on the sidewalk, Brown continued his counterclockwise stroll around the square, head down, stooped shoulders and a scowl on his face. He didn't look up until he got to the Post Office where he turned and went in, passing the wanted posters without even a glance.

As he walked into the stamp lobby, Haymar greeted him and moved to the Dutch door to let the Sheriff inside.

As they settled in the back around the table in the mail carrier room, Haymar grabbed two coffee cups and the pot off the wood burning stove. He poured both cups, staring at the Sheriff who still had a scowl on his face.

"Let me guess. You talked with Harvey?"

"Oh, that conversation was easy. It's the one I just finished with Lowell's that's got me bothered," said Brown.

Part Two

8

The Dress

Billy Nix was busy filling orders from customers when he happened to look up to see his wife Alma with her sister Stella come in the door.

Stella Erwin was Alma's much younger sister and had come down from Gilmer to help out during Alma's recent sickness and although Alma had appeared to have fully recovered, continued to stay just in case of a relapse.

"Well, this is a surprise," said Billy taking in the two. "What brings y'all to town?"

"I got to thinkin'," said Alma, "Stella's been so much help to me and I know she has lifted a burden from you while'st I was sick, I thought she needed to get out of the house for a while and go to the dance tonight. Have some fun and maybe meet a nice fella."

"Well, I think that's a bully idea," exclaimed Billy in agreement. "But that don't tell me what y'all are doin' in town."

"Well, poor Stella, she didn't bring nothin' fittin' to wear to a dance. So, I thought it might be okay if she picked out a new dress to wear tonight."

"You know, Stella, I do appreciate all your help the last many weeks," said Billy with a grin. "Don't know what I'd have done without you. There's no way I could take care of Alma and run the store at the same time."

"Oh, I don't mind a bit," replied Stella. "It was getting pretty borin' back in Gilmer any ways."

"You and Alma go on and pick out a nice new dress for you to wear. My treat and a little show of my appreciation for all you've done for us."

"Oh, I don't know about that," said Stella emphatically. "I don't hardly know nobody in town. I don't know about the dance. I'd likely be the only unattached woman there. Not sure how that'd look. Kinda embarrassin', if you ask me. I ain't met nobody in town hardly, 'ceptin' for the neighbors and that Depotti boy you got workin' for you." She glanced over at Dave Depotti and when she did, she caught him staring back at her. Embarrassed, she ducked her head and turned back to Billy.

"You need to get out of the house. We'll pick out a nice dress, go home and get you all gussied up," said Alma without giving Stella much choice.

"Well, it would be nice enough to maybe go out. I do love to dance so. I haven't danced in months. Since New Year's Eve. Lord, where has the time got to. Thank you so much Billy. I'll never forget this," replied Stella.

The ladies made their way to the back of the store and began their search through the two racks of ready-made dresses.

Returning with a floral print yellow dress, both women were giggling as they stepped up to the counter.

"Let me see what you picked out," said Billy.

As Stella held it in front next to her, Billy let out a low whistle. "Well, that'll certainly get some gentleman's attention."

"Come on Stella. Let's get home and get you all gussied," said Alma.

The pair were like some young schoolgirls as they left the store. All excited and able to leave the past weeks health concerns behind them.

After a bath and with her hair washed and her cheeks rouged, Stella strolled into the parlor, transformed from a plain country girl into something almost out of a fashion magazine. The dress, cut low enough to accentuate her bosom, would certainly attract attention. It also accentuated her narrow waist, showing just enough calf to almost be called "sexy". The yellow of the dress brought out her sparking green eyes and contrasted nicely with her long auburn hair put up with hair pins to show her long slender neck.

"Oh, my," exclaimed Alma as she rose from her rocking chair. "I'm not sure we ought to turn you loose on the single men of Jasper, Texas. By tomorrow, I'll have to guard my veranda from all the suitors."

Stella demurred, dropping her head, somewhat embarrassed of the compliment, but enjoying and reveling in the good feeling it gave her.

"Ok. I guess I'm ready. Alma, thank you so much for everthin'. And thank Billy too when he gets home. Y'all are too kind."

"Our pleasure. Billy will come get you from the dance around eleven thirty so you don't have to walk home by yourself."

"Ok. Thanks. Wish me luck!" With a smile from ear to ear and a gleam in her eye, she walked to the front screen door, looked back at a beaming Alma, pushed it open, slamming it behind her, and to the dance she went.

9

The Barber

Buford Baxter locked up the barbershop and walked next door to his wife's beauty shop. She was just finishing up with her last customer, so he had a seat, saying, "Hello Mrs. Axelrod, how are you?"

"Just fine," she replied. "Fannie Mae, I do believe you have the most talented hands in East Texas," as she admired herself in the mirror.

Fannie Mae was the only beauty operator in town and served mostly the 'well to do' of Jasper.

As she finished Mrs. Axelrod, she chatted with her about things that women find interesting and that Buford ignored as he re-read that week's *Jasper News-Boy*.

The next thing Buford knew Mrs. Axelrod was saying goodbye and waking out the door onto the wooden sidewalk.

"You 'bout ready to go home?" asked Buford.

"Yep. Been a long day. Lots of customers," replied Fannie Mae.

"Yeah. Everbody's gettin' ready for the dance tonight. I was busy all day long too."

"Yes. Seen ladies in the shop today I haven't seen in months. Wantin' to get all gussied up for the dance. Lord, you'd think the rapture was comin' tonight and all were told to look their prettiest."

As they strolled toward their home on Austin Street, the evening brought the first hints of still warmer weather ahead and thoughts of the hot humid summer to come.

Buford was the town barber and was of portly build, well above average weight at nearly 280 pounds at five feet, nine inches. He had average smarts and was average with barber shears. But, everyone like Big Buford the Barber. The one thing he had that wasn't average was his charismatic personality. People were naturally drawn to Buford and his witty sense of humor and for his ability to make them feel like they were the most interesting person in the world. And the fact that he was a clearinghouse for half the town's gossip didn't hurt his popularity.

Fannie Mae, while not pretty or beautiful, was a handsome woman, self-assured and quick with a smile that warmed everyone she came in contact with. She went out of her way to help folks in need and was one of the driving forces behind the Christian Women's Club. Most of the men in town, particularly the husbands, referred to it as the Hen Party Club where the women gossiped about whoever wasn't there that day. She also, with the operation of her beauty shop, was the other half of the gossip and rumor clearinghouse of Jasper.

As was their custom in the evening, after chores were done, they sat on the front porch, shared a glass of homemade muscadine wine and the gossip they had heard that day. Buford and Fannie Mae shared a building on the square where he had a barber shop on one side and Fannie Mae had a beauty shop on the other. As they sat and sipped, both would share the rumors they had heard during the day, trying to separate fact from lies and then to speculate about the rest.

The two had been married for eight years. Him, two years after his first wife died of diabetes, her three years after her husband had been killed in an accident in the logging woods. Neither had children during their previous marriage and as they approached 40, it looked like they never would.

"Well, nothin' much excitin' at the barber shop today," shared Buford.

"Nothin' much for me either. But, there was the beginnin's of a rumor about the mayor's wife and Harvey the ice man, which is interestin' because you never hear things 'bout Harvey. Most of it is wishful thinkin' of the part of the ladies, I believe. But, you know, I've never known of Harvey to be anythin' but nice and gentlemanly around anyone, particularly the ladies. He's in and out of most houses in town at least once a week. Most of the women that come into the shop say the same thin'. If Harvey was really a Casanova, I'm sure it would have been out by now. I'm wonderin' if maybe the part about the Mayors wife is partly true, but they've just got the wrong fella. Georgette Philpott came into the shop today and said she saw the Sheriff go into Lowell's office this mornin'. Not sure what that means, but I guess the rumor mill will be hummin' full throttle at church tomorrow."

"Well, I haven't seen the mayor in several weeks. He used to be in the shop once or twice a week just to catch up on the gossip. I guess if he's the subject, he's kinda layin' low. I did hear, though, that he's spendin' a lot more time than usual at the Texas Rose lately."

They rocked in their well-worn chairs, enjoying the soft evening, listening to the drifting sounds of the Johnny Trimble band a few blocks away. A chorus of crickets were chirping; the occasional barred owl hooted; and the stars were twinkling in the clear night sky. It was a good evening.

Finishing the wine, she rinsed the glasses, put on her nightgown and joined Buford in bed, both ready for a good night's sleep.

For the first time in months, Buford Baxter slept well.

10

The Malt

The first Saturday in June was also the first day of June. People came to town on Saturdays to buy supplies for either several weeks or a month or more. For many it was an all-day undertaking. Generally, the farthest you could travel in a wagon in a day was about fifteen miles. So, anyone living six or seven miles out would spend the greater part of the day traveling. The town bustled with people and business nearly every Saturday.

But this wasn't a typical Saturday. The dance had an excitement stirring among all the folks that had come to town. The undercurrent was almost palpable, evident among the chatters and smiles on all the faces around the square. If anyone had been studying the throng from a psychological viewpoint, it would appear that virtually everyone had been given some kind of happy pill. Anyone paying attention would be very hard pressed to see a worried face, much less a frown.

The wagon yard was full and the street around the courthouse had so many wagons parked around it you could literally step from one wagon to the next without setting foot on the ground.

The ladies that came to town were dressed in their best homemade dresses and bonnets. The children had on their best homemade clothes, dresses for the girls, shirts and trousers for the boys. The men generally had on their best set of work clothes.

Flour and sugar sacks with the prettiest patterns were picked out by the ladies for clothing. The cloth sacks, when empty, would be turned into dresses for the women and girls and shirts for the men and boys. In addition to flour, bags of coffee, sugar, salt, and other staples were loaded onto the wagons. Nothing went to waste in early twentieth century rural East Texas. Many were eating a picnic lunch under the shade of the Cedar Tree and visiting with old friends they hadn't seen in a while.

The special atmosphere on this first Saturday of June was because Johnny Trimble and his band had come to town from Beaumont to play the dance. They had guitar, bass, piano, trombone, French harp and, of course, a fiddle and could play all the latest hits published by the music houses back east. And Johnny could croon with the best of them, hitting the high notes just right and making the men marvel at the low range of his voice.

The dance was to start at 7:00PM at the Armory, four blocks from the square on College Street. The old Armory was a left over from the days of the Confederacy and was later used by U.S. troops for storing various supplies. It hadn't held weapons since the Union army emptied it of Confederate arms in the summer of 1865.

Most of the ladies in town had begun their preparation for the dance around mid-afternoon, making sure their dresses fit just so and taking extra time with their bath, makeup, hair and toilet water.

The men would take a bath, shave, dress and be ready in half an hour's time if there wasn't another man in the house needing to do the same.

Several of the folks from the country would attend and instead of trying to find their way home in the dark, would simply sleep in the bed of the wagon or on the ground underneath it.

This was one of the biggest events all year in Jasper. The other being the Fourth of July festivities. And this was one of those times where the teachings of the bible might be bent just a little bit. Things like drinking alcohol, holding hands, dancing closer than you should so both partners could feel the bulges of the other. And of course, the occasional out of wedlock he-ing and she-ing.

Spirits were high leading up to the start of the dance. A lot of the young folks would be attending, at least those that weren't Baptist. The sun was slipping behind the tall pine trees to the west and the sky was turning a pretty shade of light violet. The temperature was slowly lowering itself to be tolerable for the entertainment.

So, it was in this atmosphere Gurdon Marion slowly walked to Nix's store and bought himself the first bottle of malt of the day. He then walked back outside and took a place on the bench in front of the store, the better to watch the people moving around. He developed a taste for the malt, a smoother but more potent version of beer, and enjoyed the way it made him feel, more so than the taste. He sipped on the malt and thought ahead to the dance and hoped he would find a girl to not only dance with, but maybe leave the dance with also. Both his sisters, Valley and Minnie, were going to the dance and he hoped not to have to talk to them there.

Gurdon Marion sat on the bench outside of Nix's store watching the crowd move and enjoying the early summer day. The temperature was dropping almost into the tolerable range and folks began to venture out of the shade the trees and building awnings provided.

Gurdon was the blacksmith's son. His dad was also the wheelwright. Gurdon hated the way his dad made a living. To him the work was hot, sweaty, hard and low class. He had no truck for the profession and was always looking for a way out. He wanted a job that didn't take much physical or mental effort. But in 1901 East Texas, those kinds of jobs were far and few between. Only those with enough smarts or family connections got what Marion considered the easy jobs like at the bank, post office, telegraph, or the railroad depot. While Marion wasn't dumb, he was always looking to make a quick, easy dollar with the least amount of effort. When he struck upon a good 'idear' and mentioned to someone else, they pointed out what seemed like a hundred reasons it was a bad 'idear'.

It was getting on about six o'clock and, because of the dance, most of the folks had finished their shopping early. Billy Nix decided to call it a day and head home early.

"I'm fixin' to head on home, Dave," said Nix. "You handle the store for the rest of the evenin'. Not sure what business'll be like, what with the dance and all. Stay open as long as the folks are steady. Use your best judgement about when to close."

"Ok, Mr. Billy. What do you want me to do with the money, put it in the safe?" asked Depotti.

"Nah. I've taken most of what we made today and already locked it in there. You shouldn't have all that much more to take in tonight. Probably mostly from the sale of malt. When you close, put it behind the sacks under the cheese wheel."

"Yes, sir. You have a pleasant evenin', okay."

"Thanks, Dave. You, too."

As he stepped outside onto the wooden sidewalk, he put his hands on his hips and leaned back as far as he could, stretching muscles that had tightened during the day.

"Hey, Mr. Billy," said Gurdon.

"Hello, Gurdon. You goin' to the dance?"

"I guess so. Going stag, though. Couldn't think of nobody to go with."

"Well, I'll bet there will be a nice girl from the county there that'll get your attention."

"I sure hope so. Been thinkin' of maybe findin' a good woman and maybe settlin' down."

"I'd suggest if that's what's on your mind, you best mind how much of that malt you do," recommended Nix.

"You're probably right," replied Gurdon, smiling. "But it takes some for me to get my courage up with a girl."

"A little courage never hurt nobody. You have fun at the dance." Nix then turned and began the walk home.

As Gurdon returned to his survey of the town square, his sometimes chum Clarence Keaghey came idling by heading toward the Armory.

"Hey Gurdon," greeted Keaghey. "How ya' doin'?"

"Hey, Clarence. Doin' pert near awright, I guess. You?"

"Okay. Don't have no date for the dance tonight. Not sure I'm gonna go. You goin'?" asked Clarence.

"I think so, but not too sure. You want a Malt?" asked Gurdon.

"Sure. You buyin'?"

"No. You are, and I'm fresh out so you need to buy me one too so you ain't drinkin' alone," grinned Gurdon.

Clarence could hardly ever say no or disagree with Gurdon. He held that much sway over him for some reason. He never knew when it started, just seemed it had always been that way. Clarence reached into his pocket and pulled out the coins he had and quickly made a mental inventory. It was enough to get several Malts and have plenty left over for the dance if he decided to go.

"Ok. I'll spot you this one and that's it," said Clarence.

"Great! Next round's on me!"

They walked into Nix's store where Depotti asked if he could help them.

"Yep, a couple of Malts," said Keaghey.

"Sure thing. Y'all goin' to the dance?"

"Haven't made up our minds just yet," replied Gurdon. "Thinkin' 'bout it though."

"Hear it's gonna be good what with the Johnny Trimble band. I heard 'em one time when I was in Lake Charles. They're pretty good," said Depotti as he handed over the two Malts. "That'll be twenty cents."

Keaghey pulled a quarter out of his pocket and handed it over as Depotti took it and moved to the cash register. He rung up the sale and as the cash drawer opened, he said, "I figure there'll be plenty of girls there tonight. There's still a big crowd of country folks in town so there should be plenty to choose from."

"Thanks," said Clarence as Depotti handed back his nickel change. "What time you gonna close tonight?"

"Don't know exactly. Mr. Billy said to keep it open as long as there was decent business comin' in. So, it just depends."

"We was just wonderin' in case we want more Malt. Just want to make sure we come back before you close."

"Normally things start to wind down around eleven, so I'll probably be here 'till then anyway."

"Ok," both replied with Keaghey saying they would probably see Depotti several more times before the night was over.

By the time the two returned to the sidewalk, the sun was fully into its final throws of the day. Julius Hackner would soon begin making his normal rounds, lighting the gas street lamps around the square which would brighten the atmosphere, both literally and emotionally, especially for the country folks who were not used to lights at night.

The two sat back down on the bench, relaxed and were enjoying their Malt when Clarence spied Oscar Brown and Leo Blake in front of the post office walking their way.

"Hey, fellas," said Keaghey.

"Hey back," replied Oscar. "What're you guys doin'?"

"Getting' ready for the dance," replied Gurdon as he held out his Malt.

Oscar and Leo laughed at this with Leo saying, "That sounds like an idea I can cotton to. Oscar, you want a Malt?"

"Sure," said Oscar pulling a dime out of his pocket and handing it to Leo. "Get me one?"

"You bet," said Leo. He walked into the store and returned shortly with two bottles of Malt.

"Nice evenin' ain't it," said Gurdon, to which all agreed then asked, "Oscar, where you workin' at these days?"

"Nowhere right now. Was workin' at the sawmill up at Remlig, but I couldn't see no future in that. Got paid in company script by old man Gilmer, had to shop at the company store and lived in a company barracks with eleven other guys. Hell, when I quit, I went to old man Gilmer's store to change the script for real money and they'd only give me ninety cents on the dollar. That was the nail for me. Already had a bad taste in my mouth and that was the final nail. Never again. I wanna find somethin easier than sawmillin'."

"Got anythin' in mind?" asked Gurdon.

"Nah. Ain't thought that far ahead. Just gonna enjoy the dance tonight and I'll worry about the rest tomorrow," said Oscar.

"Well, you thought about askin' your Uncle J.M. about a job? I hear that they ain't got no jailer. That'd be a pretty easy job," said Gurdon.

"Nah. That ain't for me. I just want somethin' easy to do. I'm young and kinda smart. Don't wanna have nothin' to do with logs or lumber. A job like Dave's would be okay so long as I have a little money left over each week."

"I'm with ya' on that one," replied Gurdon. "Say, y'all ever hear the tale of Jean Lafitte leavin' treasure up at Shacklefoot? Supposedly he left a lot of loot up there. Things would get hot in New Orleans or Galveston and he'd sail up the Sabine and stay at Shacklefoot till things quieted down."

"I've heard them tales," said Clarence. "Not sure about 'em though. Sounds like the Lost Dutchman Mine to me. A lotta tale and not much else."

"How much you figure it'd take for the four of us to go up to Shacklefoot for a week and poke around to see what we can find?" asked Gurdon.

"Not sure," replied Keaghey. "We'd need coffee, beans, sugar, hardtack, flour, salt, somthin to cook in. Any y'all got a rifle or shotgun for huntin'?"

"I'm pretty sure my daddy would let me borrow his shotgun," said Leo.

"I think we need a grub stake," said Gurdon. "Ain't none of us got the dough to make a run at it. I figure it'll take somewhere north of seven dollars to be up there a week. We need to come up with a way to make some quick money so we can all be rich when we find that treasure."

And without realizing it, the other three were absently nodding in agreement. Gurdon Marion had used his charisma to its fullest and had already diverted the others' thinking in the direction of the plan that was now forming in his mind.

11

And the Music Played

Johnny Trimble and his band had already begun playing and there was a good crowd that, by all accounts, were having a good time.

Hector Henry manned the door to the armory and was taking up the admission money from the folks.

He saw Andrew Wayne approaching with Ruth Svenson. Hector had never seen Andrew so dressed up. He was normally disheveled at best, but tonight he was impeccably dressed in his new pin striped suit with the contrasting vest, highly polished Brogans and a hat that sat upon his head at a jaunty angle. While Ruth was not what anyone would refer to as beautiful, tonight she went beyond what was normally a decent looking woman to what bordered on pretty. Her light blue dress contrasted nicely with her long red hair and her bright green eyes. There will be some fellas here tonight that are gonna rethink Ruth, Hector thought to himself.

"Evenin', Hector," said the Deputy as he walked to the door.

"Evenin', Andrew. Miss Ruth. Y'all doin' okay tonight?" Hector asked.

"Yep," said Andrew.

"Just fine, thanks for askin'," replied Ruth.

"That'll be twenty-five cents," said Hector.

Andrew handed him the dime and three nickels, Hector bid them to have a good time and the two strolled into the dance.

Hector looked up and saw the most stunning looking woman he had ever seen standing in front of him. The yellow dress that was cut just so. The beautiful blond had radiant blue eyes, full lips and just a little color in her cheeks. He stood there with his mouth agape, speechless.

Finally, he heard this angel from heaven ask, "How much to get in?"

Hector stammered and was trying his best to be suave, but he just couldn't pull it together. Finally, he blurted out "Fifteen cents. Fifteen cents for one person. Twenty-five cents for a couple."

Stella opened her small purse, retrieved the money and held it out. Finally, Hector reached out his hand so she could deposit the money in it.

"Thank you," said the young woman as she walked into the Armory.

"No! Thank you!" exclaimed a nervous Hector. He turned and was admiring the vision slowly swaying away from him and thinking of the various things that would be enjoyable with this delectable young lady.

"Hector!" exclaimed George Newton. "For the third time, how much is it to get in?"

Shocked out of his reverie of a possible future with the lovely young lady, Hector came back to earth and was actually somewhat embarrassed. "That's twenty-five cents. Twenty-five cents a couple."

The couple paid and entered the armory as Johnny Trimble was in the middle of "Old Dan Tucker", singing, *"Old Dan Tucker was a fine old man, washed his face in a fryin' pan, combed his hair with a wagon wheel, and died with a toothache in his heel..."*

Gurdon Marion was leaning against the wall in one of the back corners of the armory, watching the people enter and when the vision in the yellow dress walked in the door, he stood up straight, unconsciously touched his hair and watched as she eventually made her way to the punch bowl.

He wasn't the only man at the dance that had seen Stella. She turned nearly every man's head, some to the chagrin of their wives or girlfriends.

Gurdon slowly made his way to the punch bowl just as she was turning toward the dance floor with her cup of punch. She didn't notice Gurdon until he stepped up beside her.

"Good evenin'," said Gurdon, "I'm Gurdon Marion."

Somewhat startled, Stella replied, "Hi. I'm Stella Erwin."

"Haven't seen you 'round before," said Gurdon. "Where're you from?"

"Gilmer, Texas. Been here for about three weeks helping out my sister. She's been sick."

"Who's your sister?"

"Mrs. W.P. Nix."

With recognition, Gurdon said, "So you're Billy Nix's sister-in-law?"

"That would be right. How do you like my dress?"

"I think you make the dress look lovely and beautiful. And I can say this for certain. You have made the armory much prettier than it was before."

"Well, thank you, sir. You flatter me," said Stella, slightly blushing as the pair walked away from the punch bowl and stood along the wall. They watched the people dance and had a little small talk about which couple were good dancers and which weren't.

"Hey, Stella," shouted Minnie over the music.

Stella and Gurdon studied Minnie and Oscar Brown as they strolled toward them. Minnie looked very nice in her blue print dress with the pearl necklace. Oscar appeared uncomfortable in his coat and tie. Minnie gave Stella a brief hug while the men shook hands and said their hellos.

"Didn't realize you was comin'," said Minnie as her sister Valley and her date Barney Robinson walked up.

"Hey Barney; Valley. How y'all doin'?" asked Gurdon.

"Fine, just fine," replied Valley for both of them.

"I didn't know either. Billy and Alma talked me into it. Billy let me pick out a new dress from the store," she said as she twirled around once to show off her outfit. "What do you think?"

"I think you look lovely," said Valley.

"Likely the prettiest girl here," chimed in Minnie.

Then, both girls shot their dates looks that told them they should not agree with their assessment, lest the rest of their night become miserable.

"Are y'all havin' a good time?" asked Stella.

"I should say so," replied Minnie, the more outgoing of the sisters. "This don't happen too often in Jasper. Best enjoy it while it's here."

"I swear my throat is parched. Barney, let's go over to the punch bowl," said Valley.

"Ok," said Barney as he took her arm.

"We'll come too," announced Minnie as the couples strode away.

"Well, that was interestin'," said Stella.

"Why's that," asked Gurdon.

"All I've done is nod to them in passin'. Haven't spoken a word to them or them to me. It's just strange," said Stella somewhat confused.

"You know what that was about, right?"

"I have not a clue. Please tell."

"Those are my two very nosey sisters. They wanted to size up the competition tonight in case they might get a better offer from some other fella," said Gurdon with a grin.

"Oh, my! I'm so embarrassed. What ever can I do to apologize?"

"I think proper penance would be for you to dance with me," said Gurdon hopefully.

For a brief thoughtful moment, Stella didn't reply, but considered this ruggedly handsome young man. He had dark hair, dark brown eyes, a medium build and average height. She settled on the dazzling smile that she had initially noticed. When he smiled, his eyes lit up, bright and almost mesmerizing. And there was something about the way he looked at her that gave her a sense of trust. This seemed like someone that she might have fun with for a couple of dances. "Yes. Yes, I will," she said.

Stella sat down her half empty cup of punch, took Gurdon's proffered hand and followed him to the dance floor.

One dance turned into two, then five, then ten, then Johnny Trimble announced the final song of the night. Gurdon and Stella looked at each other amazed at how the time had flown by. As they danced, they talked. They talked about their lives, growing up, plans for the future and they both seemed to want the same thing. They seemed to be compatible in nearly all things. When Gurdon asked if he could call on her, she readily agreed.

Stella, remembering that Billy was supposed to retrieve her from the dance, began looking around frantically for him. She saw him near the front door in what appeared to be a deep conversation with Hector Henry.

"I've got to go. Billy is here to take me home. I've had a nice time. You might want to talk to Billy about when would be the right time to come a callin'," said Stella.

"I will, first thing Monday," replied Gurdon. "I can't wait." They both looked at each other for a long moment, then Gurdon let her hands slip from his. She smiled at him with the warmest smile he thought he had ever seen, then she turned and walked toward the door.

Gurdon watched her go. Like every other man at the dance, it was a sight to behold and one that no red-blooded man could ignore. Everything about her either swayed, bounced or jiggled just right.

"Hey, Billy," said Stella.

"Well, how was your evenin'?" asked Billy.

"It was really nice," she replied as they stepped outside the armory and turned toward home.

"Hector told me that Gurdon Marion had you cooped up all night."

"Yep. He's such a really nice fella. I like him. He asked if he could come a callin' and I told him he needed to talk to you first."

"Let's talk about it in the mornin'. You've had a long night and you've gotta be tired."

"I am, kinda," said Stella, who hadn't stopped smiling since she and Gurdon had parted off the dance floor.

Billy could see the look of excitement and anticipation in Stella. He could see it in her face and the way she moved. This was not going to be an easy conversation in the morning.

12

The Cobbler

Oleta Goates had picked just over a peck of peaches out of their small fruit orchard and decided that a cobbler was in order. The rest of the peaches could wait until tomorrow to be canned.

She pulled out the flour bin and got a nice mound going on the counter, added some milk, just a bit of bacon grease and baking powder and began mixing the concoction for the crust. Peeling the peaches, she heard Lowell come in the front, the screen door slamming as always.

"I'm home," said Lowell with a raised voice so as to be heard.

"I'm in the kitchen," said Oleta. "How's the Barnwell's doin'?"

"They're fine," replied Lowell. "I've got their boy Sonny hired to go to work for the city come Monday. He'll replace Rayford. Him and his wife is movin' to Remlig."

"Why the Barnwell boy?"

Not wanting his authority or decision making to be questioned, Lowell responded with a sarcastic, "Why not?"

"Well, I don't know. Just didn't know you and the Barnwell's was so known to each other, that's all."

"There's lots of things you don't know about me. I don't have to explain nothin' to you. Why you questionin' me like this?"

"I'm sorry. I wasn't questionin'. I was just tryin' to make conversation." Exasperated she turned back to the stove, "Supper'll be ready in just a few minutes and this cobbler ought to be ready by the time we're through eatin'."

Lowell snorted, pulled a chair out from the kitchen table and sat down hard. Oleta knew what that meant. Lowell was in one of his moods and it was best just to let him be.

It was getting to be dusky dark when Oleta made plates of pork chops, sweet potatoes from last fall, some snap beans and some of the bread she had made the day before. When both had finished, she pulled the cobbler from the wood burning stove and set it on top.

"Best let that cool for a while," said Oleta.

"Don't think I want any," said Lowell, much to Oleta's surprise. "I'm gonna go down to the Texas Rose. Be back after a while," he said as he slid his chair back from the table.

"I'll save you some in the pie safe in case you might want some when you get back," said Oleta.

"Ok," replied Lowell as he turned, took his hat from the hook by the front door and let the screen door slam as he walked out.

Oleta pushed her plate out of the way, leaned forward, folded her arms on the table and rested her head on them. She was almost at her wit's end. She couldn't figure out how to please Lowell and more than that, she couldn't figure out how not to make him angry. Sarah and Maudine were good listeners, but they just didn't understand the situation. Both had good reliable husbands that treated them good. They were both sympathetic to Oleta's situation, but short on advice. She couldn't leave Lowell. She had no other way to survive. But the anger and the belittling were beginning to really take a toll on her. The one bright spot in her life right now was one she couldn't talk about to anybody. Nobody could ever find out about it. It was the only thing in her life that made her feel good about herself. But it was out of reach. She couldn't ever have it all to herself. But the way it made her feel was worth the few times she was able to avail herself of it. It was a powerful force. Something she had never felt with Lowell. It was exciting. Just thinking about it was exciting. She had never known such pleasure, gentleness and caring could exist.

Oleta was in depths of emotion she hadn't been to before. It was hurt. It was anger. It was disrespect. It was worthlessness. It was depression. It was lack of a future. It was no hope. It was all these emotions at the same time.

As she heard the back screen door slam behind her, she realized only then that she had a dish of fresh peach cobbler in her hands and was walking across the back yard to the back door of Frank Marion's house. She thought to herself as she went up the back steps that it felt almost like a dream, surreal if you will. Was it really her hand that was knocking on Frank Marion's screen door? It must have been, because she saw Frank walking into the kitchen headed toward her.

"Hi, Frank. I just made some fresh peach cobbler and had plenty left over. Thought I'd bring some over, just to be neighborly," said Oleta.

"Well, that's awful nice of you Oleta. Won't you come on in?"

"Oh. I don't know if I should. Where are your kids?"

"They're all at the dance. Won't be back 'till around midnight. Wife's gone to visit her sister in Nacogdoches. Won't be back till late. Where's Lowell?"

"Where else. The Texas Rose. No tellin' when he'll be home, but it'll be late, I can state that as a fact."

As he held the screen door open, Oleta looked up and down the back yards of the neighbors. Not seeing anyone, she entered the kitchen. Frank gently closed the screen door so that it wouldn't slam.

She sat the cobbler on the kitchen table and when she turned, Frank was standing in front of her. She fell into his arms and began to snuffle. They embraced for a good while, not saying a word. Frank then nuzzled the base of her neck and he could feel Oleta melt just a little. He released her, took her hand and led her through the parlor to his bedroom.

Part Three

13

The Blast

The previous night's revelry and excitement was now just a memory. But that memory was shattered in the early morning hours when the peacefulness was suddenly broken apart by an enormous blast that awoke the entire town, including Fire Chief Buford Baxter.

"What was THAT?!" exclaimed Fannie Mae.

"Some kind of explosion I think", Buford replied. "I'd better go. Sounds like it came from the square. You stay here."

"I'm not either," said Fannie Mae matter-of-factly. "I'm comin' too."

Both then rolled out of bed. He put his overalls on over his long johns, slipped on his boots and headed out the front door of his home on Austin Street, followed closely by his wife wearing the same dress she had worn the day before. The two blocks to the town square seemed farther than it had ever been.

By the time Buford got a block away, somebody began ringing the bell at the fire house just down the hill and what sounded like every church bell in town. This must be big, thought Buford as he noticed for the first time the sky around the square lit up like the sky was on fire.

As he rounded the corner at Lamar Street he came to a dead stop. He heard the clock tower on the courthouse strike 3:00AM and it all became real. As he started running once again, he could see on the other side of the Courthouse along Houston Street Billy Nix's Mercantile store and the Post Office were on fire and getting bigger by the moment. As he got closer, he could see glass scattered in the middle of Houston Street. If they hurried, they might be able to keep the fire from spreading.

Like most town squares, the businesses surrounding the courthouse were constructed of wood and built on "zero property lines", meaning that the adjacent building owner shared the "no man's land" imaginary property line separating the buildings. To stop the fire from spreading would take the effort of anybody and everybody that was showing up.

It was only moments before the fire wagon arrived with Otis Blevins and Billy Anderson pulling it along. They got it stopped and before they got all the hose pulled out, Buford was on top manning the manual pump.

Otis and Billy manned the hose, but it quickly became obvious more was needed. Many of the town folks, awakened by the blast began milling about.

Sheriff Brown arrived shortly after Baxter and was already asking people if they had seen or heard anything.

"J.M.! Tell everybody to grab a bucket, even their well bucket, and start a bucket brigade from down the hill at Sandy Creek," said Buford. "They need to fight the fire from the back alley and we'll fight it from the front."

The Sheriff began barking orders to everyone around and directing folks where to stand. All the men formed one line from the creek to the square and the women formed another, parallel line.

In what seemed an eternity, the brigade was finally formed. The men would pass the full buckets up the hill to the fire and hand the empty buckets to the woman nearest the fire and, hand to hand, send the buckets back down the hill to be refilled.

But despite the efforts of the bucket brigade and the men on the pumper, the fire slowly spread east toward the Texas Rose. If it wasn't stopped there, it would certainly destroy the rest of the buildings in the block that included Galvin's Grocery, T.M. Stone's Drug Store and on down to the end of the block to Hinson's Domino Parlor. If the fire got to Hinson's domino hall on the other end of the block, it would be too late to save any of the buildings. The whole south side of the square would be gone.

Just as the bucket brigade began to hit its rhythm, Haymar arrived. With the Post Office fully engulfed in flames, he was pragmatic about the situation. There was nothing he could do to save anything. It was too far gone. All he could do was watch it burn.

"Bob, any idea what happened?" asked Brown.

"Nope. I can't imagine. Nothing in there would explode, if that's what caused it. Even the coal oil lamp is turned off at night," he replied.

Blevins relieved Buford on the pump, who then joined the conversation with Brown and Haymar.

"Well, it's hard to tell if it started in the Post Office or Nix's store," said Brown, "but given the breeze is coming out of the west, I think it probably started in Billy's store. You seen Billy around?"

"No, but I'd suspect he'd be here anytime now," said Haymar.

"Something don't look right", said Buford. "I can't put my finger on it right now, but something just don't look right."

"You see anything Buford?" asked Brown.

"Nope. Went straight home after work. Didn't see nothin' unusual," said Buford, noticing Billy Nix walking up to the group. "Here comes Billy now."

"Any idea what happened?" asked Billy.

"Nope," replied Brown, "You have any idea?"

"I can't imagine unless that Depotti boy used a coal oil light in the feed room last night," said Nix, "But that couldn't have been it, that would'nt've exploded". The feed room was down the hill and just around the corner on Main Street and could be accessed by walking down the steps in the back of the store or the side of the store on Main Street. "I let him sleep there during the week."

"Isn't that P.M. Depotti's boy from up at Remlig?" inquired Baxter.

"Yep. A good boy. Works hard. But there is somethin' about the boy," said Nix trailing off.

"Do you have any dynamite in the store for the loggers?" asked Brown. Loggers would sometimes use dynamite to remove stumps so as to clear a straight path to move logs out of the woods, either by teamsters or a temporary tram railroad.

"Nope. Haven't had a call for that in months. Not since Gilmer opened up his store at Remlig."

"What about the Depotti boy," asked Haymar "Do you think he's still in the feed room?"

"Nope. Went in the back when I got here and woke him up," said Nix.

"You mean he slept through that? He didn't hear the explosion or all the bells ringin' or all the shotguns goin off?" asked the Sheriff incredulously.

"Sure seemed to be asleep to me," said Nix.

Looking back at the fire, Brown said, "Had to be an explosion. There ain't no other explanation. I think it's pretty obvious what with all this glass on the sidewalk and in the street. The question is what caused it."

The others agreed, nodding their heads.

"Occam's Razor would dictate that answer," stated Haymar. "A simple fire would not have caused such a noise."

"Well, Bob, I ain't got no idea about no razor but I do know all that's left to do is figure out what happened," said the Sheriff.

About this time, Deputy Andrew Wayne arrived on the scene with his shirttail hanging half out, his tie loose around his neck and hat askew.

"What's goin' on here?" asked Wayne.

Sheriff Brown rolled his eyes, then stared Wayne in the face and said, "A Sunday evenin' social and it's barely even Sunday. What the hell does it look like? I swear if you weren't the County Judges nephew, I'd…" he let it trail off. "You been home since the dance?"

"Not exactly. Me and Ruth Svenson kinda let the time get away from us."

"Well. Whatever. Go and start talkin' to anybody and everbody that might've seen somethin'. If anybody even thinks they saw somethin', I want them right here and right NOW! And if you see that Depotti boy, bring him too," commanded Brown. As he was finishing his instructions,

Nix interrupted him and pointed toward the Swann Hotel where Dave Depotti was standing. "First thing, go get that Depotti boy and tell him to come here right by-God now!"

As the trio watched the blaze slowly move eastward, helpless to stop it, each man had his own thoughts. One about what could be salvaged, if anything and whether to rebuild. One about all the reports he would have to file with the higher ups. And one considering how and where to start an investigation into how all this came to pass.

Baxter hollered at Blevins and Anderson, "Shut it down fellas. It's all gonna burn to the ground anyhow. Tell 'em to shut down the bucket brigade. Take the pumper and fill it back up and bring it back just in case we need to protect the courthouse."

The crowd stood motionless and spoke in whispers as they watched the entire south side of the courthouse square burn to the ground.

14

The Inquiry

Dave Depotti looked at the Sheriff and was attempting to rub the sleep from his eyes as he walked to where the lawman was standing.

"Any idea what happened?" he asked stopping in front of the Sheriff.

"I was gonna ask you the same. You slept through the whole thang?"

"Yep. Sure was. Mr. Billy woke me up."

"Where was you when the blast happened?"

"Asleep in the feed room."

"That's your story? You were asleep through the biggest, loudest sound this town has ever heard? You expect me to believe that?"

"Well, it's the truth, Sheriff. You can ask Mr. Billy. He woke me up."

"Awright. Let's try somethin' else then. You see anythin' unusual?"

Depotti shook his head.

"Billy said some of y'all was playin' dominoes at the store last night. Who all was there?"

"There was me, Oscar Brown, Gurdon Marion and Clarence Keaghey.

"What time did they leave?"

"I guess about 12:45 or so. We had some stragglers come by after the dance for some malt, but that was it. Mr. Billy told me to lock up when business got slow. I hadn't had a customer in quite a while. I went out to the sidewalk and looked up and down the street and didn't see nobody, so I told the fellas I was closin' up. We finished the hand and they left."

"Did they all leave at the same time?"

"Yep. When they left, I went and got me a plug of Levi-Garrett, wrote it out on my ticket for Mr. Billy, went and locked the front door, turned off the coal oil lamp and went to the feed room for the night."

"Did you see which way the fellas went when they left the store?"

"When they left, I seen Oscar and Leo roundin' the corner by the White Swan. Gurdon and Clarence went the other way toward Mr. Marion's blacksmith shop. Clarence seemed to be kinda fidgety all night, but I laid it off to his quit drinkin' last week. But he was sure tryin' to make up for it last night."

"Have you seen any of 'em since the fire started?"

"Thought I saw Oscar and Leo over in front of the White Swan watchin' the fire. Not sure though."

The Sheriff turned to Nix. "Billy, would you go over to the White Swan and see if Oscar and Leo are over there. If they are, bring them here."

As the Sheriff and Postmaster stood watching the fire burn, Deputy Wayne walked toward them.

"I was just talking to Georgette Philpott. She lives over on Milam. She said she saw two men turn onto Main Street headed for Remlig not long after the explosion."

"Where is she?" asked the Sheriff.

"Over by the gazebo."

"Can I go now?" asked Depotti.

"Yep."

"Am I in trouble?" asked Depotti.

"I don't know yet. But don't leave town without tellin' me," replied the Sheriff. He turned to the Postmaster and said, "Bob, tell Oscar and Leo to wait here till I get back." He then turned and walked toward the gazebo.

The south side of the courthouse lawn was filled with onlookers and gawkers as he made his way to the gazebo and his first lead of the night.

"Mrs. Georgette, how are you this evenin', or should I say mornin'?"

"I'm fine sheriff, how about you?"

"I'm fine. But I've got a mess on my hands. Andrew said you saw two men headed north toward Remlig."

"Yep. I did. Probably eight or ten minutes after that horrible explosion. I heard it and thought to myself, 'Oh, Lord! The world is coming to an end!'. So, I got up, got out of my night clothes, got dressed and come up here to see what all the commotion was about. When I started down my steps, I seen them comin' up Main Street and I thought to myself, 'I wonder what any soul would be doin' out this time of night.' But then didn't think no more of it until Andrew asked me about it. I don't know how he knew about it unless that hussy Gwendoline Massey told him. You know, she can't keep anythin' to herself. But she has some skeletons in her closet, let me tell you. Did you hear about her and the bank teller? Well, you see, they was…"

"Ms. Georgette, can you identify them?" asked Brown, cutting her off.

"No. Too dark. The street lamps don't go all the way up to my house."

"You have any guesses about who it might have been?"

"Sorry, Sheriff. I can't help you with that," said Philpott as she turned toward the fire. "Well, in all my years I ain't never seen nothin' like this. What do you think happened sheriff?"

"I don't know at this point. I'm just getting' started and I need to know if you seen anythin' else suspicious. How would you say the way the men seemed to be riding?"

"Whadda you mean, Sheriff?"

"I mean, was they walkin', gallopin', lopin', trottin'; did they seem in a hurry or not in a hurry?"

"I'd say more of a trot than a walk, not quite a lope though."

"And about what time was this?"

"The clock on my mantel had just struck three, so I'd say it probably took me five or six minutes to change out of my night clothes and get on this dress. So, about eight or ten minutes after three I'd reckon. You think they did this?"

"I don't know. Still not sure what happened. Could have been an accident. Maybe not. We just won't know until daylight. Thank you, Ms. Georgette. You be safe now, okay?" The Sheriff then turned and walked back to where Haymar, Oscar and Leo were standing.

Looking at the two men Brown asked, "Y'all know anythin' bout this?"

Both shook their heads.

"You have an opinion about what happened?" asked the Sheriff.

Both shook their heads again.

"Real chatty tonight, ain't you?"

Both shrugged.

"Go on. Get out of here. Get!"

"Well, that didn't accomplish anything," said Haymar.

"I'm afraid that is as close to an answer I'm gonna get from anybody tonight," said Brown as the pair stood and watched the whole thing burn to the ground.

15

Daylight

As the sun broke, the crowd had thinned considerably but the theories and speculation about what had caused the conflagration and who was involved had grown bigger and bigger.

The speculation that seemed to be taking hold the most was that Billy Nix actually did have dynamite in his store and it had somehow been set off. Speculation also settled on Dave Depotti as the person who did the deed.

However, Brown dealt in facts and not speculation.

Buford Baxter, Oscar Blevins and Billy Anderson were still manning the pump and would douse the stubborn remains that flared up. After refilling the pump two more times, the embers had cooled enough to allow Sheriff Brown, the merchants and owners of the various businesses to begin sifting through the debris to see what could be salvaged and if there were any clues to be found.

Brown had spent the evening in his office talking with several people who swore they knew exactly how it happened but not who did it. Others were swearing they knew who did it but not how it happened. Some just wanted the latest news on the investigation. He was tired. It had been a very long night. He rose from his desk, stretched, retrieved is hat from the wall peg and began the descent down the steps to Houston Street.

"Hey, J.M.! Over here!" hollered Haymar upon seeing the Sheriff.

Brown sauntered over to Haymar to where the Post Office once stood.

"Look at this," said Haymar, pointing to the large safe that had obviously been blown open. The top hinge had been torn off toward the front of the safe and the bottom hinge bent enough to allow the locking pins on the opposite side to come free. Looking inside, the safe was empty except for some ashes.

"Look at this," said the Sheriff. "Right here just above the top hinge. There was a hole bored in there. Was that there before?"

"No. See how the metal around the outer edge is pitted and flanged out a little bit? That had to be gun powder. Hole's not big enough for dynamite."

"What's goin on," came a voice that before had gone unnoticed. The Sheriff and Haymar looked up to see Mayor Lowell Goates approaching. He appeared to not have gotten enough sleep the night before. Likely he was at the Texas Rose till late last night, thought Brown.

"Well, Lowell, we got ourselves an investigation goin' on here. Did you see anythin' last night that might give us a clue?" asked the Sheriff.

"Sorry, no. I was in bed before the dance was over. Oleta told me about the blast at breakfast this mornin'. Slept right through it. Thought I'd come down here to see if I could lend a hand."

"Why don't you go over there and see if you can help Billy salvage what he can," said Brown.

"Sure," replied the mayor and began picking his way through the rubble to where Nix was stooped over picking through what was left of his store.

"He's the last thing I need to deal with this mornin'," said Brown as the pair watched him walk away.

"What are those ashes," asked Brown, pointing to one of the inside compartments of the safe.

"See how they're all in a square and the ashes are about an inch and a half thick? That compartment contained stamps," said Haymar. "See the two compartments underneath? Those contained cash; foldin' money and change. And look here under the front. Fire got so hot it melted the gold pieces and they ran out of the bottom. Didn't completely melt the silver though."

"What are you doin' with gold and silver in there?" asked Brown.

"Some folks don't like to be carryin' around much gold or silver coins, so I keep it in the safe for 'em and give 'em a receipt," replied Haymar.

"There ain't no ashes in the empty ones," said Brown.

"Right. Obviously, it was a burglary," said Haymar.

"How much cash did you have in there?"

"All of May's receipts. When I did the cash book at close of business on Friday, I had $759.48. I took $500.00 over to Joshua's bank and deposited it, leaving me a balance of $259.48 to open with for June."

"Do you remember what denominations you had?"

"Not exactly. Maybe eight or ten in tens, about fifty in fives, fifteen or twenty in ones and the rest in change. And let me show you somethin else."

Brown followed Haymar to the common wall with Nix's store, where Haymar pointed to a square steel frame standing vertically on the zero-property line. It wasn't big, but big enough at about eighteen inches square.

"You see this here. It's a pass through. It can be latched from my side, but can't be opened from Billy's side. See how the female part of the hasp that was on the door is layin over here against the wall? If it had still been latched, that part of the hasp would be layin right under the frame. Whoever did this, opened this pass through and got into Billy's store."

"What was the pass through used for?"

"Don't know. Billy doesn't either. It was put in by old man Faircloth who built and owns both of these. You'll have to ask him about it."

Going back to the safe for a closer inspection, Haymar and Brown studied it closely to see if they had missed something on their initial observation.

"Okay. That hole there. Not any normal kinda drill that can drill hard metal like that," said the Sheriff.

"You're right. I've got to get in touch with the Postal Inspectors down in Beaumont. They'll want to come up and investigate this too."

"Hey Sheriff!" hollered Nix. "Come look at this."

The summons made both men change their focus. Haymar followed Brown through the rubble to where Nix was standing next to his safe.

"This is probably where the fire started. Looks like it started here because the floor is nearly burnt through and some of the floor joists are burned pretty good right through here," said Nix pointing at the area around the safe. "And look at this hole in the safe right there. Looks like gun powder was set off in there next to the top hinge."

"Well, the hinge is definitely bent to hell," said Brown.

"Hey, Sheriff!" called Deputy Wayne, "Come take a look at this."

Brown, Nix, Goates and Haymar walked to the end of where the counter used to stand as Wayne pointed to a brace and bit.

"That ain't no ordinary brace and bit," said Wayne. "Only one I ever seen around here like that was over at Frank Marion's"

Brown took the brace and bit and was turning it so as to study the entire tool. Then, on the heel of the brace, he saw it. Someone placed the initials F.M. in the metal part of the heel. Haymar noticed it when the Sheriff did.

"Whadda you think Sheriff?" asked the Deputy.

"I think I need to talk to Frank Marion," replied the Sheriff, shaking his head in disbelief. It was hard for Brown to comprehend that a hard-working man and a pillar of the community like Frank Marion would do such a thing. Then he immediately thought that there had to be an explanation. Had to be. Couldn't have been Frank. But, then again, he never thought that Harvey Nickerson was a queer either. Just never know about some people he thought. He bade his goodbye's and walked toward Frank Marion's house.

Part Four

16

The Beginning

The sun was fully up now, but the morning was still cool as the Sheriff walked with his head down, thinking about the events of early this morning and the past three days. He was beginning to think somebody had put a curse on him or some other kind of spell as he walked along Peachtree Street toward Frank Marion's house.

This was the third hard conversation he was going to have in the last three days. The first was with Harvey Nickerson where he found out about his dark secret and one he could never repeat, then Mayor Lowell Goates and his acting out with his wife, and now there was evidence that Frank Marion might have broken into the Post Office and Nix's store to rob them and in the process, burned down the whole south side of the square.

He turned and walked up the dirt path the front door of Marion's house. It was a typical home with two front doors and one back door. This was the style to ensure good ventilation during the hot summer months. The windows and interior doors were also aligned to provide the best unobstructed breeze. The right front door to the parlor was open so he knocked on the closed screen door. He saw Frank come out of the kitchen in the rear and hollered at the Sheriff to come on in.

"What can I do for you, Sheriff?"

"I think it'd be better if we talked out here on the veranda," said Brown.

As he walked onto the porch the screen door slammed behind him. Frank Marion had a quizzical look. There's no way he knows about me and Oleta last night. His mind was racing. He began to breathe a little faster and found his palms suddenly moist. What they did wasn't against the law. It was against the church, but the Sheriff didn't have nothin' to do with that. "What's goin' on, Sheriff?" asked Frank, somewhat nervously.

Brown noticed that Frank appeared a little nervous. "Well, I hate to bother you on a Sunday, but was you at the fire this mornin'?"

"Yep. Pert near ever body in town was there I reckon."

"Where was you before that?"

"I was in bed, sleepin'. Why?"

"Well, Frank. Recognize this?" He held out the charred brace and bit.

"Yep. It's mine. See the markin' on the heel? Where'd you get it?"

"Next to the safe in Billy Nix's store. Looks like it was used to bore a hole in his safe. What I'm wonderin' is why would your brace and bit be next to the safe in Nix's store?"

"I don't rightly know. It's mine alright, but I ain't got no idea how it got there," said Marion. He began to feel some relief that it was nothing to do with Oleta and the Sheriff wouldn't be askin' about none of that. Then his concern changed.

"You keep your tools at the shop?"

"Of course."

"You got time to walk down there with me to look around?"

"Yep. Just let me get my hat." He turned, went back into his house, the screen door slamming behind him. A few moments later, he came back onto the front veranda, screen door slamming once again, settled his hat on his head and the two started down the steps toward the blacksmith shop.

As the pair strolled down Bowie Street toward the blacksmith shop on Water Street, there was a disturbing silence that didn't sit well with the Sheriff. Something was just a little off about Frank's attitude, but he couldn't figure it out. The walk continued this way until they came upon the blacksmith shop and both men stopped short as soon as they saw it.

"What the hell?" exclaimed Frank, "Beg your pardon, Sheriff. Didn't mean to cuss on Sunday. But, what the hell?"

The two surveyed the wide-open front door and the wooden window shutter to the left of the door; both of which were hanging on one hinge. They approached somewhat cautiously, but not overly concerned that someone would still be in the building.

Frank pulled the pin and slid the barn style door open so they could see better, then stepped inside, followed by the Sheriff.

"Looks like they pried the window open and climbed in. Got what they wanted and broke down the front door to get out," said the Sheriff. "Take a look around to see what all is missin'."

The normally organized shop was left in disarray with tools and metals scattered about.

"I'll have to re-organize this thing to be able to tell," he responded, still shaking his head over the mess that was scattered before him. He stooped to pick up an old brace and some old bits that lay on the dirt floor. The kiln that stood next to the bellows was still warm and would be relit the following morning to begin the weeks work. As he continued to put things back in their proper place, he was slowly able to tell the Sheriff what was missing; a medium size hammer, two premium braces and six quality bits, a pair of tongs, a pry bar and a sledgehammer.

"Frank, I've got to ask you a very serious question and you've got to tell me the truth. Where was Gurdon last night before the fire?"

"I was up when he come home from the dance. I guess it was around 12:30. Heard him go to bed. Clarence Keaghey spent the night with him. Both slept in Gurdon's room. Why you askin'?"

"Well, it's puzzlin'. See, Gurdon and Clarence was playin' dominoes at Nix's store until 12:45. But you say he got home at 12:30. About a five minute walk from Nix's store to your house. Put's Gurdon and Clarence home at 12:50. That's a ways from 12:30. But, if Gurdon was involved, why did he break into the shop? Don't make sense," said the Sheriff trailing off.

"Gurdon knows how to get into the shop without breakin' anything," said Frank quickly, trying to get the Sheriff's mind off of the times. "All he had to do was take a pocketknife and slide the latch up on the window and it would come open. Weren't no need to break it off the hinges. He's done it a bunch before. He knows how, and he knows better."

"You see, that's what's puzzlin'," replied the Sheriff. "Just don't make no sense. You see Gurdon or Clarence, ask 'em to come see me. I just want to chat to see if I can figure this thing out."

"Sure, Sheriff. I ain't seen him since the fire. I seen him down by the White Swan not long after I got to the square. He may be in his bed sleepin' right now. I'll check when I get back to the house and if he's there, I'll send him your way."

"Well, they ain't in trouble...just yet. Just want to talk to 'em. See if they might've seen anythin'. See if they can account for their whereabouts, that's all. I appreciate you helpin' me out here Frank. Been real helpful."

"Anytime, Sheriff. Like I said, if Gurdon and Clarence is at the house, I'll send them your way."

"Thanks, Frank. I guess I'll head back to square and keep lookin'. Sometimes you find stuff that helps solve a case sometimes you don't."

Brown left Frank Marion in his blacksmith shop, still sorting out the tools and metals, putting them back in their proper place. He was hungry so he headed home. It was going to be a long day.

17

The Missing Cobbler

Lowell Goates hung around with Billy Nix and Bob Haymar for a while but when he felt he wasn't accomplishing much of anything, he bid his goodbyes and began the trek home.

The breakfast Oleta had laid out earlier this morning hadn't been that appealing to him, given the number of libations he had the night before, so he was getting a little peckish. As he walked, he remembered the peach cobbler. The more he thought about it, the more it sounded like that was what would hit the spot.

He walked in the front door, the screen once again slamming behind him, hung his hat on the hook and walked into the kitchen.

"How'd it look?" inquired Oleta.

"The whole south side of the square is burned to the ground. Nix's store, the Post Office, the Texas Rose, Galvin's Grocery, T.M. Stone's Drug Store and on down to the end of the block to Hinson's Domino Parlor. Every bit of it," replied Lowell.

"Oh, Lord! Any idea what happened?"

"Looks like a robbery according to the Sheriff. Whoever it was used gun powder on the safe in the Post Office and then went through a pass through into Nix's store. They got everthing out of the Post Office Safe, but they evidently used too much gun powder in Nix's safe and that's what started the fire."

"Sheriff have any idea who done it?"

"Nope," said Lowell as he went over to the pie safe and took out what was left of the cobbler. When he took the dish towel off the top, there wasn't as much left as he thought there would be. What originally would have been about eight helpings only had about four left. He casually asked, "What happened to all the cobbler?"

"That's all that's left," she replied nervously.

"Well, how much did you eat?" asked Lowell.

"Little more than a normal helpin'. It smelled so good couldn't help myself," she replied, hoping she was believable. "You have any when you got home last night?"

"Nope."

"You sure about that?"

"Yes, I'm sure," he said firmly. "You had a little over one helpin'. I didn't have none. How come 'bout half of it's gone?"

"You must have had some when you come in. That's the only thing I can imagine," she said nervously. "I'm pretty sure that whoever burnt down the square didn't stop in here durin' the night and help themselves to some cobbler before they skedaddled out of here."

"I just don't believe I had any last night," Lowell replied, slightly shaking his head and now beginning to doubt himself.

"Well, when the Sheriff's done through with findin' who burnt down the square, maybe he can start investigatin' the case of the missin' cobbler," said Oleta huffily. "I gotta get ready for church. You comin'?"

"Not today. The Spirit just ain't moved me," replied Lowell, still not remembering that he ate that much cobbler last night.

"Okay. I'll tell Brother Lonnie you wasn't feelin' well," said Oleta as she turned and headed toward the bedroom.

"Okay." For the life of him he couldn't remember eatin' any cobbler last night. I must have been more into my cups than I thought, he decided. Well, that's the only logical explanation, he told himself. He walked to the cupboard, took down a bowl, removed a spoon from the drawer, sat down at the table and began to dish out a helping of cobbler.

As she stood before the dresser mirror, she was almost a nervous wreck. Thank goodness he came home drunk last night, she thought. She didn't think he would notice how much cobbler was gone in a million years. If he hadn't been so drunk, the lie wouldn't have worked. She realized that she was sweating a little around her neck, between her adequate breasts and her palms. Better use extra powder today, she thought. Then she quietly chuckled to herself, remembering the old saying about sweating like a whore in church. But the levity didn't last. Something had to give. Frank would never leave Inez. She couldn't leave Lowell. She didn't have anybody or anything. I really need church today she thought. I've got to pray hard. Lord, please help me figure this out, she said silently. But I don't know if I can give up the way Frank makes me feel. It was like an angel on one shoulder and the devil on the other. I need to hurry and get to the bible teaching before church begins. She had a fleeting thought of confiding to Brother Lonnie, but quickly dismissed that idea. More than once Brother Lonnie had violated confidences, particularly when it came to coveting other people's wives. Maybe I can find the answer in the bible. That's it, she thought. You can find all your answers in the bible. Just got to look hard enough. She finished dressing, placed her hat on her head, secured it with a rhinestone hat pin that was her mothers, put on her gloves, picked up her purse and bible and headed toward the front door.

"Okay, I'm gone. Be back after church."

"Alright. I may go back down to the square to see if I can help some more. Tell Brother Lonnie I said hello."

Oleta turned, quietly closing the screen door so it wouldn't slam.

18

Breakfast

Brown walked into his house, the screen door slamming behind him, took off his hat, placed it on the hook on the hall tree and walked into the kitchen where Midge was just finishing rolling out fresh biscuit dough.

"Mornin,'" said Midge. "Rough night?"

"You could say that," said Brown somewhat mischievously.

"Heard it was bad. Got the whole south side of the square, that right?"

"Yep. Burned completely to the ground. Looks like a robbery. Now ever body in town is expectin' me to figure out who did it and to get 'em to jail. Not much to go on though."

"There was nothin' around there for a clue?" she asked as she turned a drinking glass upside down and cut out perfectly round biscuits and placed them in the lard greased pie pan.

"Yep, was one thing. There was a brace and bit that belonged to Frank Marion layin' by the counter at Nix's."

"You think he did it?"

"Well, my first thought was, 'why would Frank break into the Post Office and Nix's store and rob the safes'. Didn't make sense to me. But I went over to Frank's to talk to him and he was surprised 'bout the brace and bit. Owned up to it bein' his right away. Didn't hesitate. So, we walked down to the blacksmith shop and somebody had broke into it. Wooden window and the front door hangin' by a hinge. He didn't do the robbery. I'm sure of it. Problem is, I don't know where else to look at this point."

"So, you thinkin' whoever broke into Frank's shop did the robbery?"

"That's what makes sense to me. Can't see it no other way. Whoever broke into Frank's shop is the one, or one of the ones, that did the robbery. They had to know the place pretty well too."

"How's that?"

"Did you know that there's a pass through between the Post Office and Nix's store?"

"What are you talkin' about?"

"Well, there's the hole between the two buildin's, 'bout eighteen inches square. It latches from the Post Office side so if you're in the Post Office, you could unlatch it and crawl through. But you can't unlatch it from Nix's side. So, they broke into the Post Office first, robbed that safe, crawled through the pass through into Nix's store and hit his safe next. From the way the fire marks were left, looks like they used too much gun powder or they spilled a bunch at Nix's. When either the powder in the safe was set off or when the spill was set off accidentally, it started the fire. So, at least one somebody knew about the pass through and knew to rob the Post Office first so they could use it to get into Nix's."

"You think there was more than one somebody that done it?"

"Just 'bout have to be. Don't see much other way. Probably was three or four of 'em the way I'm thinkin' about it right now. Likely broke into the Post Office and one went to the front window to keep an eye out. The first one with the brace and bit started drillin' on the safe while at least one more or maybe two more went through to Nix's store to find the safe. The first fella drilled the Post Office safe and then went through and started drillin' Nix's safe. When they were both drilled, one of 'em went back to the Post Office, loaded the safe with gun powder while another one did the same thing to Nix's. I figure they was plannin' on settin' both of 'em off at the same time so there wouldn't be two explosions. The whole thing went in their favor in the Post Office and they got everthin' they wanted from there. Somethin' went wrong at Nix's though. The powder misfired or they made a mistake or somethin'. Didn't get nothin' out of Nix's safe. But the explosion in there's what started the fire. I think they got scared and just run off."

"So instead of one fella you're lookin' for three or four? Don't ever remember three, much less four, people bein' able to keep a secret. Two, maybe. Not more than that. I think somebody'll say somethin'. May take a day, may take a week or a month, but one of 'em will let the cat out of the bag at some point."

"Well, let's hope so. I have absolutely nothin' to go on at this point. Only evidence I have is that Frank Marion's brace was used and I just do not believe he had anythin' to do with it."

"Here's your breakfast," said Midge, placing a plate of sausage, eggs, fresh hot biscuits and fig preserves on the table. "You want milk or coffee?"

"Coffee, please. I've still got a long day ahead of me," replied Brown as he dug into the delicious breakfast.

"Might I rightly assume that you ain't goin' to church?" she asked.

"You'd assume right. Tell Brother Lonnie I said hello, but I'm gonna be kinda busy the rest of today," he said mater-of-factly.

"Okay. I will. Any idea what you want for lunch?"

"Last thing on my mind right now. Don't worry. I'll eat a sandwich or somethin'. Nothin else, I can probably get Harold or Hattie to rustle me up somethin' down at the White Swan. So many people still millin' around this mornin' that they opened up. Don't do that on Sundays normally. I'll be ok."

"I'm gonna go get dressed then. You be careful today."

"I will," he replied as she walked from the kitchen into the parlor.

19

Return to the Scene

Brown finished up his breakfast, placed the dirty dishes in the wash pan, took his cup, poured the remainder of what was left in the pot into it and went to the back veranda, the screen door slamming behind him.

He sat in the chair and leaned back so the front legs were off the floor and the back rested against the wall of the house. He decided he just needed a little time to think. The breakfast had been good and the coffee was just right. He again counted how lucky he was to have Midge in his life.

The last many hours had been some of the most stressful he could ever remember. Not only was a significant part of his town burned to the ground, but everybody was looking to him to solve who did it. And fast. Problem was, there just wasn't any real evidence to go on. Frank Marion's brace and other tools, but that was it. Frank certainly didn't do it. Or did he, he began to wonder? He certainly could have. He could have staged the break in at the blacksmith shop. He was handy enough with the tools and knew how to use them well. He still made musket rifles and scatter guns, so he had access to gun powder. But why? Why would Frank Marion break into two different businesses to rob them? Could one person have done it by themselves? Yep, sure could have, he thought. Would've been a stretch, but he could have done it by himself. Could have had a longer fuse on one of the safes so they'd both go off about the same time. The more he thought about it, it seemed the only likely way it happened.

The only part that was still puzzling was why? Why would Frank do it? Was he in that bad a money shape? He knew that some people put on airs the other folks mostly saw right through, but Frank never seemed to put on any. He was always the same fella all the time. There was some reason Frank did it and he decided that if he could figure out why, he'd have Frank Marion dead to rights. He had the opportunity and he had the ability. The only thing that was missing was the motivation. I've got to figure out his motivation, he thought. But where to start.

First, he thought, I'll go back down to the square and keep lookin. Maybe I'll come up with something. The obvious reason for the robbery was money. If it were for money, whoever did it needed more than what he had. I've got to talk to banker Tidwell first thing in the morning, he decided. That would be the place to start.

He set the front legs of the chair back on the veranda, threw the rest of his coffee out into the yard and walked back into the kitchen, the screen door slamming behind him. He put the cup in the wash pan along with the other dirty dishes, walked into the parlor, took his hat off the hall tree and walked out the front screen door that slammed behind him.

As he walked back toward town, the more he thought about Frank Marion, the more he was convincing himself that Frank was at least involved in the whole thing. Maybe banker Tidwell would shed some light on it tomorrow. Still my best suspect at this point, Brown ruminated.

When he rounded the corner of the courthouse, Billy Nix and Bob Haymar were both still sifting through the debris along with all the other merchants. Nix had started piling what he could salvage where the sidewalk had been. The Depotti boy was helping. Haymar was busy doing the same thing but had to make certain everything he salvaged could be secured because of postal regulations.

The Sheriff walked over to his Deputy who had been gathering what he considered 'unusual stuff' that might be a clue to what happened and hopefully, who was involved.

"Hey, Sheriff," said Wayne. "I've gathered up this stuff over here if you wanna take a look at it," as he gestured toward a small array of odd-looking items near the safe in Nix's store.

"Well, let's take a look," replied Brown.

They walked toward where the safe remained and Brown stood, studying the items one by one.

"That's the pry bar, hammers and brace and bit taken from the blacksmith shop," said Brown.

"You talk to Frank?" asked Wayne.

"Yep, I did. We went down there to the shop and it had been broke into. Window and door hangin' by one hinge. These here were some of the things he said was missin'."

"He have any idea who might've broke in?"

"Nope. Was quick to say it wasn't Gurdon though. Said Gurdon knew how to get in without breakin' the window and door off'n the hinges."

"Why would he be that quick for Gurdon?"

"Well, I asked young Mr. Depotti over there about what time he closed last night. Said Gurdon Marion, Clarence Keaghey and Oscar Brown was there. Played the last hand of dominoes and they left at 12:45. I asked Frank what time Gurdon got home and he said 12:30. Said Clarence spent the night there. Asked him where Gurdon was this mornin' and he said he figured he was still asleep. Told him that when he saw Gurdon or Clarence for them to come see me."

"Hard to see how he got home before he even left the store," replied the Deputy.

"Brilliant deduction, Andrew," replied the Sheriff a little more sarcastically than he intended.

"Yeah, I know, but...You think Dave Depotti had something to do with it?" asked Wayne.

"Well, it's for certain that somebody's not tellin' the truth. What you got here?"

"Well, that obvious stuff from Frank's shop and this," said Wayne as he held up a folding knife. The knife was a medium sized three blade Case. The yellow bone casing had survived the fire and was barely scorched on one side.

The Sheriff took the knife and turned it over and over in his hand, studying the casing noting no obvious markings. He then opened the blades one by one and studied them for any markings. When he got to the smallest blade there was a small, rudimentary etching next to the case. He held it up for Wayne to see. "What do you make this out to be?"

"Looks like "SK" to me," said the Deputy.

"Me too. Not much to go on. Have you seen anybody around with a knife like this?"

"Pretty common. Not off the top of my head."

"Any idea who might have the initials "SK"?

"Gotta give ya' the same answer, Sheriff. Nope. I'll think on it though."

"Okay. Me too. Find anythin' else?"

"Nothin', Sheriff. But I'll keep lookin'."

"Ok. Keep lookin'. I'm gonna visit with Billy for a minute. And, don't tell nobody 'bout the knife," he instructed.

He walked through the rubble that was beginning to be cleaned up little by little and stopped where Billy Nix was picking up thread spools. "Billy. You have any clues or any supposin' who might have done this?"

"Nope. Dave and I've been talkin' about it pretty much since we started the clean-up. Neither one of us can come up with anythin' that'll point us in any kind of direction."

The Sheriff opened his palm and Nix focused on the yellow handled folding knife. "You recognize this?"

"Pretty common, J.M. Quite a few of them around. I used to sell 'em, but they raised the wholesale price too high and I didn't think most of my customers could afford 'em."

"Let me show you this," said Brown as he unfolded the smallest blade. "What do you make that out to be?"

"Looks like the letters 'S' and 'K'."

"That's what Andrew and I think. Know anybody with those initials? You have a customer with those initials?"

"Well, it'd be awful easy to tell you if all my credit books hadn't burnt up. Can't think of anybody off the top of my head," replied Nix who then called out, "Hey, Dave. Come over here a minute."

Depotti placed what could be a salvageable bolt of gingham in one of the "keep" piles and walked toward the pair. "Yes, sir, Mr. Billy. What do you need?"

"You seen a knife like this?" asked Nix.

"Pretty common. It'd be hard for me to say."

"Look closer at this and tell me what you see," said the Sheriff.

"Looks like the letters 'S' and 'K'."

"Well, that makes four out of four thinkin' the same thing," said Brown. "You think of anybody you know has those initials?"

Depotti did not immediately reply and Brown could tell he was thinking hard about the question. "None come to mind, Sheriff. I'll keep thinkin' on it and if I think of anybody, I'll let you know."

"That's all I can ask. And, Dave. Don't tell nobody 'bout findin this knife, okay?" Depotti nodded in agreement and then turned, walked back to the area he was cleaning and resumed sorting the debris.

"You gonna rebuild, Billy?"

"Good question. I'd been thinkin' about openin' up another store up at Brookeland. Was trainin' Dave to run it if and when I decided to. There's not another vacant building left around the square and any that does come open, the rent is gonna be higher than usual. All the businesses that was burnt out will be wantin' the same buildin'. I'll have to talk to Alma. We've made a lot of friends here and we love the church. It'd be hard to leave, but I've got to make a livin' somehow and somewhere," Nix said with more sadness than he likely intended.

"I'd hate to see ya' go. I mean, who's gonna do my shirts," said the Sheriff with a grin. "But, you gotta do what's best for your family. I completely understand that."

"Yeah, I just need some time to think. Everthin' has happened so quick. But I'll have to make a decision pretty quick I reckon."

"I understand. If you think of anybody that knife might belong to, let me know. Okay?"

"Sure will. And, J.M., thanks for lettin' me bend your ear for a minute."

"Don't mind a bit. If you wanna talk more, you know where to find me."

"Okay. You take care now."

"I will. Talk with you later. And, Billy. Please don't say anythin' 'bout the knife." Nix gave him a thumbs up as the Sheriff turned to walk through the slowly disappearing rubble toward the remains of the Post Office.

Haymar was busy sorting the mail that had come in on the train earlier that morning and was just finishing up when Brown walked up.

"Well, what do ya' think?" Brown asked Haymar.

"I think I've got a heck of a mess," replied the Postmaster. "Could've been worse though. If I hadn't made the bank deposit Friday, the Regional Postmaster General would probably have my butt in a sling. I'll be okay though, I think. Luckily, the 3:30AM train from Beaumont hadn't arrived yet so that mail was safe. But all the outgoing mail to Shreveport and points north and west was lost, burned up."

"Find anythin' resemblin a clue?"

"Nothing. I mean if Andrew hadn't found that brace and bit, I don't figure there would have been any clue at all."

"Well, we may have another one. You know everbody around. Don't repeat this 'cause it may be nothin', but Andrew found a folding knife in all the rubble at Billy's store. Billy said it ain't his and so did Depotti. Found what looks like the initials 'SK' on one of the blades. You think of anybody around with the initials 'SK'?"

The Sheriff could clearly see a studious look come over the Postmaster's face. "Well, there's Simon Knowles, but I haven't seen him around in months. Not too many folks with last names startin with K. Of course, there's the Keaghey's. Old man Keaghey's been dead for a couple of years now. That could be it", he said with some conviction. "Old man Keaghey's first name was Seamus. That could fit. Don't know how it could get in Billy's store though."

"I guess with all the other mysteries we've got goin' on, he could have risen from the dead," Brown said with a grin. "That would fit right in with everthin' else we don't know."

"The only other fella I can think of is Samuel Knightly, but he moved to Crockett eight or ten months ago. I just don't know. I don't think none of those fellas would do somethin' like this. Didn't know 'em well, but I think I knew 'em well enough. What happens now, J.M.?"

"To be right honest with you, I just don't know. Midge said somethin' this mornin' that I think is goin' to likely solve this whole thing. She said it's hard enough for two people to keep a secret, but if there were three or four involved, likely one of 'em will let somethin' slip before long."

"No more than what you've got to go on, I'm hoping Midge is right."

"Me too. Okay, if you think of anythin' else let me know. And, hey Bob. Please don't say nothin' about the knife just yet."

"You can bet on it."

Brown turned, strolled through the rubble, across the burned sidewalk and into the sandy street toward the jail, not knowing what his next move was going to be.

20

The Jail

Brown took the steps on the west side of the jail and when he got to the top of the landing, he was surprised to see Clarence Keaghey sitting in the corner against the half wall of the landing.

"Mornin', Sheriff," said Keaghey.

"Mornin', Clarence. You talk to Frank?"

"Yep. Said I was to come see you 'bout last night."

"Good. Where's Gurdon?"

"Don't rightly know. Stayed at his place last night. Wasn't there when I got up this mornin'. Asked Mr. Frank and he didn't know neither."

"Ok. Come on in," said Brown as he unlocked the door.

Brown put his hat on the peg and settled behind his desk while Keaghey took the round backed oak chair in the front of the desk.

"What can I do for you, Sheriff?"

"Not real sure. Let's start with you tellin' me where you was last night when the explosion went off."

"I was at Gurdon's house, sleepin'."

"You go to the dance last night?"

"Yep. Didn't stay long though. Never worked up the nerve to ask any of the girls to dance, so I left early."

"What time did you leave?"

"I guess about 11:00."

"Where'd you go after that?"

"Over to Nix's store. Dave was there and business was slow. We played straight dominoes until Gurdon and Oscar got there."

"Oscar who?"

"Your nephew, Oscar Brown."

"What time did they get there?"

"I think about 11:45. Gurdon got there first and then Oscar showed up a little later. Jesse Robinson showed up as Dave was closin' and he got a malt to go and left with us."

"What time did you leave Nix's store?"

"Don't rightly recall. Guess it was somewhere around 12:30 or 12:45."

"Well, which was it; 12:30 or 12:45?" asked the Sheriff sharply.

"Closer to 12:30. I remember the clock striking the half hour. So, yeah, I guess closer to 12:30."

"Gurdon leave with you?"

"Yep. We left together 'cause I was spendin' the night with him. Oscar and Jesse left too and walked with us as far as Bowie Street. I reckon they went on home from there."

"Him and his folks live over on Pearl Street, don't they?"

"Yeah, I think so."

"So, you left together and got home around 12:35. Is that right?"

"I s'pect so. Like I said, I'm just kinda guessin' at the time."

"What did ya' do when ya' got to Gurdon's?"

"We talked to Minnie and Valley about the dance and Gurdon kept on talkin' about Stella Erwin, Billy Nix's sister-in-law. They was together the whole time at the dance 'till Mr. Billy came and got her about 11:30. That's what Gurdon said. Minnie and Valley got to teasin' Gurdon a little bit 'bout how he had the happy eyes for Miss Stella."

"And you got no idea where Gurdon is?"

"Nope. Sure don't."

On a hunch, Brown pulled the Case knife out of his pocket. Held it in his open hand, turning it over and over, not saying a word while Clarence's demeanor changed slightly and he shifted almost imperceptivity in his chair.

As the Sheriff leaned forward putting both elbows on the desk, he held the knife up by one end for him to see it more clearly. He slowly asked "Clarence. Do you have any idea who's responsible for the fire last night?"

"Uh. No, I don't. I don't have no clue at all," replied Keaghey nervously.

"You sure 'bout that?" asked the Sheriff sternly, still holding the knife at their eye level.

"Yes sir. Dead sure."

"And you don't know where Gurdon is?" he asked again as he slid the knife into the lap drawer of his desk.

"No sir. I don't," he said, still with a little nervous quiver in his voice that the Sheriff now noticed.

"Your Grandaddy was Seamus Keaghey?"

"Yes sir."

"I hear he was a good man. When did he die?"

"Died in spring, 1899."

"He leave anythin' behind?"

"He had a couple acres up toward Remlig. My dad and his brothers and sisters sold it to Mr. Barton. That's about it."

"Didn't leave no personal affects?"

"What do ya' mean?"

"You know, like a watch, gun, skinnin' knife. Somethin' like that?"

Getting just a tad more nervous by the minute, a sheen appeared on Keaghey's upper lip. "Uh, no sir."

"So. If I was to go ask your daddy about him leavin' anythin', he would say there wasn't nothin' either?"

"Well, I reckon so. Not so leasts as I know of. If he did, I didn't know nothin' 'bout it," said Keaghey as sweat now was on his forehead.

"And you still don't know where Gurdon Marion is?"

"Naw, Sheriff. I mean, you accusin' me of somethin'? I ain't done nothin' for you to be accusin' me like this," said Keaghey who was beginning to show signs of exasperation.

"Have I accused you of anythin'?"

"Well, no sir. Not outright. But the way you're askin' them questions don't make a body feel too comfortable," replied Keaghey even more nervous than before.

"You think the Sheriff got the right to ask questions given that half the square burned down last night?"

"Yes, sir. But I didn't have nothin' to do with it. No sir. Not one bit," said Keaghey who surprised himself with the adamant tone he used, almost becoming defiant.

Brown studied the young man sitting across his desk and couldn't quite figure out whether he was telling the truth or not. "Ok. You go on now. I've got some investigatin' to do and a lot of people to talk to. You're on my list, I'm gonna tell you that much. It'd help if I could talk to Gurdon. He may be able to clear up some of this for you and get you off my list. You see him, you make sure you tell him I want to talk to him sooner rather than later."

Keaghey did not need a second invitation to leave. "Yes sir, Sheriff. I guarantee you that if and when I see Gurdon, I'll tell him."

"Okay, then. You go on now. You think of anythin' that might help solve this case or to get you off'n my list, you need to let me know, okay?"

"Yes, sir," Keaghey said again as he stood, quickly turned, and left.

"Well, hell", Keaghey thought to himself as he descended the steps of the jail. That damned Gurdon has done duped me again. I'm done with the son-of-a-bitch. May just whip his ass when I see him. Sorry bastard. If I go to jail, him and Oscar is goin' with me.

Deep in thought, he did not see Hector Henry as he stepped off the last step and they almost collided.

"Hey, Clarence. What you doin' here?" asked the reporter.

"Aw, the Sheriff wanted to know if I seen anythin' bout last night. Didn't see nothin' so I couldn't tell him nothin'."

"He got any idea who done it?"

"Don't know. He's playin' this real close to the vest. You goin' up to talk to him?"

"Yep. Gonna try and put out a special edition on Tuesday, so I need the latest he's got. I can go as late as five or six this evenin' but then I gotta get the copy to the typesetter by then."

"Well, good luck," said Keaghey as he turned east on Houston Street.

"Ok. See ya round," replied Henry as he proceeded up the steps.

Hector Henry did not knock but walked right into the west side door which opened directly into the Sheriff's office. When he walked in, he saw the Sheriff with a puzzled look on his face, staring at a knife.

"Mornin', Sheriff."

"Mornin', Hector. Now look. I ain't got nothin' and even if I did, I'm not tellin' you. You'd plaster it all over the front page and scare off any potential lead I might have. Probably scare 'em off to Arkansas or Louisiana and then I'd never solve this thing."

"Aw, come on J.M., give me somethin'. This is the biggest thing to ever hit this town. Hell, biggest thing to hit this county!" exclaimed Henry. "If I publish that you are just still investigatin', that don't tell my readers nothin. Come on J.M., give me somethin to work with here."

Brown abruptly stood, stared Hector Henry in the eye and in a stern voice filled with exasperation, not realizing he was shaking the knife at him said, "Hector. It has been a total of eight hours since the fire started. I am doin everthin' I can with what I got to work with. Billy, Bob, Mr. Galvin and Mr. Stone are down there goin' through the ruins to try and find a clue. Andrew is down there with 'em. I'm runnin' on about two hours sleep. I am tired, I am frustrated and I'm tryin' my best to figure out who done this. The absolute last thing I am concerned about is your damned readers. Now then, I have told you all I'm gonna tell you and I am now invitin' you to leave and if you do not want to leave or if you ask me one more question, I've got three empty cells back there for your comfort and enjoyment. Because one more word and I'm gonna arrest you for impedin' and investigation. Now I'm going to ask you if you understand what I just said and anythin' other than a 'yes' answer will make you a guest of Jasper County until I get tired of feedin' ya'. You understand?"

Wide eyed, Henry had never seen the Sheriff act or talk this way. This was different. Totally different. He had no reason not to believe this man. Finally, he muttered, "Yes", turned, opened the door, stepped across the threshold, closed the door behind him and stood on the landing taking a few deep breaths in an attempt to settle his nerves.

Brown watched him until he closed the door, then sat down heavily, praying that somehow, someway he could catch an early break in the case.

The more he thought of Frank Marion as a suspect, the less plausible it became. He decided that he would check in with banker Tidwell in the morning just to verify he didn't have any money woes. That left him with not a single suspect and even less proof. I'm missing something, he thought to himself. He then thought again about what Midge had said about keeping a secret. After much consideration, he decided that would likely be what solves the case. And if not, it just wouldn't be solved.

As he stood on the landing outside, Hector Henry took in the view from the high perch to survey the damage the fire had done. He could see all of the merchants in their ruined stores trying to salvage what they could. There was no telling what it would take to replace the buildings and all the goods that were inside them. Maybe that was the angle for the article. That was it. He'd get all the merchants to estimate the cost of their damages. It was liable to run to $10,000.00. A fortune. As he descended the steps, he decided the headline would be "Fire Destroys Jasper Businesses: A Fortune to Rebuild".

21

Prayers

The gawkers, rumor mill oracles and the plain curious continued to walk down Houston Street, surveying the damage and mumbling among themselves. There was a constant stream of folks, some had come from Remlig, Burkeville, Browndell and even Roganville.

The Negros from Dixie Community also came, but unlike the whites, they had their hats off and heads bowed to show respect, and that they "knew their place". They walked on the north side of Houston Street, leaving the white folks to have the closer view. A few offered to help the merchants sift through the rubble and a couple were taken up on their offer.

None of the white folks offered to help.

The clock tower on the courthouse struck ten and shortly thereafter all the church bells began to ring, calling their flock to services. With the ringing of the bells, both crowds began to thin as most made their way to their respective places of worship.

Some of the men filling the pulpit were preachers, others were pastors.

The preachers would preach fire and brimstone, quoting the bible at length, voice rising and lowering for dramatic effect, focusing on the job of preaching and saving souls. Most of their personal interaction with their flock was shaking hands as the faithful left the church hoping that at least one family would invite him for Sunday dinner. At the funeral of one of the followers they inevitably would say a few words about the departed, but mainly focus on trying to ensure the rest of the attendees would consider dedicating their lives to Jesus to ensure a heavenly hereafter and ensuring them that there was no time to waste.

In contrast, the pastors concentrated on the life events of their members. They would greet the members as they entered the church, calling each by name and maybe having a brief inquiry about something fairly innocuous such as how their crop was coming along or how were the fish biting. They would also be at the door following services to thank them for coming, and also to perhaps get an invitation to Sunday dinner. They would be there with the families for births, deaths, sickness, accidents and other situations when it was thought the pastors' attendance would be warranted. At funerals, pastors would speak at length about the dearly departed, comforting the family with reminders of what a true believer and follower of Jesus they had been and assuring them their loved one was now living in the "house with many mansions", walking the streets of gold and no longer in pain nor suffering.

With one of the preachers last spring, one of the children of his flock did a deed so dastardly that the incident became famous for its cunning and its horrible humor.

Little Archie Weathered's mother was one of the best cooks in town and certainly the best cook in the First Baptist Church. She was famous for her fried chicken and cobblers. As was the custom at the time, the adults ate first and the children ate after the adults finished, having to make do with whatever was left. The single Preacher Albert Gaston was a rotund man with an enormous girth and an appetite to match. Each Sunday after services he would thank each congregant for coming and if he hadn't received an invitation by the time the Weathered's came out of the sanctuary, he would make a point of asking if she was having fried chicken for lunch and could she spare one more plate, to which she always replied that she could. When the meal was over, all that would be left for little Archie was a spoonful of each vegetable, maybe a biscuit, and the chicken neck. As everyone knew, the neck was the least desirable part of the chicken because there was so little meat on it.

After months and months of Preacher Gaston leaving only the chicken neck, little Archie devised a plan he hoped would deter the despised man of God from ever trying to wrangle an invitation to a Sunday meal again.

After church on this Sunday, when the service was over and he and his parents were heading out of the door, little Archie overheard the preacher wrangle one more invitation for Sunday lunch. Upon hearing this, he ran on home ahead of his parents, went to his room, took of his "Sunday go-to-meetin' clothes" and changed into his regular overalls, shirt and left the house barefooted. He then went into the front yard where he climbed up the chinaberry tree alongside of the path that went to the front door. He got as far up the tree as he could and out on the biggest limb that hung over the path and waited. His parents didn't even notice him when they got home, which to little Archie was a good sign.

He saw Gaston approaching and little Archie steadied himself, unbuttoned the fly on the overalls, pulled the foreskin over the end and just as the preacher turned onto the path to the house, filled the end until it was completely full, then he let go, spraying pee all over the preacher.

Astonished and not sure what had just happened, he looked up and saw little Archie up in the chinaberry tree who had the biggest smile of satisfaction he could muster.

"Damn it boy, get down here!" exclaimed the preacher.

"No, sir," replied little Archie.

"Damn it boy, I said get down here," he shouted again as little Archie's daddy came out the front door to see what was going on.

"Your boy just pissed all over me! I've never seen such a thing. It's foul and disgusting. You best beat that boy, that's what I'm tellin' ya'. He needs a hickory stick for sure."

"Come in the house, let's get you cleaned up," said little Archie's daddy.

"Oh, no! Never! I'll never darken the door of this house ever again!" Gaston said hatefully and turned to walk off. "And you might as well find a new church home 'cause you ain't welcomed back!"

As he stormed off, little Archie's daddy said, "Hey, Archie. Come on down now. We gonna talk about why you done that. I gotta know why you'd do such a thing."

And with that, little Archie climbed down out of the tree and walked to the veranda where his daddy had sat on the porch swing. "Come sit here," he said patting the swing next to him. So little Archie sat beside his daddy on the porch swing. "Okay, tell me why you'd do such a thing."

"Well, sir. I was tired of him comin' here on Sundays and eatin' all the fried chicken. I ain't got nothin' but a neck every time he comes here. I was just tired of it. Don't like the man. I like momma's cookin' too. 'Specially her fried chicken. Just weren't right in my mind that I live here and he don't, but he gets the chicken and I just get the neck. I was just tired of it, daddy."

His daddy smiled, put his arm around little Archie's shoulders and said, "Okay. This here stays between us. Don't tell your momma. Anybody else asks, you got a whuppin' like you ain't never got before, you understand?" As little Archie nodded his head, his daddy continued, "Tell you the truth, I never liked the son-of-a-bitch neither. He ain't a good preacher and he don't care nothin' about his flock exceptin' how much is in the offerin' plate ever Sunday. His table manners was lackin' some too. I ain't disappointed he won't be back and I ain't disappointed about findin' a new church home. You done us a favor Archie. Now neither one of us has to deal with him again. I ain't sayin' what you did was right, but that look on his face was one of the funniest things I ever did see."

With that, both father and son had a good chuckle just as Mrs. Weathered stepped onto the front porch and asked where the preacher was.

"He suddenly changed his mind and left before he even got to the porch," deadpanned Weathered.

"Strange. He always bragged on my fried chicken. And I told him I had fresh peach cobbler today. He's kind of a strange fella," she lamented as she turned, opened the screen door and stepped into the house as the screen door slammed behind her.

Mr. Weathered held his finger to his lips, indicating that little Archie should just be quiet. It was all both of them could do to keep from busting out laughing.

Although the family was eventually excommunicated from their church, they found what they truly believed was a better church home with a caring pastor rather than a preacher. They again began enjoying sermons like they had not in a very long time.

The most respected pastor in town was Lonnie Furth at the First Methodist Church. He was the Nix's son-in-law who married Claudia. Lonnie was a very kind-hearted soul that was respected and loved by everyone in his church. They lavished gifts on the Furth's for their wedding anniversary, their anniversary at the church, theirs and their kid's birthdays and of course at Christmas.

Pastor Lonnie genuinely cared about each and every member of his congregation and his compassion did not stop at the church door. Member or not, Pastor Lonnie was always kind and caring to everyone he met. He was at the side of each family whenever the strength of God and the faith in Jesus was needed to help get through a crisis, whether large or small.

As Pastor Lonnie assumed the pulpit on this tragic Sunday morning, he wanted to provide his congregation a feeling of hope and a better future following the conflagration. He would tell them that what had happened overnight was a trial to be endured and learned from; one that would make everyone stronger and more resilient. He opened the service with a heartfelt prayer for those who had suffered a loss: the citizens of Jasper for their communal loss; for the strength to rebuild stronger and better than before; and to do so in a manner pleasing in God's eye.

The sermon was based on the book of Matthew, Chapter 18, versus 21 through 22 which said, "Then Peter came up and said to him, 'Lord, how often will my brother sin against me, and I forgive him? As many as seven times?' Jesus said to him, "I do not say to you seven times, but seventy-seven times."

Pastor Lonnie was attempting to tamp down the anger that many were feeling and to remind his followers of Jesus' mantra of forgiveness. He told them he was sure many in the congregation were angry at what happened to their town and were anxious to retaliate against those who did this horrible deed. But forgiveness must be the watch word, he said. Forgiveness, not hate, is pleasing in the eyes of the Lord. To do unto others; to turn the other cheek; to walk a mile in other shoes. Hate would slowly rot a person from the inside, and after all your body was a temple, made in the image of God, a kind and forgiving God who knew what was in the heart of each person. Everyone needed to let go of the thoughts of evil and of getting even. Let God shine down his countenance upon everyone, free them of their burdens, and fill them with forgiveness.

As he wound down the sermon with a final prayer, in a momentary lapse of judgement he picked the closing hymn. The piano began the introductory stanza and then the congregation rose and began an enthusiastic rendition of "Onward Christian Soldiers".

Such was the difference between a preacher and a pastor.

22

The Proposal

Alma Nix and Stella Erwin left the Methodist church and began their walk home. As they turned off of Bowie Street and onto Milam, they met Gurdon Marion walking the opposite way. When they got close, all stopped and greeted each other. Alma could see quickly that she was as welcome as an outhouse breeze, so she made her goodbye's and left the two alone.

"You're lookin' awful nice again today," said Gurdon.

"Well, thank you. You are too kind," replied Stella.

"Look," he said nervously, "I like you a lot. I'm gonna have a lots of money real soon. I can take good care of you. I think we need to run away and get married. We can do it just as soon as I get the money. It'll be a lot of money. It'll be enough that we can buy us a house and have plenty left over. It'll be good."

"Oh, my!" exclaimed Stella, the color rising in her face. "I've never considered…I mean I couldn't…I mean it's all so fast. What would people think? What would I tell my sister? I've never been married before. I don't know. I just…"

"Look, I'll have the money by Friday, Saturday at the latest. I'll hire us a hack and we'll go to Burkeville and spend the night. Then we'll go to Leesville and get married. We can change our names and nobody will find us. They won't know who we are or where we are. We can live happy."

"Oh, this is just too fast," said Stella almost exasperated. "Why would we want to change our names?"

"A fresh start. Nobody would know us. We can become new people. Make up a background about where we're from, what we do for a livin'. Brand new people," said Gurdon enthusiastically.

"I'm gonna have to think on this," said Stella as she began to walk toward the Nix home that was now only two blocks away.

Gurdon fell in beside her and said, "Don't you like me? I thought you liked me. At least, that's what I thought last night at the dance. You don't like me?"

"Yeah, I guess I do. Kinda. But goin' from a dance to bein' married in less than a day is fast. I'm gonna have to think on this real hard," said Stella with a look of consternation.

"Okay, we're getting' close to Mr. Nix's. I'm gonna go. Next Sunday I'll have a hack behind the bushes back behind the church. You excuse yourself for the outhouse when the sermon starts. We'll go by the Nix's and get your stuff and go to Burkeville. Make sure you pack up the night before so we don't have to wait around."

"Oh! I don't know! Don't rush me! I have got to think this through!"

"Tell you what, you come down to McReynolds Cafe Thursday about 1 o'clock. I'll be there waiting on you for your answer."

"Okay. Thursday at one at McReynolds. Okay," said Stella as Gurdon Marion stopped and Stella continued on to the Nix's home.

She didn't know what to think, much less what to do. He was likeable enough, good looking enough, but all he did for a living was work at his daddy's blacksmith shop and the odd job here and there. He was obviously a little older than her at twenty-six, but not that much. But her prospects for marriage and children were dimming with each passing year. If she hit thirty without marriage, she would be considered a young spinster and when you got that said about you, any chance of having a husband and children began vanishing rapidly. She could take a chance on Gurdon turning out to be better than she thought or she could wait on another suitor. However, there was no other suitor in sight. But then again, there never had been. She walked up the path to the house and when she walked through the front screen door, it slammed behind her and she heard her sister ask, "What's wrong?"

Somewhat startled out of her thoughts, Stella replied, "Oh. I'm not sure. I don't know. Why?"

"Well, you look just a little green around the gills and you seem to be just a little distracted. It have somethin' to do with Gurdon?" asked Alma.

"Where's Billy?" asked Stella.

"Down at the store goin' through the ruins to salvage what he can. Why?"

"We need to talk. And yes, you are right. It has to do with Gurdon."

"What did he do?"

"He as much asked me to run off and marry him," said Stella as she sat on the divan.

Alma walked over and sat beside her, saying, "Tell me what was said."

"He wants me to excuse myself from church next Sunday and him and I run off while church is goin' on and go to Burkeville and spend the night there, then go to Leesville the next day and change our names and get married," said Stella as fast as a rushing creek. She continued to sit with her elbows on her knees and her hand pressed against her forehead. "He says he'll have plenty of money later this week and that we can buy our own place and nobody will ever know who we were."

"That's just plumb crazy."

"I know. It don't make much sense to me. But I ain't got no beau and no prospects back home in Gilmer neither. If I don't do this, I'm gonna wind up bein a spinster. I do wanna have kids. Havin' a place of our own sounds nice, a place to raise our young'uns," shaking her head slightly, she turned to Alma and asked, "What do you think?"

"I think the whole thing in crazy. My opinion is he's got a big hole in his screen door and he's too lazy to fix it. Gurdon Marion has never had a reputation for nothin' cept' for bein' lazy. Why, a man his age still livin' at home with his momma and daddy. Most boys have moved out, started an apprenticeship or went to work by time they's fifteen, sixteen at the latest. The boy is a no-account. And how's he gonna pay for all this? He say where he got the money from?" asked Alma, becoming a little agitated.

"No, he didn't. He ain't got it yet, but he said it like it was a sure thing. I understand what you're sayin', but I'm lookin' at the rest of my life. I'm not getting' any younger. I don't have any prospects back home and I ain't met none here, 'cept Gurdon. He may be a little hard around the edges, but sometimes bein' married can change a man," said Stella in her defense.

Alma was becoming more exasperated with her sister's attitude and tried a different approach. "Okay, so let's say you do this. You run away with Gurdon, you go to Leesville, change your names and get married. What happens then? What happens when 'all this money' he got runs out. What you gonna do then? Huh? What happens if he starts hittin' on you? You think 'bout that? What if he turns out to be a steer instead of a bull and you can't have kids? What're you gonna do then? You gonna come back here after everbody knows what happened? You won't be able to go back to Gilmer. Word always travels with you. Always has. Somebody'll find out. Then what're you gonna do?"

Stella began to whimper, shaking her head from side to side. She knew her sister was right, but this was the first time anybody had asked her to marry. And it might be the last. She was caught right between that figurative rock and a hard place.

"I've got a few days to make up my mind. I ain't gotta decide right now. I got time to think on it."

"A week's not much time."

"Not that much time. I told him I'd give him an answer Thursday. Don't say nothin' to Billy, okay. I don't want him knowin 'bout this just yet. Promise me," pleaded Stella.

"Ok. I promise. Don't know 'xactly why, though. You run away with Gurdon, he's gonna find out then for sure. But if you leave church early next Sunday, I'm gonna tell him ever detail."

"That's all I can ask. Thank you, Alma. You know I love you and I need your advice on this. I just got a lot to think on. If you don't mind, I'm gonna go lay down now. I'm mostly wore out."

"You go ahead. I'll call you for lunch," said Alma as she rose and headed to the kitchen.

"Okay. Thank you, Alma. You know I love you."

"I love you too," said Alma over her shoulder. "Just hate to see you make a mistake this big."

Stella rose from the divan and walked to her room. She needed to lay down and think. It turned out sleep would be hard to come by for the next several nights.

23

A Brotherly Visit

As church let out and the faithful left their houses of worship, most went directly home, but many came back by the disaster area or came by for the first time. Most everyone agreed it was a disaster. There was speculation about the future of the town itself; whether it would, or could, rebuild and if so, how and what would it look like?; what would it be like?; would it have the same businesses or new ones? Even on this Sunday, following worship services, there was a great deal of anxiety among the citizens. If the businesses didn't reopen, would there be a future for the town itself? How would the lack of businesses affect them in the short term? The anxiousness of the unknown in the long term was almost palpable.

Sheriff Brown stood in the window of his office and watched the people stroll through the sandy streets. Ladies dressed in their best, the more well off had hats and those that were putting on pretentions carried parasols. The men were mostly in suits, but all were in hats. The more prosperous men wore three-piece suits with a gold chain draped across the vest for quick retrieval of their pocket watch. All had a studious look about them as they surveyed the ruins of the town.

Brown took in the scene and decided that he had to do something, anything to try and drum up a break in the case. He was on the brink of dismissing Frank Marion's involvement entirely and even the notion of questioning banker Tidwell. He thought again about his and Frank's conversation earlier that morning and the discrepancy of the times that Gurdon and Clarence got home. He was pretty sure that he got Clarence Keaghey's attention with the little talk earlier and was hoping that Clarence might be frightened enough to make a mistake he could begin building a case on. But he couldn't count on that. Not much he could count on about this case right now. Gurdon. I need to find Gurdon Marion. Maybe nothing. Maybe something. Maybe Midge is right. If those two were involved, one might talk.

He began reviewing everything that had happened and all that he had been told, from the time he arrived at the fire until now. He talked to Buford, Bob, Billy, Mr. Galvin and Mr. Stone the druggist, Dave Depotti,

Clarence Keaghey and Hector Henry. A thought occurred to him that he had talked to two of the four domino players from last night but still hadn't talked to Gurdon Marion or Oscar Brown, his nephew. *I don't know where Gurdon is, but I can bet I know where Oscar is.* He walked toward the west door, took his hat off the peg, walked through the door, turned, locked it and went down the steps to the street.

Oscar was J.M.'s brother, R.W.'s boy, who still lived at home. The Sheriff began walking toward his brother's house on Peachtree Street. He passed several folks on his way, each stopping to ask who did the dastardly deed. To each he replied that he was investigating as hard as he could and if they thought of anything to let him know.

He turned and walked up the path to R.W.'s house, stepped onto the porch and knocked on the door. Mildred, his sister-in-law, was coming out of the kitchen, wiping her hands on her apron as she came to the door.

"Hey J.M. It's good to see you, come in. You're just in time for dinner."

"I appreciate that, and I think I'll take you up on it," he said with a grin as he stepped inside and removed his hat, "It's been a long day so far."

"Good. R.W. went to the square to see if anybody needed any express freight to rebuild. He should be back in just a bit."

R.W. Brown had a freight company that ran goods and supplies from Bevilport over on the Neches River to the west, Beaumont and Orange to the south and Sabinetown northeast on the Sabine River. He hauled to all points in between and as far north as Lufkin, Nacogdoches and San Augustine. He had more than two dozen wagons, scores of mules to pull them and a semi-parade of muleskinners to operate them.

"OK. Oscar or Olivia around? I ain't seen them in a month of Sundays."

"Olivia went home with a friend, but Oscar's out back gatherin' eggs."

"Mind if'n I go out there to help?"

"Not at all. One of them settin' hens likes to peck. I keep tellin' him if he'll throw a little hen scratch out there that they'll come off the nest."

"Awright. I'll be back in a minute," said J.M. as he walked out the back screen door he put on his hat, the door slamming behind him.

He could see Oscar in the chicken coop and he walked that way. As he opened the gate, he said, "Hey, Oscar. How ya' doin'?"

The young man, startled, turned to see his uncle standing just inside the gate. "Hi, Uncle J.M. How are you?"

"Doin' pretty good. They layin' good?"

"Yeah, they's beginnin' to pick up some since the weathers got warmer." Oscar said this without much thought and his mind began racing about the fact that his uncle was here in the chicken coop with him, and he didn't know why. Uncle J.M. didn't come by that often, usually just special occasions. Most other times was when they happened to run into each other when they were out and about. This was the Sheriff and he knew his uncle well enough to know that it didn't matter who you were when it came to enforcing the law. If he thought you were guilty, he'd arrest you and let the judge and jury figure out the rest.

"Hey, Oscar. I need to ask you about last night."

"Okay. What?"

"You go to the dance last night?"

"Yes, sir. Went with Minnie Marion, Gurdon's sister."

"You take her home?"

"Yes, sir. Walked her home. Got there a little before Barney Robinson and Valley got there. Barney went with Valley."

"What time was that?"

"I reckon bout 11:45."

"Then what did you do?"

"I started for home and ran into Gurdon and Clarence and they was headin' to Nix's store for some malt, so I went with 'em."

"Well, I talked with Dave Depotti and Clarence Keaghey. Both of them said that they and you and Gurdon played dominoes in Billy Nix's store till 'bout 12:30. That right?"

"Yes, sir. That sounds 'bout right. Think I recall hearing the clock tower on the courthouse strike the half 'bout the time I left," said Oscar who as beginning to get a little nervous about the direction this conversation was headed.

"All of y'all leave together, you, Clarence, Jesse and Gurdon?"

"Yes, sir. 'Ceptin' for Dave. He stayed behind to close up the store."

"What'd y'all do after you left?"

"I come home."

"You leave again before the fire?"

"No, sir."

"Anybody see you when you got home?"

"No, sir. Everbody was in bed."

"You know where Gurdon is?"

"No, sir. I ain't seen him since. Might want to talk to Mr. Billy. All Gurdon could do whil'st we was playin' dominoes was talk about Mr. Billy's sister-in-law, Miss Stella."

"Why's that?"

"Well, to hear him tell it, him and her danced every dance last night and said he had eyes for her and that he wanted to marry her. Said she was as sweet as muscadine wine and finer than frog hair. Said she was as beautiful as a field full of daisies. I'm tellin' you Uncle J.M., he's got it bad for her."

"Okay. But you ain't got no idea where he's at right now?"

"No, sir I don't."

"You see him, tell him he needs to come see me right straight, okay?

"Yes, sir. I'll do it."

"Okay. You need any help with them eggs?"

"No, sir. I got it okay."

"Not sure what your momma's cookin', but it smells delicious."

They both walked toward the gate, J.M. unlocked it and stepped through, followed by Oscar and the Sheriff locked it again. They both walked to the back porch and through the screen door into the kitchen with the sound of the slamming door following them inside.

"Y'all wash up now," said Mildred. "Dinner's almost ready."

"Sure smells good," said J.M. earnestly as he walked back outside, screen door slamming again. He went to the washstand on the back veranda and washed his hands, drying them on the cloth from an old sugar sack. He then went back into the kitchen, the screen door making its normal sound, and took a seat at the table. It was then that his brother R.W. came in the front screen door, it slamming closed.

J.M. rose from the table and greeted his brother warmly with a firm handshake, saying, "It's good to see ya'."

"You too," replied R.W. Brown.

"Mildred invited me to dinner. It smells so good I'd invite myself."

"Hard for me to turn down any of Mildred's cookin'. Gotta be one of the best around," R.W. said.

"Well, from the looks of it," said J.M. gazing at his brother's belly, "you ain't been missin' too many of her meals."

They smiled at the gentle teasing that was always a theme between them.

"Y'all go on and sit down now. Dinners ready," said Mildred.

All sat at the table, bowing their heads as thanks were returned. It was the same prayer offered at the table when the boys were growing up and likely the same one their dad heard growing up at their grandparents' table. Now, at least a fourth generation would hear the same words at each meal. R.W. intoned, "Lord, bless this food to the nourishment of our bodies and our souls to thy service. Amen." To which he quickly added, "Pass the biscuits."

24

Where is Gurdon Marion

Following a delicious meal of fried ham, black eyed peas with chili sauce, cabbage, fresh tomatoes, biscuits and banana peppers, Sheriff J.M. Brown sat with his brother on the front gallery catching up on the various family happenings along with what they knew about the burning earlier that morning.

"So, you got nothin' so far 'bout who done the burnin'?" asked R.W.

"Nope. Not a clue, not even a good 'spicion. First thought Frank Marion might have done it, what with his tools and all bein' there and him admittin' they was his. But the more I thought on it, it didn't make no sense he'd do such a thing. Did find a knife close to the counter at Nix's, but it's as much a mystery as a clue. I think Midge is likely to be the rightest 'bout this whole thing. Likely more than one person done it and it's hard to keep a secret when more than one person knows it and even harder when the law's been broke and there's money involved."

"I agree. With nothin' to have for evidence, Midge is likely right about it. But if she is, it may be a while before anybody says somethin'."

"Yep. And everbody wantin' me to arrest whoever done it right now. Hell, if I was to arrest somebody this afternoon, they'd be a crowd at the jail in the mornin' wantin' a trial before noon and a hangin' by sundown."

"You're likely right. Most folks just don't understand. They don't want nobody accused of a crime to have no rights unless it's them that's broken the law, then they can't have enough."

"What's Oscar been up to lately?"

"Nothin' much. Picks up a little work here and there. I get him to drive a team when I'm shorthanded, but he ain't the best skinner I've seen," said R.W. about his son.

"Who's he hangin' around with these days?"

"Same bunch as always, I reckon. Clarence Keaghey, the Robinson boys, Leo Blake, Gurdon Marion and a few others. Why you ask?" inquired R.W. with a quizzical look.

"No reason, really. Just goin' out on a limb here and thinkin' that if he's hangin' out with some of the fellas that done this or the fellas he's hangin' out with are hangin' around some other folks that done it, he might hear somethin'. And if he did, I'd appreciate him lettin' me know 'bout it."

"Hey, Oscar," R.W. hollered toward the screen door. "Come here."

Stirring was heard in the house as Oscar made his way to the brothers. He stepped onto the veranda as the screen door slammed behind him.

"Yes, sir," said Oscar facing his daddy.

"J.M., you tell him what you told me."

"Oscar, I need your help. I need your help in tryin' to figure out who done the burnin' last night. Your daddy tells me you're hangin' around with pretty much the same fellas you always have. I need you to keep your eyes and ears open about the burnin' and if you hear anythin', anythin' at all that might help point to whoever done this, I need you to let me know right straight."

"Yes, sir. I'll do that," said Oscar as sincerely as he could.

"Now don't get it in your head that any of them fellas you know done it. I don't know who done it. But they may hang with some fellas that did do it. So, if some of the fellas you know hint around 'bout they may know somebody that done somethin', I need to know 'bout it. Okay?"

"Yes, sir. I understand. I'll keep my ears open, sure 'nough," said Oscar who hoped his sense of relief that he wasn't under arrest wasn't showing.

"Thank you, Oscar. You datin' anybody these days?"

"Naw, sir. Danced with Minnie Marion last night. She seems right nice. Walked her home after," said Oscar with a slight grin of accomplishment.

"Well, lookie here," said his Uncle, "Tell me, you hold hands did you?"

Oscar flushed just a little, ducked his head slightly, nodded his head up and down and said, "Just a little."

"Ok. You go on. Me and your uncle has stuff to talk about," said R. W.

"Yes, sir. I'll keep my ears open Uncle J.M.," said Oscar.

"I'd appreciated it. Thanks."

Oscar turned to go back into the house and had opened the screen door when his daddy said, "Oscar, I need you first thing in the mornin'. Got freight to pull from Bevilport for some of the folks in town. You be up and ready 'fore daylight, okay?"

"Yes, sir," said Oscar, who then stepped into the house, screen door slamming shut behind him.

"He's a pretty good boy, ain't he R.W.?"

"He is. Needs a little better attitude 'bout work, but it's still better than a bunch of folks I know."

The two brothers fell into silence as they leaned the straight back chairs against the wall of the house, taking in the warm cloudless afternoon. It would have been another quiet peaceful Sunday if the burning hadn't have happened. The pair remained this way for quite some time. They had been very close growing up, being only a year apart, with J.M. being the oldest. The silence between them was never awkward. There was always an unspoken feeling between them that if they would admit it, was the deepest kind of brotherly love there could possibly be.

So, it was with this mutual feeling of contentment that J.M. leaned forward to set all four legs of the chair on the porch, pulled his pocket watch from his vest pocket, opened the lid and noted the lateness of the approaching afternoon.

He stood, stretched, and said, "Well, it has certainly been a long day and I am bushed. I'm fixin' to go back down to the square and see if there's anythin' new. Please tell Mildred that I really did enjoy the dinner. It was really, really good. You know, you and I have been very lucky to have both married such good cooks."

"You're right 'bout that," said R.W. with a grin patting his stomach. "You take care now. If I can be of help, just let me know. And I'll remind Oscar 'bout keepin' his ears open."

"Awright. Thanks. I'll see you next time," said the Sheriff as he stepped off the gallery.

"Tell Midge we all said hello."

"Will do. Y'all take care now." The Sheriff started up the path to the street, turned right and headed back to the square. He was really hoping nothing new had been found so he could head home where he hoped he could find some peace, some quiet and some time to think.

Part Five

25

A Glimmer of Hope

This Monday was different. Not only was Jasper missing half of its businesses, but there was a palpable difference in the attitude and outlook of the people. Folks had come from miles around on Sunday to gawk at the damage done by the fire and they were back again this morning. Staring, shaking their collective heads they wondered who could have done such a thing and why as they muttered to themselves in low, respectful voices.

The fire would be a marker in time for the current and next generation of citizens when talking of events. They would be tagged as either before the fire or after the fire. Such was the distinction of its significance.

These were some of the things that Haymar pondered as he set up the Post Office inside Sorrells Mercantile on the north side of the square. Carl Sorrells had made the offer when he stopped by after church yesterday while Haymar was still salvaging what he could. It was a welcomed offer and one that was readily accepted. The town could do with one less dry goods store, saloon or ice cream parlor, but people depended on the mail and as the Post Office's creed said, "The mail must go through."

Haymar had ridden to Burkeville Sunday afternoon to see Postmaster Sharpe where he got some stamps and other supplies so he could resume service. It had been a long and stressful day yesterday with little time to rest or sleep. He had gotten home shortly after sundown and after stalling his horse, he took a "whore's bath" and went directly to bed, not rising until after sunup this morning.

It was about midmorning when Sheriff Brown came through the door removed his hat and without saying a word, sat down in the chair next to the table the Postmaster was using for a desk.

"And good mornin' to you too," said Haymar smiling.

"That, sir, is the only half fact that I have been told in the last twenty-four hours. It is in fact mornin', just not sure if it's good," said Brown light heartedly.

"Sorry I can't offer coffee. Havin' to run a bare bones operation here."

"I had my coffee at the house this mornin'. Tryin' to avoid the White Swan for a while. Too many folks got questions. Problem is, some of them got the answers too. They don't know a damned thing, which is just as much as I know right now. But they want me to do somethin' 'bout it and they mean right damn now."

"I don't envy you and I damned sure wouldn't want your job right now. You've got a lot of pressure on you. But, to sound like everbody else, any progress on the investigation?"

"Nope. Not a thing. I'm at a dead end. Kinda dependin' on Midge's philosophy to get a break on the case. You got time to sit under the cedar tree for a bit and talk without big ears listenin' in?"

"Well, I can't. Don't have a way of securin' everthing. What about lunch? Sorrells is shuttin' down an hour for lunch. He's got an appointment with Doc Davis."

"Sounds good. I'll bring sandwiches. We can sit under the Cedar Tree. The spit and whittle club ought to be gone by then anyway."

"Alright. Sounds good. See you then," said Haymar as Brown rose from the chair, settled his hat back on his head and headed out the door.

Brown looked at the sky as he stepped onto the wooden sidewalk and thought to himself that it was as gloomy as the mood of most of the town folks. Overcast, humid, and with no breeze to speak of was enough to cast a kind of pall over one's attitude. All this on top of the fire yesterday was enough to make even the most optimistic revival preacher depressed.

He looked down the street to Tidwell's bank and debated whether or not to inquire about Frank Marion and his financials. Without any other leads, it was best that he go ahead and do it. Anybody ever asked, he could say he'd left no stone unturned and do it with a clean conscience.

Looking around, nobody was hardly stirring on the north side of the courthouse. Anything worth seeing was on the south side. So he walked slowly down the street, his boot heel making a sound like someone knocking on a door as his foot hit a loose board. He opened the door to the bank and a small bell rang as he did.

"Mornin', Oliver," said Brown to the teller behind the counter. He was peering out through the bars that ran from just above the counter to the ceiling where they disappeared into a decorative ceiling joist.

"Mornin', Sheriff. You here to see Joshua?"

"I am." Is he in?"

"Yes, sir. Go on back. He's back there in his office."

"Thanks, Oliver," said Brown as he walked through the swinging half gate at the right end of the counter. He could see Tidwell sitting behind an enormous desk with a green eye shade affixed to his head.

"Well, mornin' Sheriff. This is a surprise. What can I do for you?" asked the banker.

"I'm investigatin the burnin' and the only possible lead I've got so far is actually pretty far-fetched, to my way of thinkin'. But I was wonderin' if you might help me to rule it out," said the Sheriff as he began lowering himself into the barrel backed chair across from the banker's desk.

"Whatever I can do, J.M. What do you have?"

"Frank Marion. He havin' any money problems that you know about?"

"Not to my knowin'. He's got a little money. Not rich by a long shot. But I don't see him doin' the deed yesterday. Just can't see it."

"I'm grabbin' at straws right now. You just confirmed what I was thinkin'. I appreciate your time, Joshua," said Brown as he began to rise.

"If I think of anythin' that might possibly help, I'll be sure to let you know J.M."

"Thanks. I need all the help I can get at this point," said Brown as he turned to leave the office.

"Have a good day, Oliver," said Brown as he walked through the lobby to the door.

"You too, Sheriff," he replied.

Brown stepped back out onto the sidewalk, taking in the gloom once again. He looked at the clock tower on top of the courthouse and it was 11:20. Better get on home so Midge can make those sandwiches. He turned right and when he got to the corner at Main Street, a teenage negro boy stepped out onto the sidewalk, stopped and looked at the Sheriff.

"Can I help you, boy?" asked Brown.

"Naw, sir. But maybe perhaps I can help you," said the young man.

"What's your name, boy?"

"Luke. Luke Simpson from up at Remlig. My daddy's Bonaparte Simpson," said the teenager.

"Really? I been knowin' your daddy for years. Your daddy's a good, fine man. He still preachin'?"

"Yes, sir. He am. Still at Mount Horiah CME up there."

"Well, you said you could help me. Help me with what?"

"I seen 'em, Mr. Sheriff. I seen 'em comin' out the back door of Mr. Nix's sto'," he quickly stammered.

"Wait. What? What are you sayin'?" the Sheriff asked confused.

"I seen them fellas runnin' out of Nix's sto' yesti'dy monin' right after'n the 'splosion. There'n were three of 'em. They hightailed it out of there right straight. Didn't waste no time a'tall. No, sir. None a'tall."

"Well, young Mr. Simpson, did you recognize any of 'em?"

"Yes, sir. Yes sir, I did. I did recollect seein' two of 'em. Yes, sir. Could see 'em clear as day from the gas light on the street. Yes, sir. Sho 'nuf seed 'em Mr. Sheriff."

"Okay. Who was they then?"

"That one, he's that Marion boy. I know'd him from the blacksmith shop his daddy got down there by the crick. The other boy was Mr. R.W. Brown's boy. Can't call his name, but it were sure 'nuf him."

"How would you be so certain sure it was them two?"

"They's down at Mr. W.J. Simms livery pretty reg'lar. I work's down there helpin' Mr. Simms. That Marion boy helps his daddy and they come's to the livery ever once in a while and Mr. R.W.'s boy, he always in and out of the livery what with his daddy haulin' freight and such. Always a needin' somethin' for the hosses an' mules or rentin' one or somethin. Yes, sir. I know'd 'em alright."

"You dead sure 'bout this Luke?" asked the Sheriff solemnly.

"Yes, sir. Deadist I could ever be. No doubt, Mr. Sheriff."

"You didn't know the other fella though?"

"Don't know his name. But he be a tall, lanky fella. See him around all the time. Don't see him work none too much though. Seed him mostly with that Marion boy."

"What was you doin' out that late yesterday mornin?"

"Mr. Simms, he a good man. He let me sleep in the livery and pay me fifty cent a week. I goes home to Remlig on Sunday mornin's. Mr. Simms lets me use a mule. I goes back and goes to daddy's church to listen to him preach the word. When it's over and we gets through with dinner, I come on back to Jasper time enough before dark. Any ways, I 'as a sleepin' in the livery when I heard that terrible racket like the world was comin' to an end. I thought to myself, 'It's the rapture fo' sho', but t'wern't. I ran outside to see and that's when I seed them three white boys runnin' out of the back of Nix's sto'. Yes, sir. Just like that."

Brown was stunned. He suspected that Gurdon Marion was involved, but his own nephew. Just didn't sound like Oscar. The third fella had to be Clarence Keaghey. He did appear a little nervous when he was in the office yesterday morning. Then the legal issues began to creep into his mind.

"Okay, thank you Luke. But here is what you can't do. You can't tell nobody what you seen. You understand me? You can't tell nobody. Even Mr. Simms. If'n you do, word might get back to them fellers and they'd run for the hills and I'd never find 'em. You understand, don't you?"

"Yes, sir. I understands. I ain't told nobody else neither and I promise I won't. No, sir. Didn't wanna tell nobody but you. That's a fact, Mr. Sheriff."

"Well, you done the right thing. You comin' and tellin me like you did. You're a good boy. You at the livery ever day?"

"Yes, sir, 'ceptin Sundays. I goes to daddy's church on Sundays."

"Okay. Good. Here," said the Sheriff as he pulled a nickel out of his pocket and handed it to the teen. "You go on over to the drug store and get you a soda and some candy with this."

"Wow, Mr. Sheriff! Thanks a bunch!" With a smile as wide as the Angelina River, he took the nickel and rushed away.

Well, this complicates things, he thought. My only eyewitness was a teenage negro boy who isn't allowed to testify in court against any white folks. Couldn't even use what he saw as evidence. He began pondering how he could get enough on those three boys to throw them in jail without having to disclose anything about the Simpson boy. Weren't going to be easy. But at least he had suspects. But, how was he going to handle Oscar's involvement. It would tear his family apart. If I ever needed to talk with Haymar, it's now. So, he began walking briskly toward home to retrieve the sandwiches.

26

Lunch Under the Cedar Tree

The Postmaster was waiting on the bench under the cedar tree when Brown arrived. He had pushed the dominoes that were always on the table over to one corner so it could be used for their lunch.

"Midge fixed ham and cheese sandwiches. The bread was just comin' out of the oven when I walked through the door. Fresh sliced tomatoes, sweet pickles she put up last week, and a whole jar of canned peaches for dessert. Brought along some lemonade too," said Brown proudly.

"Sounds great. I'm feeling pretty peckish," said Haymar as he took the offered sandwich and fixings. "So, what's new?"

"Not sure what kind of news you got, Bob, but I'll bet my boots that mine will top yours."

"Well, do tell then."

"You know that negro works over at Simms livery. That Simpson boy?"

"Yes, I do. Bonaparte's boy from up at Remlig. He comes to the Post Office every once in a while to give me a few cents or a nickel to keep in the safe for him."

"Well, he stopped me on the way home after I talked to you. Said he seen three white boys run out the back of Nix's after the explosion. Said there was Gurdon Marion and Clarence Keaghey, but didn't know the other'n," said the Sheriff, hoping his delivery was smooth and gave no hint of him telling the fib.

"Well, I'll be. Think on it a bit and it kinda starts makin' some sense."

"I talked with Clarence yesterday mornin' at the jail. He seemed a bit fidgety but didn't seem real nervous. Said Frank told him that I wanted to talk to him and came on over. Beats me why he would do that. Come over to the jail to talk with me when he's one of the one's that done it."

"Most likely tryin' to throw you off the scent. A nice little psychological move, you ask me. You already doubtin' he did it just a little bit, aren't you? Yep. He's playin' some mind games with you."

"Well, I'm through playin'. I'm sure he's probably left town by now and nobody knows where Gurdon is, includin' his daddy. I'll bet if I find one, I'll find t'other."

"I wouldn't bet against that, Sheriff," said Haymar as both men turned to their meal.

They were just finishing the peaches when there was the distinctive sound of someone riding a horse hurriedly toward the square. When both men looked up, they saw Deputy Wayne rounding the corner at Austin Street heading for the jail. The Deputy happened to look up and see the Sheriff and quickly turned the horse, kicking up a cloud of dust as he did so. He barely got the horse stopped before he shouted, "Lowell's dead!"

"Do what?" asked the Sheriff incredulously.

"Lowell's dead," repeated the Deputy excitedly. "Out toward Jamestown, just this side of the Little Sandy. Looks like he got throwed out the wagon."

"How far out?" asked Brown, rising from the bench.

"'Bout two miles. I just happened up on it. Been out to the Barton place lookin' for Samuel. Me and him was headin' back to town and found Lowell layin' in the road. Hit his head on a big rock. The right front wheel was off the wagon. I left Samuel there with him and come to town to find you," said Wayne still excited and nervous.

"Okay. You head on back out there. I'm fixin' to go saddle Molly and I'll be right there. Don't let nobody move or touch nothin' till I get there, you understand?"

"Yes, sir. Anythin' else?" inquired the Deputy as he was already turning his horse back to the east.

"Nope. Don't be surprised if Samuel ain't there when you get back. Just don't want none of them animals getting' to Lowell. Bob, I need your help. You mind fetchin' Pastor Lonnie over to my house? I'm gonna get him and Midge to go over to Oleta's to be with her."

"I'm on my way right now," said Haymar, starting toward the parsonage.

"And go over to Burl Easley's mortuary and have him bring his hearse," hollered Brown as they both headed in separate directions. "And go down to Simms livery and ask him to come out with stuff to fix the wagon too."

"Got it," shouted Haymar over his shoulder, not slowing his brisk walk.

As Brown walked briskly toward home, he thought about the reality of the situation. There was nothing else that could be done for Lowell, if he was dead like Andrew said. The aftermath would certainly be bad. Oleta would be devastated. But she had a really strong faith and Lonnie was as good a pastor as there was anywhere around. Just what else is going to happen, he thought. Half the town burned down yesterday. The mayor gets himself killed today. Finally got an eyewitness to the burning and it turned out to be a negro boy that, under state law, can't testify against a white man in court. Which, given Oscar's likely involvement, is not a bad thing. But he was sure that the other two prime suspects had done fled the country. They might be in Arkansas by now. So, I'm almost back where I started. Well, wonder what crisis tomorrow's going to bring.

Brown strode briskly into his house, didn't remove his hat, and as the screen door slammed behind him, he hollered, "Midge!"

"Out here," she said from the back yard where she was hanging clothes on the line.

Brown walked out the back screen door, and it began to slam just as the front had stopped. "Midge! Quick! I need your help! Lowell's been killed in a wagon wreck. Front wheel came off, threw him out of the wagon and he hit his head on a rock. Andrew found him 'bout two miles out toward the Little Sandy. I got Haymar to go fetch Lonnie over here and I need you to go with him over to Oleta's and stay with her until I get back."

"Oh, Lord. Oh, Lord, no. Oh, Lord," was all Midge could say as she stood there holding wet clothes in her hands.

"Put them clothes back in the basket and take 'em back inside and get ready for Lonnie. Go on now," said Brown in as soothing and gentle voice as he could muster. "I'm fixin' to saddle Molly and ride out there. I'll be back soon as I can."

Midge wasn't moving. She was frozen in place with only her head shaking back and forth in disbelief. Brown walked over to his wife and put his arms around her and gently whispered in her ear, "I need you to be strong right now, Midge. Oleta needs you to be strong right now too. You go on in the house and I'll hang the rest of the clothes. I'll be right in behind you in two shakes of a lamb's tale." He released her, placing both hands on her shoulders and looking her in the eye. "You'll be okay, now. You've got important work to do. Oleta is really goin' to need somebody to lean on right now. I need you to be strong and so does Oleta. Go ahead. Go on in and get ready."

She stood on her tip toes, tilted her head up and gave him a soft brief kiss on the cheek. "I'll be awright now." She then stepped around her husband and went into the house, screen door slamming once again.

He finished hanging the rest of the clothes on the line, went in the house, with the ever-present slamming screen door doing its normal job, and set the empty basket on the kitchen table. He went into their bedroom where he found Midge had changed clothes and was brushing her hair.

"You okay?" asked the Sheriff.

"I will be. You're right. I've got to be strong now. I'll be fine. You need to get goin'. I hope he just got knocked out and not killed," said Midge.

"I'm afraid it's wishful think' at this point," he then stood behind her, put his arms around her waist and gave her a light kiss on her neck. "I'll see you at Oleta's, okay?"

"Okay. You need to get goin'," she replied.

He turned and walked back through the house and out to the small barn, opened the door and walked over to Molly's stall. "Hey there old gal," he said as he gently stroked her neck. "Come on now. We've got work to do." He walked her to the tack room door, went in, got the tack and began the process of saddling her. He then led her outside, mounted, and started a fast walk. When the pair got to the courthouse square, Molly was warmed up and he increased the pace to a lope.

27

The Notification

Midge heard the knock on the door and knew it was the pastor. She hollered "Come on in Lonnie." She was in the bedroom finishing putting her hair up when she heard the screen door slam. "I'm 'bout ready," she said loud enough to be heard.

She was adjusting her bonnet as she walked out of the bedroom and saw Lonnie standing in the parlor. "This is terrible business, just terrible," said Midge.

"I agree. There's nothin' good 'bout it a' tall. All we can do is try to comfort her the best we can. We can't make the pain go away or make her bein' frightened go away. All we can do is be there and offer what help and support we can."

"Oleta is a good friend. My heart aches for her. Lord, I don't know what she's gonna do now. It's awful. Just awful."

"Well, we best be getting' over there. I'd hate for her to hear it from Georgette Philpott or one of the other gossips."

"Okay, let's go," said Midge as they walked to the front door, Lonnie holding the screen door open for her and after stepping through, letting it go to slam shut.

They walked the three blocks to Oleta's house, not saying a word and barely looking up. The silence gave them both time to think and hopefully come up with something comforting to say.

"I think you ought to be the one to tell her," said Midge. "I don't think nothin' hardly is gonna comfort her hearin' the news, but comin' from a pastor might soften the blow just a bit."

"Okay. I guess so. This is the worst part of my job. Havin' to tell somebody that the Lord has taken one of their loved ones. They don't understand why and for the life of me, I can't ever rightly explain it to nobody. Most times, my words feel empty to me. But I just have to trust in the Lord to guide me to be the best comfort I can to the bereaved," said Lonnie just as they arrived at the path to Oleta's front door.

Midge took the path first, followed closely by Pastor Lonnie. Midge gently knocked on the door and quickly saw Oleta coming from the back of the house, wiping her hands on her apron.

"Well, I'll swun. Y'all come on in now," said Oleta as she pushed the screen door open.

They followed Oleta into the parlor. "Can I get y'all some tea or lemonade?"

"No thank you," said Lonnie. "Oleta, we need to sit down."

Oleta and Midge sat on the divan while Lonnie continued to stand. He then went over and kneeled in front of Oleta. Reaching out and taking both her hands he said, "Oleta, I'm very sorry, but this isn't a social call. I'm afraid we have some terrible news. It's about Lowell. He's been in a wagon accident and I'm afraid he's been killed."

"Well, I'm right sure you don't know what you're talkin' 'bout," replied Oleta with a wild look in her eyes. "That just can't be true. What kind of cruel joke is this any way?" She had no more gotten the words out of her mouth than her hands began to tremble and her bottom lip began to quiver.

Midge put her arm around her shoulder and when she did, Oleta began deep, long sobs. Continuing to hold her hands Lonnie said, "Oleta. We are here to help you. Whatever you need, we are here to help. Is there someone who we can get for you or can we get you anything?"

All Oleta could do was sob and shake her head.

All Midge and Lonnie could do was be there for her, hoping it would bring her some comfort.

It was going to be a very long afternoon.

28

The Wreck

Brown rounded the curve past the Reed place and that's when he saw it. It was basically just as Andrew had described it. He rode up to the back of the wagon, dismounted and tied Molly to the left rear wheel.

He walked over to where his Deputy was standing with Samuel Barton, close to where Lowell Goates, the late mayor of Jasper lay lifeless, covered with a blanket.

Nodding to both men in turn, Brown acknowledged them, saying, "Andrew, Samuel." He then bent down and pulled the blanket back, beginning at the head until the whole body was exposed.

There was no doubt about what had happened. The right front wheel of the wagon laid partly under it. There was a good-sized rock under Lowell's head. Lowell had bled enough that blood had run down the rock into the dirt. He covered Lowell back up.

He turned to the Deputy and asked, "When you first got here, you see any tracks or footprints around the wagon or around Lowell?"

"No, sir. Didn't see nothin'. Them prints the horses made, you can see where we come from the east, then you can see one set goin further east, that'd be me goin' to town to get you. Then there's two sets comin back from town, one of 'em's mine and the other'n is yours."

"Well, it's pretty clear to me it was definitely and accident. Don't rightly know of nobody that would go to this much trouble to kill nobody. What with buryin' a rock half in the ground and takin' a wheel off the wagon and then pickin' up the wagon and puttin' it under there. Definitely an accident. I asked Bob to get Burl Easley out here with the hearse and to get Simms livery out here with stuff to fix the wagon, so all we got to do now is wait."

"What about Mrs. Oleta," asked Wayne.

"Had Bob to tell Lonnie to get over to our house so's he and Midge could go over and give Oleta the bad news. Midge was pretty upset, but she's a strong woman. I don't know what Oleta'll do. I 'spect she'll fall apart. But, I'll tell ya' one thing. This part right here is a whole lot easier than what Lonnie and Midge are doin' right now."

They all stood around for a few moments looking at the late mayor and finally the Sheriff said, "Not doin' nobody no good standin' here like this. Sun's getting' hot. Let's get in the shade over there under that chinquapin tree." The trio then ambled over and sat a fallen log and began making small talk among themselves.

"Samuel, Andrew never said what he was out here getting' you for. What is it?"

Wayne interrupted and said, "Old lady Turner came to the office this morning and said she seen Samuel stealin' one of her goats. Seen him leadin' it off with a rope 'round its neck. So, I told her I'd go out there and see about it. Rode up to Samuel's place and there he is, skinnin' a goat out behind the barn. Kinda "red handed" as they say."

"Well, Samuel, you admit you done it?" asked the Sheriff.

"Yes, sir. I done it awright. I was hungry, Sheriff. Man can't live off peas and tomatoes all the time. We's dirt poor and just wanted some meat."

"You know what. I think that you admittin to it and the fact that you didn't run away when Andrew left you here is mightily admirable. You stayin' here to guard our mayor speaks very highly. Some might call you a minor hero. I think that this here good deed is payment enough for any crime you might have committed involvin' any goat. You're free to go on back home whenever you like."

"Really, Sheriff? Wow. Thank you. I really do appreciate this, I really do," said Samuel as he rose from the log and offered his hand to Brown.

The Sheriff stood, took his hand, shook it vigorously and added, "But no more stealin' goats, right?"

"No sir, Sheriff. None at all," replied Samuel with a grin. He then stuck out his hand to the Deputy. Wayne took it saying, "No hard feelin's, okay?"

"Naw. None at all. Thanks, fellas." He walked to his horse, mounted and with a wide grin, waved to the pair of lawmen as he rode back east.

About an hour passed when the pair heard a wagon coming from towards town. As it rounded the curve, they could see it was Burl Easley with his hearse. Easley pulled up close to the body and dismounted.

"Afternoon, gentlemen," he said as his feet hit the ground.

"Afternoon, Burl. What do you need us to do?" asked the Sheriff.

"Let me get this stretcher out of the back here," he said opening the rear door of the hearse. Once he removed the stretcher, he walked over to where Lowell lay and laid it down parallel to the body.

"Okay, fellas, I need the two of you to roll him over on his side away from the stretcher. When you do, I'm gonna slide the stretcher under him far as I can and then y'all roll him over on it. Okay?"

"Awright, whenever you're ready," said Easley as he squatted down next to the stretcher.

Brown and Wayne were on the other side of the body, the Sheriff on the shoulders and Wayne on the hips. They pulled the body toward them as Easley moved the stretcher under it with a single smooth move. "Okay. Let him down," said Easley. The pair complied, gingerly allowing the late mayor to roll completely onto the canvas.

"Okay. Now then you fellas get the end at the head and I'll grab the feet. Your end goes in first," said Easley as they all moved into place. "Okay, on three. One. Two. Three." All lifted at once and moved to the rear of the hearse. The lawmen laid their end of the stretcher inside as Easley pushed from his end until the entire thing was inside.

"Whose blanket?" asked Easley.

"Oh. That was Samuel's. Guess he forgot it, he was so quick to leave," said Wayne.

"Mind if I keep it to get back to town?" asked Easley.

"Not at all," replied the Sheriff. "If he wants his blanket back, he'll figure out where to find it."

"Awright, gentlemen. There's nothin' left for me to do here. Anybody tell Oleta yet?"

"Yeah. Midge and Pastor Lonnie are with her now," said Brown.

"Gonna be a real rough patch for that woman. Might just be a little bit of relief, way Lowell's been actin' lately," opined Easley.

"Might be," said the Sheriff without any real conviction.

"Awright, I'll be seein' you gentlemen," said Easley as he mounted the hearse and snapped the reins to urge the horses on.

"Take care, Burl," said the Sheriff as Easley drove away.

As Easley and his hearse entered the curve toward town, Simms and the Negro boy passed him headed toward the lawmen. They watched as the hearse disappeared around the corner and the livery wagon got closer.

Simms pulled the livery wagon alongside the wrecked one, stopped the mules and he and the boy dismounted.

"Afternoon fellas," said Simms.

Both men replied with the same greeting.

Simms and the Negro boy silently went to the right front of the wrecked wagon to see what had caused the wreck, followed by both lawmen.

"Whadda ya' think?" asked Brown.

"Looks like the pin come out," said Simms. "Bet you go back down the road a piece, you'll find it. Shame bout this. Just a real shame. Lowell was a decent fella. Been kinda out a sorts lately, but deep down a good decent fella."

"I think everbody will agree with you on that," said Brown.

"Okay. Luke, get that fulcrum out the back of the wagon and I'll get the lever. Hub looks okay enough and the wheel looks awright. I think all we need to do is put another pin in it and it'll be good. You fellas mind helpin' Luke hold down the lever so's we can get the wheel back on?"

"Not t' all," replied Wayne.

The repairs were made in short order and Simms drove the repaired wagon up the road a piece and back to make sure it was okay, then studied the pin to make sure this one wouldn't fall out.

"Who's gonna drive this rig back to town?" asked Simms.

"I am," said the Sheriff. "I'll take it to Lowell's house. I'm sure Oleta's gonna have questions 'bout what happened from somebody that was out here. Not lookin' forward to that conversation, though."

"Don't envy you a bit. Well, we done all we can do here. I'll see y'all back in town." He snapped his reins and the mules began their trek back toward Jasper, the teenage Negro sitting alongside.

Brown tied Molly to the back of the wagon and mounted it. "Andrew, it's gonna be close to dark by the time we get back. You go on home and I'll take care of everthing else for the rest of today. I'll see ya' at the jail tomorrow."

"Sure thing, Sheriff. You don't mind I ride ahead so as not to have to eat your dust all the way back, do ya'?"

"Not a bit. You go on ahead. I'll see ya' tomorrow."

"Okay, then. You watch out for that pin so's you don't wind up like Lowell, now," said Wayne with a grin.

The two parted ways, with it not taking long for the Deputy to disappear ahead of the Sheriff. There wasn't much for him to do on the way back to town except to think. Damned if I don't need one more thing to happen to make me go off my chump he thought. Then he began thinking about the conversation laying ahead of him with Oleta. He went through dozens of scenarios and finally decided all he could do was offer his sympathies and to tell her the truth about what happened. Finally settling on how to handle one more stressful situation, he looked up and realized he was already in town.

29

The Town Comes Together

The funeral for Mayor Lowell Goates was a fine affair attended by an overflow crowd that spilled out of the Methodist Church. There were common folks and uncommon folks in attendance. Most of the merchants in town were there along with community leaders, county officials and even Congressman Samuel Cooper was there to honor the late Mayor. Pastor Lonnie Furth did an admirable job of recounting the late Mayor's best qualities and avoiding those that were not quite so flattering. As always, he did his best to try and comfort the family and loved ones. He studiously avoided trying to save souls or encouraging everyone to find Jesus now.

The pallbearers were dressed in their finest dark suits all with ties and polished shoes or boots. They were some of the leaders in the community and included Sheriff Brown, District Judge Matt Davidson, Dr. Charlie Davis, Hector Henry and County Judge Lester Bartlett. Burl Easley did a masterful job on making the mayor presentable so as to have an open casket.

Oleta Goates had been inconsolable for the last three days; she wouldn't eat and couldn't sleep. She would sit silently just staring off into nothing and then without any provocation that anyone could discern, would begin to cry, light sniffles at first and gradually increasing to wails of despair. She couldn't sit still and she didn't want to move. She hadn't smiled at anything since the news on Monday. Nothing anyone said was comforting. Her sister, Pauline Anderson, had arrived the next day from San Augustine and even she couldn't assuage her grief. Pastor Lonnie tried his best but couldn't get through to her, and neither could her closest friends. She was absolutely distraught.

The entire attendance walked behind the hearse and pallbearers to the cemetery, located about a quarter mile north of the square on Main Street. It was a nice plot that was shaded by a large red oak tree. Pastor Lonnie, as everyone would later remark, did a fine job not only at the service, but the final prayer at the graveside was one of the best many had ever heard.

Following the service at the cemetery, the majority of the crowd walked back behind the church where several church ladies had prepared food for everyone. Fried chicken, fried ham, chicken and dumplings, fresh peas, corn, tomatoes, cornbread, several different pies and a few cakes along with sweet iced tea and lemonade were spread out on the long narrow tables between two oak trees. Oleta sat next to her sister with a plate in her lap, just staring at it, making no move to avail herself of the nourishment it could provide and that she needed so badly.

Judge Matt Davidson walked over to Oleta to once again express his and his wife Eddie Mae's sincere condolences which she seemed to scarcely acknowledge. Noticing this, Judge Davidson looked at Pauline and indicated with a look and movement of his head that he wanted to speak with her privately. He turned and walked closer to the back of the church and stopped under a pine tree to wait for her to arrive.

"You wanted to talk to me?" asked Pauline, stopping near the Judge.

"Yes. I'm really worried about Oleta. I've seen things like this before and if somethin' isn't done right straight or somebody's not with her all the time, it could be real bad. Are you goin' to be stayin' with her for a while?"

"I talked to my husband long distance last night. I told him how Oleta was doin' and I told him I was afraid to leave her alone. He said to take her back home with me to San Augustine and that's just what I'm gonna do. You think the house will be okay while she's gone?"

"It'll be fine. Neighbors will keep a good eye on it. I'm just worried about Oleta, though. You know, Lowell hadn't been actin' too husbandly-like lately and Oleta was on the edge already."

"Didn't know nothin' 'bout that. Oleta's always been pretty private. Never said nothin' in any of her letters. What was it he'd been doin'?"

"Well, not to speak out of turn or ill of the dead, but Lowell had taken to drinkin' a whole lot more than he probably should have. He'd get liquored up and then start accusin' Oleta of all kinds of things that, in my opinion, Oleta not only would never do, but would never even dream about. The Sheriff even went and talked with him last week' 'bout his drinkin' and his behavior toward Oleta. Didn't do no good, though. No good a 'tall."

"Well, I think maybe a change of scenery might do her some good. Get out of that house. Got to many memories in there. From what you're tellin' me some of them memories probably ain't very good."

"I think you're doin' the right thing by Oleta. I know she'll be in good hands. When you think y'all will head back to San Augustine?"

"A few days. Maybe on Monday. Give her a chance to say goodbye to her friends and her church family on Sunday. Think I'll phone my husband long distance and get him to head this way with our wagon so we can carry whatever she wants to take with her."

Judge Davidson took one of Pauline's hands, held it with both of his, looked her in the eye and said, "I want you to promise me that if there is anything I can do, anything at all, you will let me know. Lowell was a good friend of mine and Oleta is one of the best people I've ever known. Will you promise me that?" he asked sincerely as he looked her in the eyes.

"Your offer is very generous and very kind and it is much appreciated. I will certainly take you up on it if the need arises," she said as he let go of her hand. "Thank you Judge, you are very kind." She turned and walked back to her sister.

30

In the Judge's Chambers

After the tragedy with the Mayor, Brown put the explosion investigation on the back burner. But, just because he hadn't been actively investigating the burning didn't mean he wasn't thinking about it every waking hour.

He had decided that he was going to do all he could to keep Oscar's name out of all of it. After thinking on the whole picture for the past few days, he had decided that the colored boy had probably seen Dave Depotti run out of the back of the store instead of Oscar. Depotti was about the same size and height, and from a distance and without good light, it would be hard to tell, even for a white man.

With this mindset, he decided that his primary suspects were Gurdon Marion, Clarence Keaghey and Dave Depotti. He hadn't been able to find Gurdon since the fire and after talking with Keaghey that Sunday, he had also disappeared. Depotti was still working with Billy Nix so he wouldn't be hard to find. He decided that Depotti likely wasn't going anywhere anytime soon and that before talking to him, it would be best to find Gurdon and Clarence and interrogate them first.

The only problem with this plan was that he didn't have any proof that any of them were involved. Only the word of a teenage colored boy.

He thought on this while leaned back in his chair with his feet propped up on his desk. If there was just a way that Simpson boy could testify in court, it would surely help his case. There had to be a way around the law on that. Someway that would allow a Negro to testify against a white man.

The only person in Jasper County that might know a way around it would be Judge Davidson. And as that thought crossed his mind, he swung his feet off the desk, walked to the door, shouted to the reception area over his shoulder, "Andrew, I'll be back in about an hour." He picked his hat off the peg settled it on his head and stepped outside into a pleasant morning breeze.

He walked across the grass to the south courthouse door and up the stairs to Judge Davidson's office. He opened the heavy oak door that had a large opaque glass panel in the top half that had 'Matt Davidson, Judge, First Judicial District' written on it in gold leaf. He opened the door and stepped into the reception area, finding the Judge's secretary, Horace Ebarb working busily behind the desk.

"Mornin', Sheriff," said Ebarb.

"Mornin', Horace," he said, taking off his hat. "Judge in?"

"Nope. He's in court. Got several cases this mornin'. Shouldn't be long though. You want to wait in his office?"

"Nah. I think I'll sneak into the courtroom and watch till he's through. Thanks Horace."

Brown walked back into the second-floor hallway and removed his hat again as he pulled on the courtroom door. There were several men sitting on benches behind the defense table, but no lawyer on that side of the courtroom. Gilbert Powell, the District Attorney was standing behind the other table for the prosecution and very earnestly addressing Judge Davidson. Powell was a stern looking fellow in his mid-forties with his most distinguishing feature being his huge nose. It was long, crooked, bulbous and pock marked.

"Your honor, Mr. Sawyer is charged with aggravated assault. The Grand Jury saw fit to indict him on that charge as he admitted he willfully shot Charles Cawthorn on the night of July fourth and ended up wounding Mr. Cauthorn in the left thigh," said Powell.

Judge Davidson looked over at the defendant and asked, "You care to explain why you shot at Cawthorn?"

"Yes, sir, Judge," said Sawyer, "See, he come over to the house late after all of us had gone to bed just a beatin' on the front door and hollerin' to let him in. I went to the door and asked what he wanted and he said he wanted to go to bed. I didn't know the fella and wasn't 'bout to let him into the house, much less spend the night. He started getting' real mad and I had my pistol and then he starts like he's gonna attack me, so I shot him in the leg to stop him. I did."

"So, you were trying to protect your family is really what you were tryin' to do. Is that right?" asked Davidson.

"Yes, sir. That's right Judge."

"Well, you can't go around shootin' people. You got your crops laid by?"

"Yes, sir Judge."

"Okay, then. Seven days in the county jail and the next time you shoot somebody I won't be as easy," the Judge admonished.

"Yes, sir, Judge. Yes, sir."

"I see Sheriff Brown in the back there. You go on home and get your business straightened out and report to the jail in the mornin' first thing," instructed Davidson.

"Yes, sir, Judge," he turned and walked through the bar gate and out the west door of the courtroom, nodding to the Sheriff on his way out.

"You have another case?" Davidson asked the District Attorney.

"Yes, your honor. One more. Mr. Nathan Nesbitt."

"Mr. Nesbitt, rise and be sworn in by the bailiff," ordered Davidson.

Nesbitt rose, walked to the witness box, was instructed to raise his right hand and was given the oath to tell the truth by John Capps, an old frail stooped gentleman who had been the court bailiff as long as memory would serve. Nesbitt said 'I do' and then sat down.

"Mr. Nesbitt, you are accused of the theft of a full-grown sow from Mr. Bernard Self. After being caught with the stolen hog you admitted to the crime, is that correct?" asked Powell.

"Yes, sir."

"You want to explain to the court how we came to know it was Mr. Self's hog?"

"Had Self's notches in her ear."

"You want to tell the court why you stole the hog?"

"No, sir. Don't rightly think I do."

"The state rests, your honor," said Powell.

"You got anything to say in your defense?" asked the Judge.

"No, sir. I don't reckon," replied Nesbitt.

"Okay, then. I find you guilty and sentence you to thirty days in the county jail," said Davidson with a bang of his gavel.

In astonishment, Nesbitt jumped up, and looking at the Judge incredulously, said, "Judge, that other feller shot somebody and he got seven days. All I did was steal a hog and I'm getting thirty days? That just don't seem fair, Judge. Ain't fair at all. A feller that tries to kill somebody gets fewer days than a feller does that just steals a hog? Ain't fair, Judge. Ain't fair. Why come?"

"It's simple," replied the Judge, "I've known a lot of men that needed to be shot, but I ain't never known of a hog that needed to be stole. You report to Sheriff Brown at the jail first thing in the mornin'."

Nesbitt stepped down from the witness box, still stunned at what had just happened and, without acknowledging the Sheriff, walked out of the courtroom.

"You got anything else, Gilbert?" asked Davidson.

"No, Judge. That's it for today."

"Okay, then. Court is adjourned," he said with a final bang of the gavel.

Davidson took the two steps down from behind the bench and headed to his chambers' door. As he did, Brown followed him into the office. The pair shook hands and after removing his robe and settling in his chair asked, "Guess you need to see me about something. What can I do for you, J.M.?"

"Well, Judge. I need some help. I actually need a legal opinion, I think. Nope. More likely an opinion on how to get around a law," he said, studying the law books along one wall.

"Okay," said the Judge slowly. "You're gonna have to tell me a little somethin' about what you're talkin' about."

'It's about the burnin'. I don't have no proof of nothin'. However, I got an eyewitness that says he seen three suspects run out of the back of Nix's store right after the s'plosion."

"Don't sound like a problem to me. You just put him on the stand and let him testify. You got an eyewitness, you pretty well got a sewed-up case," opined the Judge.

"See. That's the problem. The way I understand it, he can't testify 'cause he's colored."

"Who did he see run out the store? White folks or Negros?"

"Three white boys."

The Judge stared at the Sheriff as the Sheriff stared back. The Judge then reached to the front corner of his desk and removed a briar pipe from the pipe stand, opened the tobacco box, stuffed the pipe, took out a match, struck it on the bottom of the middle desk drawer and lit his pipe. He then turned sideways in his swivel chair and stared at the law books the Sheriff had been looking at earlier. Nothing was being said between the two. The magistrate was obviously thinking of a legal way to allow a colored man to testify against white men.

Finally, the Judge said, "How old is this colored man?"

"Sixteen. He's Bonaparte Simpson's boy from up at Remlig."

"Damned if this ain't a fix," said the Judge shaking his head and gesturing with his pipe, "J.M., you got two issues you got to get around. First is that no colored person can testify against a white man in a court of law in the state of Texas. Now, they can testify against another colored man, but never a white man. And even if you was to get around that, cause he ain't eighteen he isn't allowed to testify regardless if he's white or colored. You got yourself an eyewitness. That's all the evidence you got and you can't use it in court. I'm real sorry J.M., but there's absolutely no way around it. Wish there was. But even if I ruled you could, the defense would object and even if I overruled his objection and you got a conviction, it'd more than likely be overturned on appeal. It's a no-win situation. Yep. You're goin' to have to get some other evidence. I'm really sorry but I just don't see a way around it."

The Sheriff sat with his head down, staring at the hat in his hands and was slowly shaking his head. "I was afraid of that. I knew that if anybody anywhere would know how to get around it, it'd be you. You was my best hope. But I appreciate you tellin' me like it is so's I don't waste any time tryin' to figure out some kind of other way to get it done."

"You know, I feel pretty certain that if a boy of Bonaparte Simpson said he saw somethin', it would be the truth. Bonaparte has raised his whole family right. Problem with the law is, even if it'd been Bonaparte that seen them, even with him bein' a preacher and all, he still wouldn't be allowed to testify. Damned shame too. Most of these colored's is good people. They work hard, don't cause no trouble, keep to themselves and, for the most part, are in church ever Sunday. I know a lot of colored folks I'd rather be with, talk with and work with than a whole bunch of white folks. Yes, sir. Actually wouldn't mind if Bonaparte and his family was my next door neighbors. They're such good, honest, hard-workin' folks. But damnit, the law's the law and I can't change it."

"I understand that he can't testify, but is there any way to get what he seen into evidence durin' the trial?"

"I can't think of any."

"What if the Simpson boy was to tell a notary what he seen, the notary wrote it down word for word and the Simpson boy signed it with an "X". We could use that as evidence. Wouldn't nobody know who signed it," said Brown trying to circumvent the law.

"Won't work. First thing the defense lawyer will do is call the notary to testify and simply ask him who it was that made the statement and who was it that signed with an 'X'. Besides, knowin' Bonaparte, that boy can read and write. He's not gonna be illiterate. Just won't work."

"Well, it was worth a try. Anyways, how's Eddie Mae doin'?"

"She's doin' right well, thanks for askin'."

"So, what about the kids?"

"They're fine. We got thirteen grandkids now. Need a list to remember all their names."

"Where's they all at these days?"

"They's all scattered all over hell and half of Georgia. Don't get to see 'em much. They pretty much all come back for Christmas and for the family reunion next week. But, other than that, that's 'bout all we get to see 'em."

"Yeah, we're fortunate we got half ours here in town, so we get to spoil 'em quite a bit. At least Midge does," said the Sheriff as he rose from his chair. "I just wanted to stop by and see if there were anything could be done bout lettin' the Simpson boy testify. I appreciate you settin' me straight. Now I gotta work out just how I'm gonna get enough evidence to arrest them boys."

"J.M., if there's one thing I know about you to be the absolute truth, if there is a way, you will figure it out and it will be the right way."

"Thanks Matt. Hopefully I'll be seein' you in court soon with these boys as guests of the county," replied the Sheriff with a half-hearted grin.

"On that I would bet. Good luck to you. Let me know if I can help."

"Thanks again, Matt. Tell Eddie Mae that Midge and I said hello," he said as he turned toward the door.

"I will. And you tell Midge that we said hello also."

Brown was closing the door to chambers and he looked at Horace and said, "See ya', Horace."

"Awright. Good luck to you, Sheriff."

He walked into the hall and down the steps to the first floor and stepped out the south side door of the courthouse into a drizzling rain. 'Bout right, he thought. Matches my mood right now. He pulled up the collar on his shirt, pulled his hat tight on his head and walked to the jail.

31

McReynolds Cafe

Thursday afternoon had all the evidence of a rain that wouldn't let up. The clouds were rolling in from the north, even though the wind was blowing from the south. Early summer rains were unpredictable. Sometimes they brought brief showers that quickly passed. Other times they would produce deluges that would slack off after a few hours but leave lingering showers that might last for days.

Gurdon Marion was careful on his way to McReynolds Cafe, walking through the backyards and keeping to the alleys behind the stores. He'd been hiding in plain sight at home. His folks and his sisters were in on the conspiracy. His daddy, Frank, had told him the Sheriff wanted to talk to him. Clarence had stopped by after he had the conversation with the Sheriff at the jail last Sunday. No telling who else the Sheriff had told about wanting to talk to him. But he had to take this chance. He had to meet Stella. This might be their destiny.

Gurdon walked in the front door of McReynolds as the small bell attached to the facing above the door signaled there was a customer.

He took a seat as far from the front window as possible, just in case the Sheriff happened to walk by.

"Afternoon. Can I help you?" asked the young waitress.

"Not just yet. I'm meetin' somebody. We'll order when she gets here," he replied.

He had a wait alright. It was only twelve thirty, so he again went over in his mind what he wanted to say to her. He didn't think she put much stock in the love side of the equation but did in the prospect of being taken care of and maybe having children. She wasn't getting any younger even though she was just twenty-two, she was in the waning years of her childbearing window. That window had just begun to start closing and he figured she might be getting a little anxious about not turning into a spinster.

He heard the bell on the door tinkle and looked up to see Stella, resplendent in a modest blue dress with small flowers imprinted on it. She walked to the back of the cafe, parasol in hand. Gurdon stood and said, "My goodness you look pretty," to which Stella blushed just slightly.

"Let's get some iced tea," he said as the waitress approached. "We'll take two iced teas. Sweet, please."

"You ready to order?" she asked.

"Not just yet. Let us look at the menu for a minute."

"Okay. I'll be back with your drinks in a jiffy."

"You look awful pretty today, Stella, at least as pretty as you was at the dance. Maybe prettier," said Gurdon, stumbling with words.

"Thank you," she replied.

They were conversing in small talk about the coming storm, the fire and the tragedy of Lowell Goates.

Finally, Gurdon said, "Stella, you thought anymore bout what we talked about on Sunday?"

"It's all I been thinkin bout. Can't rightly think 'bout nothin' else. Nothin' else would come in my head."

"Well. What do you say?"

"I can't. Not now, at least. This is all too sudden like. I ain't got no money and you don't neither. Don't rightly know what we'd do to live on," she said looking down at the table.

"Oh, I got my money. I told you I was gonna get it and by golly I did. Got plenty of it. Plenty enough for both of us and I didn't have to work for it neither," he said excitedly. "Got enough for us to make a stake. Maybe to buy us a little house with some acreage. Enough to have a garden, chickens, hog pen and a milk cow. We're not gonna be rich, but we ain't gonna be poor neither."

"I just ain't known you too long. I don't know you good enough to know what kind of man you'll be if we get together. I can't risk my reputation not knowin' if you're good and then it turns out bad."

"I'm as good a man as you gonna find in all of Jasper County. I ever lie to you? Even get close to a fib? No, sir. Not one bit. Wouldn't do it to you. You'd find out right straight enough if'n I was to do that. Told you I was gettin' me some money and I did, didn't I? Yes sir, sure did."

"It just ain't agreein' with me right now. Alma still ain't got all her strength back yet. Billy's talkin' 'bout leavin Jasper and movin' to Brookeland and openin' a store up there. I don't think it'd be right for me just to up and leave them be if they move up there. I ain't sayin' never but I am sayin' it can't be right now."

Somewhat dejected, Gurdon began looking at the table and barely shaking his head back and forth. "Well, it's my fault. Yes, sir. Shouldn't have tried to rush you into it. Should've properly courted you before makin' that offer. That's what I'll do so's we can get to know each other better, then you'll see. We'll court a while. If'n that's alright with you."

Feeling relieved from having to make a life changing decision to go with him or lose what hold she had on him, she said, "That sounds good, Gurdon. I think I like that better than just up and runnin' off. Wouldn't be fair to Alma and Billy."

"Okay, then. It's settled. I gotta go to Silsbee for a week or so. When you movin' to Brookeland?"

"Billy said it'd be a week or two before he done that. Had to go up there to find a somethin' to rent for the store and a place to live."

"Okay, then. Next time I see you it'll likely be in Brookeland, huh?"

With the topic of running off concluded for now, they again slipped into small talk and while doing so, Gurdon slid his hand across the table and took one of hers. They talked and stared at each other for a very long time, holding hands as they did.

Stella was startled when she heard the clock strike three. The time had flown by. It was then she heard the rain for the first time. They both looked at the clock and out the front window in unison.

"I best be getting' back," said Stella as she rose from her seat. "Alma's liable to be worried since the rain started. You want to walk me home?"

Thinking fast to avoid the walk home with her and the chance of being seen, he quickly said, "I'm sorry, but I've got to run some errands for my momma. I reckon she 'spected me back some time ago now. I'm sure you'll be okay. Any other time I would, but the time got away from me today."

"Don't worry. It's okay. I got my parasol and it ain't rainin' too hard."

They walked through the door, bell tinkling, and onto the sidewalk.

"Guess I'll see you in Brookeland next time then," said Gurdon.

"Guess so. You take care now on your errands and your trip to Silsbee."

"I will. And you quit getting' prettier. I don't want no new suitor sniffin' round while I'm gone," he said with a large grin.

"That's somethin' you won't have to worry 'bout in either case," she said, returning his grin.

They looked at each other for another moment then walked away in separate directions, each with different thoughts.

32

Lack of Resolution

Weeks passed since the fire and things in Jasper returned to semi-normal. The debris left from the fire was nearly cleared. Some businesses moved into other buildings, some closed for good, and a few moved away, including Billy Nix and his mercantile store that moved to Brookeland.

Sheriff Brown was still investigating and after following several leads, still couldn't locate Gurdon Marion or Clarence Keaghey. Dave Depotti had gone with the Nix's to Brookeland to work in his new store up there. But nobody seemed to know the whereabouts of Gurdon or Clarence. It was like they dropped off the face of the earth, never to be seen again. Brown kept reminding himself that patience would likely win the day, but that commodity was getting harder and harder to believe in.

A group of businessmen and community leaders, known as the Jasper Senate, met with Brown weekly to get an update on the investigation. He told them everything he knew about the case and any new leads. However, he never mentioned the names of the suspects he couldn't find, or the one he could. After all, he didn't have any proof. Only the word of a teenaged Negro boy who, by law, had no credibility and couldn't testify in court.

Hearing the lack of progress, the Senate inquired to the Sheriff of the assistance a reward might provide in bringing the culprits to justice. They agreed it was a good idea that certainly couldn't hurt the investigation. An amount was discussed and it was agreed that all parties would contribute an equal amount of the five hundred dollar reward for information leading to the arrest and conviction of the person or persons who committed the crime. The money would be held in trust by banker Tidwell and an executive committee of the Jasper Senate was appointed to make the determination of who, if anyone, should get the reward if and when the perpetrators were arrested and convicted. If nobody was ever convicted, the money would be returned to the original contributors in equal amounts.

Even with the reward in place, a month later there was still no progress. It was beginning to appear that the case would never be solved. Such was the lack of progress that speculation on the investigation began to wane. It was in this tenor of mind that a discussion took place some weeks later involving Postmaster Haymar, Judge Davidson, Sheriff Brown, County Judge Bartlett and the newly appointed mayor, Cotton Mathers. The discussion centered around how to get the investigation back on track and how to pry information out of folks that may know something. It was decided that Haymar, Davidson and Bartlett would travel to Austin to meet with Governor Joseph Sayers about the state possibly offering a separate reward. The trio returned triumphant with a proclamation the Governor had signed approving an additional five-hundred-dollar reward for the conviction of the perpetrators.

Word quickly spread that the total reward had doubled from five hundred to one thousand dollars and as quickly as the reward had increased, the speculation as to who caused the fire increased proportionally. Telephone lines stayed busy. More people showed up for morning coffee at the White Swan to hear the latest from the Sheriff. The spit and whittle club increased in size as evidenced by the mound of shavings left in front of the cedar tree bench. And members of the Jasper Senate that hadn't been seen at a meeting in months, began regular weekly attendance.

Once again, the burning was the main topic of conversation, almost to the exclusion of all others. Even talk of the weather took a back seat to the status of impending arrests for the burning. Although Sheriff Brown did his best to tamp down expectations, there was no way to keep track of all the rumors and gossip surrounding suspects and how a lucky person would get their hands on that thousand dollars and be rich. The speculation even went so far as to how the recipient would change their life, what they would buy and even if they would turn snooty and look down on their former friends. Rumors abounded that one of the business owners started the fire intentionally. Others said that it was an accident. Another stated that no money was stolen and yet another that thirty thousand dollars was taken. The rumors seemed to compound weekly.

The investigation dragged on with no progress until the sheriff got the best lead he had gotten since the Simpson boy, and danged if it wasn't the Simpson boy that did it again.

Part Six

33

Found

Sheriff Brown was sitting on his front porch early that Sunday afternoon in the straight back chair, tilted backwards against the wall and relaxing. Things in his world weren't as speculative as they were with everyone else. His world revolved around facts and not speculation. Things had slowed down for him quite a bit over the last couple of months following the burning. With no new leads, there was nothing to chase. With nothing to chase, there wasn't much to do. Everything had pretty much returned to normal for the Sheriff and he was beginning to accept the fact that the case might never be solved.

That thought was creeping more and more into his mind. He hadn't fully accepted it yet, but it was gaining ground on his way of thinking. He didn't like it and didn't want to accept it, but the facts told him otherwise. The likelihood of solving the case would depend not only on a big break, but for the trio to confess. He still believed the colored boy and had no reason to doubt him. Why in the world would he lie about who he saw that morning? He had no reason at all that the Sheriff could think of.

It was in this frame of mind that Midge walked out the front door, catching it so it wouldn't slam shut. She looked at her husband who was staring off into the distance. "Penny for your thoughts."

He looked around at her as she sat in the chair next to him. "My thoughts right now are worth a lot more than a penny," he said grinning.

"What are you thinkin' 'bout?"

"What else. The case. Thinkin' it might never be solved. Whoever done it might be in California by now, never to be found," he speculated.

"I'm sure everbody will blame you for not solvin' it. May be the last time you get elected. Wouldn't be such a bad thing, not gettin' re-elected."

"Yep. At this point, that don't sound too bad."

They both felt the closeness they had always felt on occasions like this. appreciative of their life together and knowing the other's thoughts without having to speak. It was always easy for them when they were together, a quiet mutual respect and a deep love and trust that few couples find. It was in this relaxed mood that he saw a Negro riding a mule up the street. When he got closer, he could tell it was the Simpson boy.

Luke Simpson stopped, hitched the mule to the fence by the street, turned up the path to the Sheriff's house and stopped at the foot of the steps. "Evenin' Mr. Sheriff."

"Evenin', young Mr. Simpson. How are you?"

"Doin' right good I reckon. I come to tell you somethin' Mr. Sheriff," as he looked at Midge sitting on the porch.

"Whatever you got to say you can say in front of Mrs. Brown."

"Evenin', Mrs. Sheriff," said Luke addressing the Sheriff's wife.

"Evenin'," she replied with a smile at being called Mrs. Sheriff.

"What you come to tell me Luke?"

"I seen two of 'em. Two of them white boys that blew up the town."

The Sheriff rose from his chair and walked down the steps to where Luke stood, "Where?"

"I went to daddy's church this mornin' and as I was goin' through the loggin' camp at Remlig, I seen that tall lanky feller comin' out'n the outhouse. Yes, sir. Sho 'nuf did. Seed him real clear. He didn't pay me no mind though. Yes sir, seed him clear as day."

"You say you seen two of 'em?"

"Yes, sir. I did. 'Stead of ridin' straight back, decided to ride back through Brookeland and I'll swun if'n I didn't see Gurdon Marion on the front porch of Nix's store up there. Sittin' there pretty as you please with this white girl. They was all talkin' and makin' eyes at each other. She seen me but not sure he did or not."

"You sure certain 'bout this?"

"Yes, sir. Flat sure," he replied adamantly. "I seen that lanky feller and knowed I need to come see you right straight. Then when I seen that Marion feller, I come fast as I could."

The Sheriff reached into his pocket and retrieved a quarter, extended it to the young man and said, "Here, Luke. You take this for your trouble. If I catch them boys up there, I'll give you a whole dollar."

The young boy's eyes got wide with excitement and anticipation, and he said, "Mr. Sheriff, I didn't do this for no reward. It's just the Christian thang to do."

"You're right. It is the Christian thing to do, but you're the only Christian that's got me a lead. You go on and take this now. And I'll be true to my word. You'll get a dollar if I'm able to catch them fellers up there. You come by the jail 'bout Wednesday. I should have 'em by then."

The teenager took the quarter with great humility and thanked the Sheriff repeatedly. "You go on now, Luke. I got work to do."

"Yes, sir. Good luck, Mr. Sheriff." Luke remounted the mule and began to ride away as Brown ascended the porch steps.

"Well, looks like you caught a break in the case," said Midge as he stepped back onto the porch.

"Looks like it," he said as he reached for the screen door.

"I'll look for you when I see you comin'," said Midge, knowing that her husband was heading north to arrest a couple of suspects in the biggest case to ever hit Jasper County.

Brown didn't say a word of acknowledgement as the screen door slammed behind him. He walked over to the phone hanging on the kitchen wall, picked up the receiver and turned the crank handle three times and waited. It wasn't long before Maybelle answered, "Hello, Sheriff. Who can I get for you?"

"I need to talk to Andrew, Maybelle."

"Sure 'nough, Sheriff. I'll put you right through," she said as he heard a click over the phone.

"Yhellow," said Deputy Wayne.

"Andrew, it's me. I need you to meet me at the jail as quick as you can get there."

"What's goin' on?"

"Tell you when you get there," said the Sheriff who hung up.

He immediately went to the bedroom, got the Navy Colt out of the dresser, headed out back, got Molly, hitched her to the surrey and started off toward the jail.

34

Southbound

Gurdon Marion saw the young Negro boy ride by on the mule but thought nothing of it. He was more interested in talking with Stella, holding her hand and imagining future intertwining activities they would enjoy once they could finally be alone. On the bench in front of Nix's store in Brookeland certainly wasn't the place to carry out those imagined activities. He looked back at the colored boy riding toward Jasper. The boy looked sort of familiar, but he couldn't place him. At this moment, he had better things to do and to think about than where he knew some colored boy from.

"I'm fixin' to go down to Jasper today to get me a barber chair," said Gurdon. "Why don't you ride along with me?"

"I would but I promised Dave that I'd go to church with him this afternoon," she replied. "I hate missin' the preachin'. Brother Hollis ain't near as good as Pastor Lonnie, but he's tolerable."

"I already got the wagon and horses from old man Miller over yonder. Ain't nothin' holdin' us up. You know," said Gurdon with a flash of an idea, "You could go with me and we could just go on to Burkeville to spend the night. Then we could go on over to Leesville and get married there on Tuesday."

"I don't know. It's still all just so quick," she said with a look of concern.

"Okay, then. If I'm gonna get to Jasper and back before the sun goes down, I gotta get goin'," he said as he rose, releasing her hand.

"Dang you, Gurdon. You got me so confused. You go on now and I'll see you when you get back," she said huffily.

"Okay then. I'll be back soon as I can," he said as he turned and walked toward Miller's livery stable.

Stella continued sitting on the bench and shortly after Gurdon had left, Dave came out and asked, "You ready?"

"Is it time already?"

"Yep. To walk all the way over there, we need to start now."

Stella rose, smoothed her dress and the pair stepped off the porch and into the dirt road toward the church. When they got within about 200 yards of the church, Gurdon came down the road meeting them in a wagon. When he got even with them, he pulled the reins and the horses stopped. "That offer I made is still good if you've changed your mind."

Stella stared up at him for a long moment, not saying a word. Dave was also silent but clueless about what was going on. "Alright then. Let's do it. You go get the hack and I'll meet you at the bushes on the other side of Bob Bell's. Go on now 'fore I change my mind."

"Whoopee!" cried Gurdon. "I'll be there in a jiffy!" He slapped the reins on the backs of the horses, turned them around, and headed back to Miller's livery.

"What's goin' on?" asked Depotti, confused. "We gotta get to church."

"I ain't goin' to church. I'm runnin' off with Gurdon and we're gettin' married."

"What?" asked Depotti incredulously. "You do that, Stella, and you're makin' a big mistake. You been takin' on such over him and if he left the country, you wouldn't be losin' any great thing. Tell you what. If you won't run away, I'll marry you. You gonna regret it if you leave with Gurdon. You gonna regret it somethin' fierce. Stay here and marry me. You won't regret nothin' with me."

"I've made up my mind," she said as she turned and began walking back to the store.

"Stella! I promise! If you'll just come back, I'll marry you!" shouted Depotti at her back as she walked away. "I will! I promise I will!"

When she got back to the store, she climbed the stairs and went into the small room upstairs where she slept, gathered some of her things into a sack and headed back down the stairs.

"Where are you headed?" asked Alma, surprised.

"Me and Gurdon is runnin' off to get married," said Stella tersely and firmly in an attempt to avoid any argument or discussion on the matter.

"Oh, no!" exclaimed Alma. "Stella, don't do that. It'd be a horrible mistake. That boy ain't never been good for nothin' and never will be. You gotta listen to me. Stella. Stop. Stella, where you goin'?"

Stella kept walking and replied over her shoulder, "Burkeville."

She continued on toward Bob Bell's and was surprised she had so quickly decided her future.

When she got there, Gurdon was waiting with the hack and horse. She threw her sack in the back and Gurdon helped her onto the seat.

"Wasn't real sure you'd come," said Gurdon with a smile.

"I wasn't either," she replied with a grin. "Dave and Alma both told me I was makin' a mistake runnin' off with you."

"We's doin' the right thing for us. I ain't worried none 'bout them. They can judge all they want. Makes me no never mind. We get to

Leesville, I can change my name and they'll never find us."

"What about the money?"

Gurdon patted his breast pocket and said, "I got plenty of money. Don't you worry none 'bout that. Didn't have to work for it neither."

As Gurdon started the horse, Stella stared at his profile and began the faintest of smiles. Soon, she scooted just a little closer as they bounced along the dirt road. They talked about their future and when they got to Browndell, they turned southeast toward Burkeville.

35

Northbound

When Deputy Wayne arrived at the jail, Brown was there waiting.

"So, what's goin' on Sheriff?"

"I got an eyewitness that has seen Clarence Keaghey at the loggin' camp up at Remlig and also seen Gurdon Marion up at Brookeland. Simms is comin' with a hack for you and I want you to go to Remlig and find Clarence and I'm fixin' to go Brookeland to get Gurdon and I'll meet you back here."

"What are we gettin' 'em for?"

"For burnin' down the damned town," said Brown matter-of-factly.

"Really? You reckon they done it?"

"Best suspects I've had all along."

"Who seen 'em?"

"That's gotta stay a secret right now. But he's tellin' the truth. I'm gonna head on out. When Simms gets here, you get on up to Remlig and bring Keaghey back and just put him in the jail. We'll get with Judge Davidson about arraignin' them in the mornin'.''

"Awright. This is excitin'! This is the most excitin' thing ever happen since I got this job."

Brown bounced along in the surrey toward Brookeland and just as he approached Browndell, he could see a wagon turn off to the east on the Farrsville road. Looked like it had a man and a woman in it but it was too far off for him to be certain.

He continued on, finally pulling to a stop in front of Nix's store. He dismounted, walked onto the porch and knocked on the front door. Through the glass he could see Billy Nix coming down the stairs from their living quarters.

"Well, ain't you a sight for sore eyes," said Billy as he opened the door and the Sheriff stepped inside. Nix turned toward the stairs and hollered, "Alma! We got company!"

"It's good to see you too," said Brown. "Ain't a social call this time though. I'm lookin' for Gurdon Marion. I got word he was seen out on your front porch with a woman."

Brown looked back at the stairs and saw Alma taking the last step as she began walking toward the two men. Billy gave Alma a look and said,

"You tell him, Alma."

"He ain't here, J.M. Him and Stella done run off to get married. Left here maybe twenty, thirty minutes ago," she said with her head down and shaking from side to side. "She's makin' a terrible mistake. Told her so too. Told her that boy ain't never been good for nothin' and never would be."

"She say where they's goin'?"

"Said to Burkeville. That's all I know. She dashed off quick like. She's on a mission awright," said Alma disappointedly. "What you wantin' him for?"

"He's a suspect in burnin' down the town."

This news obviously surprised and shocked the couple from the stunned look on their faces. They were both taken aback and didn't say anything.

"What you gonna do when you catch him?" asked Billy.

"Take him to jail and see what Judge Davidson wants to do with him."

"Tell you what, why don't you go back to Jasper and I'll make a trip to Burkeville and save you and Judge Davidson some trouble," said Billy.

"Don't do that Billy. Don't be sayin' nothin like that. I'm gonna forget you said it and I'd suggest Alma forget it too. Anything happen to that boy before I get to him and you're gonna be my prime suspect," said Brown mater-of-factly and the look on his face supplemented his warning.

"Damnit, J.M, that ain't right. He single-handedly nearly ruined that town. Run me all the way up here to start over. I had a good business back in Jasper. I'm gettin' too old to be startin' 'over."

"Oh, I'm sure he'll get justice when he gets in front of Judge Davidson. I'll bet on that."

"Well, whatever's done, won't be enough in my book."

"Well, ain't no catchin' 'em from here if they got that big a jump. You got a phone?"

"Sorry, J.M., can't afford one right now. Just now gettin' my business up and runnin' kinda fair."

"Any place in town I could use a phone?"

"The switchboard is up yonder other side of city hall. You can likely use one over there."

"Thanks. It's good to see y'all. Wish it'd been a social call and not business. Keep an eye on the *News-Boy*. I'm sure Hector will have the story in this week's edition."

"Will, do," said Billy as the two shook hands and Brown left the store. He walked to the switchboard building and the front door was unlocked so he went in. He walked up to the counter and could see a middle-aged woman in the back of the room sitting in front of the switchboard that looked to have a hundred connections.

She looked up, saw who it was and walked to the counter.

"Hello, Sheriff. What brings you to Brookeland on a Sunday afternoon?"

"It's a long story. Right now, I need to talk to Sheriff Anderson in Newton. Can you get him for me?"

"I'll try. Sometimes the lines ain't that dependable. The call will have to go through Jasper and then over to Newton. Who do I bill this to, Sheriff?"

"Bill it to the county."

"Awright. You can use that phone there at the end of the counter. Just wait till I tell you we're connected," she said as she turned and went back to the switchboard.

In a few minutes, she gave the Sheriff the signal that the call had gone through and to pick up the receiver.

"Sheriff Anderson?" Brown asked.

"Yes, who's this?" Anderson asked.

"This is Sheriff J.M. Brown over at Jasper County. I'm needin' a favor. I'm needin' a fella arrested. I've been told he's headed to Burkeville in a hack and has a woman with him. I was wonderin' if you could find him and hold him there, then I'll come get him."

"Glad to Sheriff. What's this fella's name and what's he wanted for?"

"Gurdon Marion. He's about five foot seven, medium build and curly brown hair. He's the prime suspect in burnin' down the town of Jasper."

"Whew! This one is big, then. What about the woman?"

"She ain't involved, 'ceptin' makin a poor choice in men."

Anderson chuckled and assured Brown that he would travel to Burkeville the next day to look for the fugitive.

When Brown hung up, the switchboard lady asked excitedly, "So you know who done it, huh?"

"No. He's just a suspect at this point and I'd appreciate it if you'd not spread rumors 'bout this," said the Sheriff sternly.

"Okay, but you understand that's 'bout too much for a body to keep hid."

Brown gave her another stern look and said, "I'd hate to have to arrest a fine woman, such as yourself, for interferin' in an investigation."

The woman looked just a little stunned and decided that her flippant remark was just a little too much for the Sherriff. "Oh, no! No, sir! I ain't gonna say a word!"

Brown gave her another stern look, turned and left.

He walked back to Nix's store and rather than bother them again, mounted the surrey to head back. But before moving the surrey, he had a thought. He dismounted and knocked on the door of the store once again. Again, Billy came down the stairs and opened the door, this time stepping onto the porch.

"Billy, I wanted to let you to know. I called Sheriff Anderson over at Newton County. He's goin' up to Burkeville tomorrow to try and find Gurdon. If he finds him, he's gonna call me and I'm gonna go get him from the Newton jail. I'll inquire 'bout Miss Stella and find out what's goin' on with her and I'll call up here to the switchboard office to leave you a message. More'n likely, you can start out for Burkeville in the mornin' to fetch her, but I'll let you know soon as I do."

"I'd really appreciate that. Damned if that gal ain't gonna cost me a dollar and a half to rent a hack. But, on the other hand she was sure enough some good help while Alma was sick. So, I guess it's worth it."

"I understand. I best be getting' back to Jasper now. I'll call soon as I know somethin'."

"Again, I'd appreciate it. Thanks J.M."

Brown mounted the surrey once more, settled in the seat, grabbed the reins, tipped his hat to Billy and turned for Jasper. That's all he could do for today. Everything else was up to somebody else right now. Andrew and Clarence; Sheriff Anderson and Gurdon. He'd go back to the jail and wait on Andrew. He just hoped that Andrew was luckier than he was in finding his fella.

36

Triumphant Deputy Returns

Brown drove the surrey straight home. Unhitched Molly, put her in her stall and hung a bag of oats on her while he gave her a quick grooming. Finished, he locked the barn behind him and stepped onto the back veranda where he poured fresh water into the wash basin, pulled the lye soap off the shelf then lathered and washed his hands. After drying them on an old sugar sack, he walked through the back screen door which slammed behind him, removed his hat, hung it on the back of his chair at the kitchen table and sat down heavily.

"You back?" cried Midge from the parlor.

"Yep. Just got back."

Midge came into the kitchen, asking, "You hungry?"

"Yep. Feelin' real peckish right now."

"Got left-overs from dinner, if that's awright," she said as she put another stick of wood in the stove and began removing things from the ice box and pie safe.

"Sounds good. Gotta go down to the jail to meet Andrew."

"You find who you was lookin' for?"

"Nope. Missed them by twenty or thirty minutes. By the way, Billy and Alma said tell you hello."

"Well, good. They doin' awright?"

"Said they was. I think business is a little slower than what Billy was 'spectin', though."

"You know where they went?"

"Yep. Alma said Gurdon and Stella run off to Burkeville. Gonna go on over to Leesville and get married. So I went to the switchboard office and called Sheriff Anderson in Newton. He's gonna go up to Burkeville tomorrow mornin' to see if he can find them."

"You send Andrew after Clarence?"

"Yep. Hope he had better luck than I did."

"Let's hope so," she said as she put the plate in front of her husband.

"That hit the spot," said Brown, sopping up the last of the pea juice with the last bite of biscuit. He then stood, took his hat off the chair, kissed his wife and told her would see her as soon as he could but not to wait up. He walked through the parlor through the slamming screen door and stepped onto the front veranda. The sky was showing the first hints of dimming for the day and he noticed the slight cooling of the temperature as he looked around. He paused, took a deep breath, settled his hat on his head and began walking toward the jail.

As he rounded the corner onto Houston Street, he saw the Simms hack tied up in front of the jail. He walked up the east steps, stepped inside and saw through his office door, Andrew sitting behind his desk and a handcuffed Clarence Keaghey sitting across from him. Brown couldn't help the slight grin that was beginning to spread across his face as he walked into his office and hung his hat on the peg by the door.

He acknowledged the Deputy saying, "You have any trouble?"

"Naw, Sheriff. Meek as a lamb this boy was. No trouble a 'tall," he replied as he stood and walked to the side of the desk.

"Well, Clarence. Know why you're here?" asked Brown as he sat behind the desk.

"No, sir. I don't think I rightly do. I don't have no clue. No clue a 'tall. No, sir," he replied shaking his head vigorously.

"Well, I 'spect you do. I 'spect you know exactly why you're here, so why don't you go ahead and tell us. Why would we go to all the trouble to go all the way to Remlig and bring you back here if we didn't know what you done. Now it stands to reason that if we know what you done, that you'd know." And turning to the Deputy said, "Now don't that sound logical to you, Deputy Wayne?"

"Yes, sir. It certainly does, Sheriff. Yes, sir. Makes all the sense in the world to me. I can't figure if we know why he's here that he don't. Now that part is the part don't make no sense to me. No, sir. Don't make no sense why he don't know why he's here."

"So, Clarence. Why don't you go ahead and tell us why you think you're here," said Brown.

Keaghey was getting more and more nervous. He didn't know exactly what the Sheriff and his Deputy knew. For all he knew, Gurdon was already in jail and he'd spilled the beans. "Sheriff, all I 'spect is that it has somethin' to do with what we talked about that mornin' of the fire. And to be right honest, I'm not sure what that conversation was 'bout. No, sir, I don't. Didn't know then and don't know now."

Brown remembered the Case pocketknife. He opened the lap drawer to his desk and removed it, palming it so his suspect couldn't see it.

"Andrew, this boy have any weapons on him when you arrested him?'

"No, sir. Nothin'."

"Not even a pocketknife?"

"No, sir. Nothin'."

Without looking at his Deputy, Brown lifted the pocketknife, once again holding it by one end and resting his elbow on the desk while starring at Keaghey, saying "Not even the one his granddaddy give him?"

The expressions on the faces of the other two changed immediately. Wayne was confused and Keaghey suddenly became noticeably nervous, and very fidgety.

"This was the knife your granddaddy Seamus gave you. Ain't no man round these parts don't have a knife. Might be a pocketknife or a scabbard knife, but ever man's got a knife. Am I right, Deputy?" asked Brown with his stare continuing to be locked onto Keaghey.

"No, now wait a minute. Just hold on. I lost that knife. Just don't know where I lost it. I swear, Sheriff." said Keaghey shaking his head.

"Well now ain't that interestin'. You want to take a wild guess at where it was found?"

"No, sir. Don't have no clue. No, sir I don't. Wouldn't rightly know."

"Deputy, you want to explain to our primary suspect in the robbery and arson of Jasper, Texas where you found this knife?"

Warming to the conversation now and with a great sense of finally figuring out what the Sheriff was aiming for, Wayne began. "You were in Nix's store the night of the fire, right?"

"Yeah. Bought a couple of malts. Ain't no crime in that," said a nervous Keaghey with as much indignation as he could muster.

"What time was you in the store?"

"Don't rightly remember."

"How many times was you in the store?"

"Two or three, I guess."

"Which was it? Two or three?"

"I don't know. Why does it make a difference?"

"You were there. You were in the store. Now which was it two or three?"

"Okay, three then," he replied becoming more nervous.

"You sure about that?"

"Yes sir, right sure."

"What if I told you we had somebody that'd testify that you was in there four times?"

"He'd be lyin'," he replied adamantly.

"Who said it was a he?"

"Well, who was it then?"

"I'll ask the questions here," replied the Deputy who glanced over at the Sheriff who was reared back in his chair with a slight grin on his face, obviously enjoying himself. He was beginning to gain a little respect for Andrew's interrogating ability.

"Well go on then, ask," said Keaghey defiantly.

"You see, I know what time you was in there the fourth time. I know it and I can prove it. Don't need no eyewitness a 'tall. No, sir. You was in that store the last time around two o'clock Sunday morning. Yes, sir. You was."

"I don't rightly know what you're talkin' 'bout. I weren't in that store after it closed."

"Was you not, now? Let's see here," said the Sheriff as he opened the knife's longest blade, examining it closely. "Come here Andrew and look at this real close. What do you see?"

"Looks like some black powder residue," said the Deputy after studying it closely.

"And look down here in the recess of the spine here," said Brown as he took out his own knife and began delicately removing some dark debris from the recess. Gently removing the debris, he asked Wayne, "What does that look like to you Andrew?"

"Looks like fuse cord to me, Sheriff."

"Now, Deputy where would a fine, upstanding gentleman like Mr. Keaghey come across some fuse cord, and more than that, why would someone of Mr. Keaghey's stature need to come across some fuse cord to begin with?" asked the Sheriff sarcastically.

"I'm sure I wouldn't know, Sheriff."

"Now, Clarence. How do you suppose that fuse cord got into the recess of your knife?" asked Brown holding the open knife by the end again.

"Whoever done the fire must've found my knife and used it to cut the fuse cord I reckon," said Keaghey now with the first beads of sweat beginning to run off his forehead and not realizing that he had just admitted the knife was his.

"You got an alibi for where you was when the fire started?"

"I wasn't in that store! No, sir I wasn't! I was spendin' the night with Gurdon. You can ask him if you don't believe me," said Keaghey earnestly.

"Well, you see that's a problem. Not for me. For you. Cause you see, Gurdon can't be found nowhere. And since he can't be found, he can't verify your alibi. So since there ain't nobody to vouch for your whereabouts, it looks like you just become a guest of the Jasper County jail," said the Sheriff with more than a little satisfaction.

"You can't do that! This just ain't right. I didn't do nothin'!"

"But you see, Clarence, I CAN do this. I've got evidence. See, you just admitted this is your knife then you said that you lost it. Now am I mistaken about that Deputy?"

"No sir, Sheriff. You sure ain't."

"Well, let's review what we got here," said Brown holding up a finger each time he stated a fact. "We got you admittin' it's your knife and admittin' you lost it. We got fuse cord residue in the recess of your knife. You don't have an alibi for when the explosion happened. And your supposed alibi can't be found. Now then. Tell me what I'm missin' here."

"This ain't right, Sheriff. This ain't right," said Keaghey shaking his head and now sweating more profusely.

"Andrew, why don't you escort Mr. Keaghey to his new room."

The Deputy walked to where Keaghey was seated, grabbed him under the arm and helped him stand. "Come on. Room comes complete with room service. Don't even have to go nowhere to eat. We'll bring your meals right to ya'," he said as they walked to the stairs. "Got a decent view too. You can look out the window and see what all you burned down. Yes, sir. Somethin' for you to ponder on while you're here."

Brown, still reared back in his chair, began to go back over what had just happened. The little bit of evidence he had was logical. The only flaw in it would be when Gurdon got back here to the jail and if the two of them began talking and came up with an alibi good enough that Judge Davidson would let them go. The whole thing seemed to be going to rest on Gurdon and what he has said and done since the fire. Nothing he could do about anything else until he got Gurdon in custody.

Brown could hear the Deputy coming back down the stairs and looked up when he came into the office.

"He admit to anything on y'all's stroll?"

"Nope. Just kept sayin' he didn't do nothin' and that we can't do this. Kept sayin' it right up till I locked the cell door," said the Deputy, smiling.

"Well, we're just now catchin' a break on this whole thing. A lots gonna depend on what Gurdon's got to say." Rising and moving toward the door, Brown said, "I think I've had enough for one day. Know anybody that wants a jailer job startin' tomorrow?"

"Might. Let me think on it."

"Don't make nobody no offers till we talk about it. Okay?"

"Sure. You headin' home?"

"Yep. You need to get on too. Clarence'll be alright by hisself tonight. I'm tired and tomorrow's likely to be a bigger day than today so you need to go on too," said Brown taking his hat off the peg beside the door.

"You're likely right. I'm fixin' to head out too soon as I shut down the lamps. I'll lock up."

"Thank you, Andrew. You done good today. You go on home and get some rest. I know I am."

"Will do, Sheriff. See you in the mornin'," he replied as Brown shut the door on his way home and hopefully to a good night's rest.

37

The Burkeville Jumble

As Gurdon and Stella drove the hack toward Burkeville, they talked back and forth about their future together and what each wanted from their lives. The trip was long and they continued after the sun had shed its last bit of light of the day. When they reached Farrsville, Gurdon knocked on a farmhouse door just outside of town to inquire about feed for the horse. The kindly farmer agreed, took a lantern from the front gallery, lit it and showed the pair the way to the barn. He opened the barn door and pointed to the feed, saying, "There is a creek just down the road about a hundred feet. Can't miss it as the road goes right through it. You can water the horse there."

The farmer was thanked by the pair for his kindness and help with the horse. The farmer left the lantern with the couple and told them just to put it back on the gallery and turn it off when through. The pair took the feed bag off the wall, filled it with oats, took it to the horse and hung it around its neck. They then waited for the horse to finish, returned the empty feed bag and locked the barn. After they took the lantern back to the gallery and turned it off, they remounted the hack and proceeded on to Burkeville. They stopped in the creek as long as the horse needed, and then started up again.

"Should make it there a little after daylight," said Gurdon.

"Good. My bones could use a rest. This old hack is nice, but it sure does rattle one's bones."

They rode in silence while Stella was thinking about how they were going to do all the things they had been talking about without money. She had no real reason to doubt what Gurdon had said about having plenty of money, but she didn't know how much 'plenty' was. His idea of 'plenty' and her idea of 'plenty' might be a long way apart.

"So, all these things we been talkin' bout, how we gonna afford them?" she inquired gently.

Gurdon, patting his chest pocket once again, said "Don't worry. I've got plenty of money."

"Well, how much is 'plenty'?"

"More'n enough. I got six five dollars and two ten dollars currency. That ought to be enough to get us started real good. I hear things is much cheaper in Louisiana anyways."

"Well, that is a right smart. But it ain't gonna last forever. You gonna have to find some work somewhere for us to keep goin'."

"We run out'n of this, I might just do again what I done to get this," he said, patting his chest pocket again.

"Well, just what did you do to get that?"

"Don't want to rightly say. I know lots of people gonna suspicion me about the burnin', but I didn't have nothin' to do with that. Don't care what folks says. I didn't have nothin' to do with it. But I got money awright and if I have to, I'll do it again."

"Did you have anythin' to do with the burnin?"

"Best not be askin a man everthing 'bout his business. No, sir. Shouldn't be doin' that. This here what I done is man's work. Ain't no business of a woman, not even a wife."

"If that be your thinkin', awright then," she said and dropped the subject.

The pair continued on in silence and watched as the morning sun came slowly up in front of them as they trudged along in the bumpy hack. The sun was full up when they got to downtown Burkeville. It was a bit smaller than Jasper and didn't have a courthouse square, with Newton holding that distinction for the County. There was an array of businesses along the main street that were typical in East Texas during the time; hardware, mercantile, livery, blacksmith, general merchandise and feed stores, along with the always present café, saloon, and domino parlor.

Gurdon pulled the hack to a stop in front of Windom's Hotel in the middle of town, climbed down, tied the horse, and helped Stella to the ground.

"We'll stay here tonight. I know Mr. Pike Windom and I think he'll give us a cut on a room," he said.

Stella didn't reply but followed him into the small lobby where she saw a slightly built and balding man behind the counter with garters on his long sleeves to hold them in place while they were rolled up.

"Mornin', Mr. Pike," said Gurdon smiling as the screen door slammed behind him.

"Hello, Gurdon," said Windom flatly, not returning the lilt in Gurdon's voice.

"Say, Mr. Pike, I need a room for tonight. For me and Miss Stella."

Eyeing the two suspiciously, Windom asked, "You two married?"

"Not yet," said Gurdon, taking Stella's hand and holding it tightly. "We're gettin' married tomorrow. Goin' over to Leesville."

"I got one room left for one of you. If you ain't married, you can't stay in the same room."

"Aw, come on, Mr. Pike. We's as good as married. Yes, sir. All we don't got is the license and that's cause we ain't got to Leesville yet. Please Mr. Pike, let us have a room together just for tonight. Just one night, that's all I'm askin'," pleaded Gurdon.

"Nope. Firm and fast, that rule is. I'd get run out of the church somebody find out I was lettin' unmarried folks share a room. Probably end up havin' to close up, a business get that kind of reputation. No, sir. Not gonna do it. No exceptions," said Windom firmly.

"Okay, then. Let me and Miss Stella talk on it a bit to see what we're gonna do."

Gurdon and Stella walked back to the front gallery and sat on the bench.

"It feels good to sit down on somethin' that ain't movin'," said Stella.

"Yep, it does. Okay, here's what I'm thinkin'. You stay here and I'm gonna take the hack back to Brookeland or see if I can find somebody else to drive it back. Pay him a dollar to do it, then I'll be back and hire us another hack and we'll strike out for Leesville. Here's ten cents so's you can get somethin' to eat and do a little shoppin' while I'm gone, if you want," he said handing her the silver.

"I'm just not knowin' 'bout this now," said Stella dejectedly.

"'Bout what?" asked a stunned Gurdon.

"'Bout this runnin' away. I mean, here I am thirty miles from where I was and over a hundred and fifty from home and I'm 'bout to be here all by myself and all I have to get by on is a dime. I'm scared, Gurdon."

Gurdon took her hand and held it tightly, looking into her eyes. "Don't you be worried 'bout nothin', now. No reason to fret. I'd leave you more but all I got is a fiver. I'll make it good with Mr. Pike and if you need anything for him to credit it to you and I'll pay it when I get back."

"I don't know. Don't guess I don't got no choice. Sure ain't startin' out like I thought," she said sadly with her head hung.

"You wait right here. I'm gonna go in and talk to Mr. Pike and get everthing fixed up. I'll be right back," he said as he rose and strode back inside, screen door slamming behind him.

"Mr. Pike, I need a favor. Since you won't let us stay in the same room, I'm gonna take the hack back to Brookeland and Miss Stella is gonna stay here. Credit her whatever she needs and I'll pay you when I get back. She's gonna need board too."

"For the life of me, Gurdon. I have no idea why I'm doin' this. Oh, wait. Yes, I do. I ain't doin' it for you, I'm gonna do it for that poor girl out there. I didn't like the way you fooled that other girl you brung here and I don't cotton to whatever it is you're up to with this one. But you go ahead. I'll make sure the girl is took care of. But when you get back, y'all both gonna have to leave. Don't want you around here," said Windom solemnly.

"Thank you, Mr. Pike. I appreciate it. I won't let you down. I'll be back late today or tomorrow at the latest. Depends on whether I have to take the hack all the way back or if I can maybe find somebody else to take it."

"You go on, now. You tend your business and I'll tend mine."

"Yes, sir. I'm goin' on now," said Gurdon who then turned, went back out of the always slamming screen door and sat back down beside Stella.

"Okay. It's all set. Whatever you need you just tell Mr. Pike and he'll credit me for it and I'll pay it when I get back."

"Gurdon," she said and looked at him sternly, "I want to see the money. You've told me about it but then you say all you can give me is ten cents. I want to see the money or I'm goin back to Brookeland with or without you. You know Dave Depotti said he'd marry me if I'd come back to Brookeland and right now that's beginnin' to look like a better offer."

Gurdon was stunned and taken aback by her demanding tone. Especially with the threat of leaving him thrown in for good measure. He blinked a few times and then reached into his inside coat pocket and pulled out what appeared to be a woman's small cloth purse with a design of stripes running diagonally and a snap at the top. He opened the snap and turning toward her to be as close as possible and deny any passerby a glimpse of what he was about to pull out of the purse, he reached in and revealed the currency. "See. Just like I told you. Six fives and two tens."

"Awright then. But you be quick 'bout bein' back here," she commanded.

He put the money back in the purse, snapped it shut and put it back in his coat pocket. Then he abruptly pulled it back out and opened it again, saying, "Open your purse."

Stella looked at him quizzically but did as he said. She watched in amazement as he put five fives and both tens in her purse. "This is all I'll need. You hang onto the rest 'til I get back. I trust you and you gotta trust me. People gotta do that if they're gonna get married. You can give it back to me when I get back. Don't be showin' none of it to nobody. Anybody asks you where you got the money, you tell them it's yours and that I didn't have none. If you tell folks I gave you the money, they really might start suspicionin' that I had somethin' to do with the burnin'. Then I might get arrested and we couldn't get married. I want to marry you somethin' fierce."

"Please don't be long. I don't like bein' here all by myself."

"I'll be back in a bit. You go on up to the room. I'm gonna get Kate to keep you company 'till I get back. You go on now and wait in the room."

"Who's Kate?"

"A girl I know. She'll keep you company. We'll sneak up the back stairs. You leave the door open a bit so I'll know which room you're in."

"Okay. Don't be long though," pleaded Stella.

Gurdon squeezed her hand tightly, looked her in the eye then rose, untied the horse, mounted the hack and drove south.

38

The Other Sheriff

True to his word, Newton County Sheriff Henry Anderson left Newton at sunrise and headed north to Burkeville. Anderson was a huge man at five inches over six feet and the two hundred and fifty pounds he carried was lean and muscular. He had ham like biceps and the two Colt .45 revolvers he carried looked small in his huge hands. He rode briskly but not hurriedly as he wanted to get to Burkeville and get back home before dark. He brought a change of shirts with him just in case but was counting on finding the Marion fella and getting him back to Newton so as not to need it.

He rode into town from the south side, looking at both sides of the street to see if there was anyone he didn't know that might fit the description that Sheriff Brown had given him. He had already decided that the Windom hotel would be his first stop. He figured that since he had a woman traveling with him, they wouldn't spend the night on the road sleeping on the ground. If he had no luck at the Windom hotel, then he would go over to Mrs. Lawrence's boarding house.

He stopped his horse in front of the hotel, dismounted and hitched it to the railing. Stepping inside, he removed his hat. When the screen door slammed behind him, Pike Windom turned to see the Sheriff standing in the lobby.

"Well, Henry," Pike exclaimed as he started from behind the counter, "It's sure good to see you! What are you doin' here?"

"Mornin', Pike."

The pair shook hands and exchanged a few pleasantries, then Anderson said, "Say, I'm lookin' for a couple likely came in here last night or this mornin' from Brookeland. Fella's name of Gurdon Marion and the woman is Stella Erwin."

Pike frowned just a little and said, "Should've figured that. Yep. She's here but he left. The woman is upstairs in room two. I wouldn't let them both stay in the same room. Them not bein married and all. Gurdon left not long after they got here this mornin' to take the hack back to Brookeland. Don't know much else. He did tell me before he left to give the woman credit for whatever she wanted and that he'd make it good."

"Well, I don't 'spect the woman's goin' nowhere. I'll ride on out toward Farrsville to see if I can catch him. You got a telephone?"

"Sure. Right over there," said Pike pointing to the end of the registration counter.

"I need to call Sheriff Brown over in Jasper and let him know his suspect is headin' back toward Brookeland, just in case I don't catch him."

The Sheriff cranked the phone, told the operator to charge the long-distance call to the county and asked to be put through to the jail in Jasper. The phone was answered on the other end by Sheriff Brown.

"Hey, J.M., it's Henry. Listen, I'm here in Burkeville. The woman is at the Windom Hotel, but the Marion fella has left headin' back toward Brookeland takin' back the hack, accordin' to Pike. He told Pike he was comin' back here for the girl. I'm gonna head on out toward Farrsville and see if I can catch him. Pike said he might try and hire somebody to take it back. If he does, he may be headin' back here pretty quick."

"Henry, I really do appreciate this and I hope I can return the favor one day. I'm gonna send my Deputy on up to Brookeland to wait and see if he shows up there. If we get him, I'll call you back. Where are you?"

"At the Windom Hotel right now."

"Okay if I call back and leave a message there?"

Anderson covered the receiver and called over to Windom, "Hey, Pike. You mind takin' a message from Sheriff Brown for me if need be?"

"Not at all, Henry."

"That'll be fine, then. Pike'll take the message. If I find him or not, I'll stop back by here and either get your message or call you and let you know what's goin' on."

"It's much appreciated and I'm much obliged."

The two hung up, Anderson thanked Pike Windom and walked out, the screen door slamming behind him. He untied the horse, mounted and rode just down the street to the livery stable.

"Howdy, Posey," said the Sheriff to the owner of the livery stable.

Posey Baily looked up from the harness he was working on to the mountain of a man standing in the livery door. "I'll be. How you doin' Henry?"

"Good. Good. How 'bout you, Posey?"

"Doin' right well. No complaints. No, sir. No complaints at all. What brings you to these parts?"

"I'm lookin' for a feller named Gurdon Marion. He's wanted over in Jasper County. You seen him?"

"Yep. He's in here this mornin' askin' 'bout hiring a hack to go over to Leesville. Said he'd need it today or tomorrow. What's he wanted for?"

"Well, he's suspicioned in burnin' down Jasper."

"I heard 'bout that. Terrible that happened. Just terrible," said Posey shaking his head.

"Word I got was Marion is headed back to Brookeland. I'm fixin' to head out toward Farrsville to see if I can catch him. If he comes back here, I'd appreciate it if you could delay givin' him the hack 'till I get back. Tell him the hack's gotta be fixed or somethin'."

"Don't have to make up no lie, Henry. This here's the harness that goes with the hack. I'm tired of workin' on it anyways. So, there you go. Done," said Posey as he threw the harness on the work bench.

"I appreciate it. I'll see ya' when I get back. Thanks Posey."

"Never a problem Sheriff. Always glad to help."

Anderson mounted his horse once again and turned northwest toward Farrsville.

The Sheriff had gotten about two miles out of Burkeville and was about to cross Little Cow Creek near Wiergate when he saw a man walking toward him. Anderson didn't slow down but kept the same pace. When he got closer to the approaching man, he pulled up, held the reins in his left hand and let his right drop by his side near the holster.

"Mornin'," said the man nervously as he kept walking, not wanting to stop and visit.

"Well, you see. That depends," was Anderson's reply. "I'd invite you to stop for a spell and answer me some questions if you don't mind."

"I've got to get back to Burkeville and I'm in a hurry," replied Gurdon.

"Well, you see I invited you real nice to visit for a spell, but you act like you don't want to. So now I'm tellin' you to stop which you will do either voluntarily or involuntarily. Now, which is it gonna be?" asked the Sheriff as he removed the pistol from the holster.

"Okay. I'm stoppin'. But make it quick. I need to get back."

"You Gurdon Marion, ain't you?"

"So, what if I am?"

As Anderson dismounted, still holding the pistol at his side, he said, "Boy, you got kinda smart mouth on you, don't you?"

When Gurdon saw how much of a man he was dealing with, his attitude changed to one of compliance.

"No, sir. My apologies to you, Sheriff. I just now realized who you was," said Gurdon apologetically.

"Okay, let's try this again. You Gurdon Marion?"

"Yes, sir. I am."

"Where's the hack you was drivin'?"

"I paid a colored boy in Wiergate a dollar to take it back to Brookeland for me. What's this all about Sheriff?"

"Sheriff Brown over in Jasper County wants to visit with you 'bout some business that took place over there back in June. You reckon what that might be?" asked Anderson to see just what this jackanapes would say.

"No, sir. I don't rightly think I do."

"Well, don't make no never mind. You stand still now, you hear me," said Anderson as he walked over to Gurdon, "I'm gonna search you now." He proceeded to pat all of Gurdon's pockets and around his waist looking for a knife or a gun. He felt something in the inside breast pocket of the coat and said, "Take that out of your pocket."

Gurdon removed the purse from his pocket and handed it to the Sheriff. The Sheriff opened it, saw nothing of interest, closed it and handed it back to him.

Holstering his pistol, Anderson said, "What do you say you just keep on walkin' toward Burkeville and I'll just follow behind to keep you company. You don't mind that now, do you?"

"No, sir. What's gonna happen when we get back to Burkeville," he asked nervously.

"Well, I'm gonna call Sheriff Brown over in Jasper and we're gonna sit in the lobby of the Windom Hotel until he comes and gets you."

He remounted his horse, and the pair began the trip back to Burkeville. The Sheriff was thinking that he would make it back to Newton about dark and was relieved at the notion.

Gurdon's mind was racing about what to do about his situation and how to handle Stella. She could blow the whole thing wide open if she started talking. Especially about suspicioning his involvement in the burnin'. This was not good, Gurdon decided. Definitely not good.

39

Gurdon Returns

Word spread quickly through Jasper that the prime suspect in the burning had been arrested and that Sherriff Brown was escorting him back to town.

It was getting late in the day with a few hours of good daylight left when Brown and Gurdon Marion began their approach up Houston Street to the jail. A small group had gathered in the hot afternoon, including some of the merchants who had lost businesses, a few politicians from the courthouse, and Postmaster Haymar. Of course, the two biggest town gossips Georgette Philpott and Gwendoline Massey were there. Andrew was standing on the third step on the east side of the jail. Front and center of the group was Hector Henry. He was standing beside the tripod that held his new wet plate camera. He was hoping to get a good photograph of the Sheriff and his prisoner.

Sheriff Brown evaluated the scene as he drew closer to the jail. His initial thought that the crowd might be unruly and try to take his prisoner from him was fleeting after he began to recognize who composed the crowd. The group parted silently as Brown directed the surrey to the hitching post in front of the jail.

"Evenin' everbody," said Brown as he stepped down from the surrey. Nobody replied.

He walked around to the other side of the surrey and helped Gurdon down. He was shackled with handcuffs and hobbles.

"Gurdon the man who done it?" asked Georgette Philpott of Brown.

Looking back at her sternly, Brown replied, "Gurdon Marion has been arrested as a suspect in the burnin' of Jasper on June second. Whether he done it or not will likely be up to a jury. My job is to investigate and gather evidence."

"I need to get y'all's picture, Sheriff. What's he charged with?" asked Henry.

"I'm fixin' to charge him with robbery and arson," said Brown as he and the suspect stood in front of the camera then said, "Deputy Wayne, you come down here and join us for this."

The Deputy came down the steps and stood next to the prisoner on the opposite side of the Sheriff.

"Y'all be still now and don't move 'till I tell ya'," said Henry as he disappeared under the cape behind the camera.

As he stood next to Gurdon waiting for the picture to be taken, Brown noticed a young colored boy across the street in front of where Hinson's Domino Parlor had stood. He thought to himself that it sure would have been a whole lot easier on everbody if that boy could have testified. An eyewitness made the case open and shut. He had a passing thought and wondered if the Negro's would ever have some of the rights the white folks enjoyed. Probably not, he decided.

Holding the flash pan high with his left hand, Hector counted, "One, two, three." The flash pan made a bright flash and the camera made a dim click. He came out from under the cape and without a word, began disassembling the setup.

"Well, I guess we can move now. Okay, let's go," said Brown to Gurdon. The pair turned toward the steps which, with the hobbles, he had a struggle to negotiate. Led by the Deputy they entered through Brown's outer office door, went to the hallway, where Brown took off the hobbles. They then proceeded up the stairs to the jail cells. When the pair entered the outer door of the cell block, Clarence had an expression of genuine surprise on his face which Brown noticed immediately.

"Somethin' wrong, Clarence?" asked Brown to a silent reply.

Brown placed Gurdon in the cell next to Clarence. Both cells had bars across the front but there was a solid wall between the cells. "Turn around and put your hands through the bars," said Brown who then removed the handcuffs. "Okay, now your feet."

"Got anythin' you want to say, Gurdon?" asked the Sheriff.

"Yep. What's for supper," said Gurdon sarcastically.

"Who said you're gettin' any," said Brown as he turned on his heal and headed out of the cell block.

40

Jailhouse Plans

"How long you been here?" asked Gurdon standing and facing the front of the cell with his arms through the bars.

"Since yesterday," replied Clarence who was standing the same way.

"How'd they catch you?"

"That damned Deputy come in the dormitory while I was sleepin' and afore I knowed it, he had handcuffs on me and I was headin' back to Jasper. What about you?"

"It's a long story, but I almost got away. I was this close," said Gurdon holding his thumb and index finger barely apart, "Got me some though. If I'd made it back to the hotel in Burkeville, I'd sure enough have got me some more. If not, I'd by golly got me some again the next day after we was married."

"Who's the girl?"

"Stella. You remember Stella from the dance?"

"You almost lucky bastard," said Keaghey with a grin and slight giggle.

"You're right. But close only counts in horseshoes."

"What's our story gonna be?"

"Stick with the original story. It's worked this far. Ain't no sense in changin' it. Best thing to do is keep our mouths shut. Don't say nothin'."

"You tell the girl anything?"

"Nope. Not a word. I think she 'spicioned. But 'spicion ain't no proof."

"How long you think they'll keep us?"

"Probably long as they want. The town folk are wantin' somebody to blame and to pay for the burnin'. So, we're just gonna have to go along with their doin's and see how it's gonna play out."

"I don't like it. I only been here a day and it's already getting hard."

"Here's the way you gotta think on it. We can spend some time here and stick to the plan and get found not guilty, or we can say fuck the plan and maybe get found guilty and sent to Huntsville for years. For me, I'd rather take my chances here than in Huntsville."

"I've always heard bad things bout Huntsville."

"Yep. From what I hear, this here is a spring social compared to Huntsville. You really think they ain't gonna feed us?"

"Not sure, but I think they will. The Svenson's at the White Swan feed the prisoners. Pretty good food, too," said Clarence who walked over and stretched out on his cot, "Think I'll have a nap before supper."

"Awright, then," replied Gurdon as he walked to the back of the cell to look out the window at the courthouse. That building was holding the key to his future. It would determine what kind of future he had. One of years of incarceration or of freedom and getting all he wanted of Stella. His mind began drifting to the girl and wondering how she was and where she was. He hoped she would keep her mouth shut about the money. If she told anybody, it could spell Huntsville for him and Clarence. If he had to go to prison in Huntsville, then he wasn't going alone. Everbody would go with him. Everbody.

41

Additional Company

When Brown got back to his office, Andrew was sitting in one of the visitor's chairs in front of his desk.

"Andrew, I need you to high tail it up to Brookeland and bring back Dave Depotti. Take my surrey. I'll wait here 'til you get back."

"Am I arrestin' him?"

"Yep. Sure are."

"What for?"

"Arson and robbery. He's the third suspect in the burnin'."

Stunned, he slowly rose from his chair. "You sure 'bout that, Sheriff? He always seemed like a decent enough feller to me."

"Yes. I am dead sure. Now go on. Daylight's burnin' and I want to wrap this thing up soon as possible," said the Sheriff in his no-nonsense manner.

"Yes, sir. I'm gone then," said Wayne as he took his hat off the peg by the door and left.

Brown sat behind his desk, reared back in his chair and took several deep breaths staring at the ceiling. Now it begins, he thought. He realized that what he did in the next several days could either make or break the cases against the three. He had two of them in jail already and he had no worries that Andrew would bring back Depotti. Depotti wasn't going anywhere. He didn't know he was a suspect. He was going to stick around Nix's store hoping that Stella would leave Gurdon and come back to him. Him disappearing wasn't a real concern. His real concern was being able to show that it was Depotti and not his nephew that was involved with the burnin'. Well, he had a few hours to figure it all out before the Andrew got back. He pulled a pad and pencil out of the desk and began the paperwork the District Attorney would use to indict the trio.

Deputy Wayne arrived back at the jail a little before midnight with Depotti in tow. As they walked into the outer door of the Sheriff's office, Brown stood and looked at the pair. Both appeared tired and haggard.

"Any trouble?"

"Not a bit."

"You look wore out. Go on home and I'll take care of our new guest."

"Not gonna argue with you, Sheriff. I'll see you in the mornin' then," said Wayne who turned and left the same way he had come.

"Sit down Dave," said Brown motioning to one of the chairs in front of his desk. "Gonna ask you the same question I've asked the other two fellas. You know why you're here?"

"No, sir. I don't, rightly. What other two fellas?"

"Your partners. Gurdon Marion and Clarence Keaghey. Here's what I know. I know that you were involved in the burnin' and robbin' back in June. I can prove it. Got an eyewitness who identified all three of you. What've you got to say to that?"

"Ain't true," he replied, not elaborating.

"You're tellin' me that what a man seen with his own eyes ain't what he saw? Let me ask you another question. How stupid do you think I am?"

"Don't think you're stupid at all Sheriff. That ain't what I said. All I said was it ain't true."

"You know it's gonna go a whole lot better for you if you'll just admit what you and the others done. I'll put in a good word with Gilbert, might even put in a word with Judge Davidson. Now, why don't you start by tellin' me who was it that planned the thing."

"Wouldn't rightly know, Sheriff. If I weren't involved, I wouldn't know who done the plannin'. And I'm tryin' to tell you, I wasn't involved."

"Well, let's try a simpler question then. Other than you, Gurdon and Clarence, who all else was involved in the caper?"

"Wouldn't rightly know, Sheriff. I wasn't involved."

"I'm beginnin' to think you really do believe that I'm stupid. Do you remember me talkin' to you the mornin' of the fire?"

"Yep. Sure do, Sheriff."

"Remember you tellin' me that you slept through the 'splosion and that Billy woke you up?"

"Yes, sir. That's the truth. That's what happened."

"You mean to tell me that an explosion that woke up the entire town, then had every church bell in town ringin' to beat the band and with shotguns goin' off to wake people up, that you slept through all that and had to be shook awake? Do you really expect me to believe that? Even more, do you expect a jury to believe that?"

"It's the truth, Sheriff. Anybody says different ain't tellin' the truth. Like I said, whatever your eyewitness seen wasn't me," he said unmoved by the accusations.

"I've had enough. Get up," said the Sheriff rising. "Let's go."

The handcuffed suspect and Sheriff moved up the stairs to the cell block where the handcuffs were removed and he was locked in the last empty cell. Brown closed the door hard and locked it. Looking at Depotti he said, "Have a nice evenin'," and walked out of the cell block.

Clarence spoke first. "How'd they get you?" he asked Depotti.

"I was workin' at Nix's up in Brookeland and the Deputy walked in and said I was under arrest for the burnin'."

"Fellas, it's late. Y'all settle down and we'll talk 'bout this in the morning. Just stick to the plan. That's all you gotta remember. Just stick to the plan," said Gurdon, "Now go on to bed and shut up."

None of the three rested easy. They all three understood on some level that their future and their freedom depended to some extent on what any of the other two might do or say. They certainly had to have each other's backs or they would all go down for the burnin'. Each was trying to figure out how to ensure the role the other two played would protect himself. They were also trying to figure out how to make sure the other two believed that he wouldn't canary on them. One little slip up or perceived disloyal act could send them all to Huntsville. All it would take would be for one of them to get a crack in their wall. If that happened it could be over with for all of them. Each, in their own way, decided to stay strong. The strength of determination varied among them, just like the physical strength varied among men. Only the future would determine who among them, was the strongest.

Part Seven

42

The Buildup

The *Jasper News-Boy*, Wednesday, September 18, 1901:

BURNING SUSPECTS CAUGHT, JAILED!
By Hector Henry, Publisher/Editor

Shown in the photo above are Jasper County Sheriff J.M. Brown (left) and Gurdon Marion, one of three suspects in the burning of Jasper on June 2, 1901, and Deputy Andrew Wayne (right).

Jasper County Sheriff J.M. Brown has confirmed that three suspects have been arrested and charged with arson and robbery in the burning of all the businesses on the south side of the courthouse square in Jasper on June 2, 1901. Charged are Gurdon Marion and Clarence Keaghey, both of Jasper, and Dave Depotti of Brookeland. All remain in the Jasper County jail without bond as none have yet appeared before a magistrate.

However, it is anticipated that all three will appear before Justice of the Peace Clyde Carson sometime today in the second-floor courtroom of the courthouse.

The suspects all fled Jasper shortly after the burning. Gurdon Marion was arrested just outside of Burkeville by Newton County Sheriff Henry Anderson as he attempted to escape. Clarence Keaghey was arrested without incident in Remlig and Dave Depotti was arrested at Nix's store in Brookeland. Both Keaghey and Depotti were arrested by Deputy Andrew Wayne. None of the miscreants resisted the badge of Sheriff Brown nor Deputy Wayne.

Asked if any of the scalawags had said anything about the burning or had confessed, Sheriff Brown said they had not mentioned a word about the burning and had not confessed. He said, in fact, all three denied knowing why they had been arrested and denied any involvement in the burning.

Sheriff Brown stated that some evidence had been recovered from one of the burned buildings to implicate at least one of the suspects. He declined to say what the evidence was or exactly where it was found.

The highly anticipated trial will take place in Judge Matt Davidson's courtroom. Judge Davidson has stated previously that when the suspects were apprehended, they would be provided a speedy trial. When asked about whether or not a jury would be empaneled, Judge Davidson replied that it would be up to the suspect's lawyers to request a jury trial or a bench trial.

It is not clear yet whether all three will be tried together or will have separate trials, which is their right according to Judge Davidson. When asked to clarify how soon a speedy trial would start, he anticipated between four and six weeks, depending on defense lawyer's motions and if a jury had to be empaneled. He also said that he did not see a need to move the trial to another location outside of Jasper County.

As a business victim of the trio, Jasper Postmaster Robert Haymar was asked his opinion about the trio receiving a fair trial. He said, "I believe that regardless of what type of trial is held that the good citizens of Jasper County will hear the evidence and come to a conclusion based on the evidence presented. I do not believe that a jury in another location could begin to fathom the impact the burning had on the town's business community nor its overall melancholy as a result. I know Judge Davison well and fully believe that he will be fair and impartial at trial and will not bow to the influence of others."

Wilford Hinson, the owner of Hinson's Domino
Parlor that burned was more pointed about what he
wanted to see happen. "I think the Judge ought to let
all of us who lost a business or a job sit on that jury to
judge them. Ain't nobody else as close to understanding
what kinda hard wallop this has had on all of us. It's
had a pretty big wallop on all the town folks too. It just
ain't fair them boys gonna have more rights than all of
us that lost our livelihood."

From all the antidotal evidence, most of the citizens
of Jasper are more agreeable with Mr. Hinson than Mr.
Haymar. Sheriff Brown said that he does not anticipate
having to deal with any kind of riot with citizens trying
to break the trio out of jail and provide them their
own type of justice. "If they come, they'll sure enough
have a fight on their hands. Ever man has to stand for
something, and ever man has to be willing to die for
somethin'. I'm willing to do whatever it takes to get
these prisoners to trial. The question folks have gotta
ask themselves is, are they willing to do the same to
keep them from justice."

Mrs. Georgette Philpott summed up the feelings of
many when she deemed the burning and upcoming trail
the biggest things to ever hit Jasper. She anticipated that
hundreds of people will turn out to watch the trial and to
hear the three suspects found guilty. The only question
in her mind was how severe the punishment would be.

The *Jasper News-Boy* will continue to cover this
story in depth as events unfold. Look for special
editions when significant events occur.

43

Pretrial

The following morning, Sheriff Brown separately escorted each of the prisoners to the second floor of the courthouse where Justice of the Peace Carson presided over the bail hearings. The benches were already full of spectators long before the first suspect ever arrived.

Appearing for the people was District Attorney Gilbert Powell. Powell was late in his first term as District Attorney and depending on whether or not he won the burnin' cases, would likely easily be re-elected for as many terms as he wanted. He was a middle-aged man, very slender, bespectacled and with an air of authority and intelligence despite the large, pock marked nose.

Appearing for each suspect was Cecil Farmer, much the opposite of the District Attorney in every way. He was young, rotund, loud and brash with an air of arrogance that annoyed most people. He had been practicing law for just over three years and had lost more cases than he had won. But as the only lawyer in town that wasn't a Judge or the District Attorney, he always got the indigent cases before Justice Carson and Judge Davidson.

Judge Carson asked each suspect for their plea, to which each pled not guilty. First was Gurdon Marion, then Clarence Keaghey and then finally Dave Depotti.

Then, in each hearing, Powell called Sheriff Brown to the stand, asked the same open-ended questions about the evidence gathered on each suspect and then dismissed the Sheriff, calling no other witnesses.

Without any fear, Justice Carson set each man's bail at five thousand dollars. He knew that none of the men could possibly have the five hundred dollars cash needed for the bond. It was that and the fact that he had already spoken to Harold Breasley, the only person in the county who did bail bonds. Breasley said there was, "No two ways in hell, and not a single chance in heaven" he would offer any of them a bond, even if it was only a dollar.

After each hearing, each suspect was returned to the jail to await a trial date in Judge Davidson's court.

The three suspects never said a word when anyone else was in the cell block. This raised suspicions with the Sheriff that the trio were conspiring to get their stories straight. It was the next afternoon following the bail hearings that he phoned Sheriff Anderson in Newton County and asked if he could transfer a couple of prisoners over there for detention until the first trial was over. After a little discussion about reimbursement, the two settled into an agreement. Brown instructed his Deputy to get a hack from Simms livery and take Keaghey and Depotti to the Newton County jail forthwith.

While Wayne had gone down the hill to Simms', Brown went up to the cell block and unlocked the cells for Keaghey and Depotti.

Depotti asked, "What's goin' on, Sheriff?"

"You're both gettin' out of here." When asked for further clarification, the Sheriff remained mum. He silently walked the two prisoners out of the cell block and as he did so, glanced back at the lone remaining prisoner who had a very confused and concerned look on his face.

Keaghey and Depotti were told to sit in the chairs in front of the Sheriff's desk. Brown placed handcuffs on each and put one side of a hobble on one leg of each man, effectively tying them together at the wrist and ankle.

Andrew came into the office shortly thereafter and he escorted the pair down the stairs telling them at the top, "You know it would be a real shame if one of you was to trip and fall down them stairs. Yep. A real shame. One of you falls, the other'n will too. Yep. Be a damned shame."

"Where's we goin'?" asked Depotti.

"Out of town," was all the Deputy would say as they loaded into the hack. They then headed east toward Newton.

Gurdon sat on the cot with his head in his hands wondering what had just happened. Did both those boys fink on him? What did they tell the JP? What did they tell the District Attorney? Did they tell the Sheriff anything? There was just too much to ponder. He could feel his confidence begin to slowly slip away and the thought of Huntsville became more and more real.

44

The Trial

It was finally here. It had taken over four months, but it was here. It was now mid-October and the first hint of cooler weather always arrived on the north winds this time of year. Everyone that farmed had their crops laid by except for the sweet potatoes, mustard, and turnip greens that are always harvested in the fall. Enough firewood had been cut, split and stacked to get through most of the winter and there were four cords on the south side of the courthouse for the stoves that were in each office.

Because Gurdon Marion was the first to go to trial, everyone believed he was the ringleader.

There was an excited buzz swirling around the town as speculation ran more rampant even than it had been immediately after the burning. These horrible people that had burned down the town were about to get their punishment and nothing could ever be too severe. There had been a little whispering going on among some of the younger men that they ought to storm the jail, take out the prisoners and then just hang them right there on the courthouse lawn. But the conversation eventually turned to Sheriff Brown's warning about being willing to die so they'd see justice, and that is when the testosterone filled conversations would begin to wane.

Both District Attorney Gilbert Powell and Cecil Farmer, the attorney representing Gurdon, had agreed on a jury trial. Accordingly, County Clerk V.L. Hefner sent out summons to sixty-three people. After mailing the summonses at the still temporary Post Office, he went to the third floor of the courthouse to ready the dormitory for those who might be chosen to serve. The dormitory could accommodate up to eighteen men. Anyone chosen that lived more than a two-hour ride from the courthouse would likely stay in the dormitory each night of the trial. Otherwise, they would have to leave home before daylight and get home after dark. With sixty-three summonses sent out, there would likely be at least fifty who would show up that didn't have a valid reason to be excused. The County had reserved ten rooms each at the White Hotel and the just finished Swann Hotel for those held over if needed for a second day of voir dire.

The area around the courthouse looked busier than a Saturday on the first of the month. The wagon yard was full and it looked as if every hitching post for a block around the square was full.

The spit and whittle club held court with many of the folks who were seeking the latest news about the trial. The group stated with absolute authority that they had the inside information that nobody else had other than the Sheriff, Judge and District Attorney. Turned out they knew nothing factual other than the date and time the trial would begin.

Court would begin promptly at nine o'clock, not one minute before and not one minute after. And woe be unto anyone with business before the court that was not in their assigned place and ready to begin in Judge Matt Davidson's court. The withering tongue lashings that Judge Davidson could give were legendary. There were some attorneys that, after being on the receiving end of one of his diatribes, refused to practice in front of the Judge ever again. Such was the command of the language that Judge Davidson possessed. He tolerated neither fool nor trick in his courtroom. The proceedings were run like a finely tuned Swiss watch and he would let nothing gum up the works.

The trial days would end as near to three o'clock as possible so the men on the jury who lived close enough could return home to do what chores could be done before dark.

Gurdon Marion watched the gathering of the crowd out of his cell window. Lawyer Farmer had been told that Keaghey and Depotti had been sent over to the Newton County jail, but he still wasn't sure why. Then he was told that Depotti had his bail lowered and that Stella Erwin had bailed him out. When he found out about this, he knew where she got the money. She had used the money he had given her in Burkeville. He decided to write Stella a letter and request she return the picture he had given her and tell her that he had no hard feelings. He also sent a letter to Depotti informing him about his letter to Stella and telling him he had no hard feelings toward him and guessing that he would be true to his word and marry her.

The trial, Stella, Keaghey, Depotti, the money, and the jail were all weighing heavily on Gurdon as he sat in his cell waiting to be taken to the courthouse where he would find out about his future. If he was lucky, he would get off with the whole thing like he did back in '97 on that other arson charge. They didn't have any real proof then, but this time just felt different.

Men were milling about on the courthouse lawn and inside the courthouse waiting for the courtroom doors to open. Promptly at eight o'clock, Bailiff John Capps opened the doors and only let in the men who had a jury summons. He also let in Hector Henry so he could have a front row seat to report the proceedings. When he was satisfied that all but maybe a few stragglers with summonses were present, he then let in the men who immediately took seats on the benches. When the benches filled up, the men began standing around the walls two deep. Loud groans were heard when, after calling for quiet with his deep resonant bass voice that was startling for a stooped old man, Bailiff Capps announced there would be no smoking, chewing or dipping during the trial. Three spittoons were passed around for all the chewers and dippers to deposit their used merchandise. One each to the benches on each side of the courtroom and one beginning on the right to be passed around for the ones standing.

After all the white folks were let in, the group of Negroes that had been waiting on the southwest corner of the square began to file into the courthouse. They then climbed three flights of stairs to the balcony reserved for Colored's only. Luke Simpson took a seat in the front row against the railing. He was anxious to see the results of his part in this spectacle. After all, it was him who identified the three white boys that done it. Still puzzling to him though was why that Oscar Brown fella hadn't been arrested with the rest of them.

Ladies were dissuaded from attending trials as many times it was just no place that a respectable lady should be. It was the prevailing belief that legal proceedings were simply too complicated for any woman to possibly understand. After all, they didn't understand politics and that was why they couldn't vote.

Negroes were not even allowed to serve on a jury even when the case involved Negro plaintiffs and defendants. The Negro's were, however, allowed to attend the trial of whites from the balcony of the courtroom. If the trial involved only Negro participants, any Negro wanting to watch still had to do so from the balcony. They could not witness the proceedings from the second-floor benches of the courtroom. That was reserved for whites, even though there would be no whites in attendance. Today, the balcony was standing room only.

Capps, in his deep baritone voice, announced that anyone with a summons should go through the bar gate and stand in the bar area. There was much shuffling and a little groaning at this, but all complied. He then gestured to the front five benches on the right side and announced that everyone must move.

Facing the potential jurors and holding open the bar gate, Capps said "Okay, I'm fixin' to call out the summons numbers in numerical order and I want the first number to sit on the front bench next to the center aisle, then the next number will sit next to him and so on." He then began the process of lining up the jurors in order.

The courtroom ran the whole width of the courthouse from north to south with windows in front and back that were twelve feet high. They were curved at the top in symmetry to match the curved pine board ceiling. Multicolored stained glass topped each window for the last foot and a half and cast interesting color patterns on the whitewashed walls. The Judge's bench was on the south side of the room and faced north. On those days in court when the afternoon sun got to just the right place, it allowed anyone paying attention to imagine a large halo being cast around the Judge. There were two oak double doors on each side of the courtroom with glass in the upper half and, depending on which door was entered, the bench would be either to the right or left. Two rows of long wooden benches began a few feet away from the rear wall and filled the spectator's area of the room, leaving a small aisle along each wall with a larger aisled in the middle and another just behind the bar.

The bar had an oaken half gate in the middle that separated the spectators from the participants. The prosecutor sat at the long oak table in front and to the right of the bench and the defense sat at a replica to the left side of the bench.

The crowd became instantly quite when shortly before nine o'clock, Gilbert Powell and Cecil Farmer walked through the west door, proceeded through the swinging gate at the bar and took their respective places. The tension in the room was almost palpable. If anyone spoke it was in a quiet whisper, if at all.

Then the room became deadly silent when Sheriff Brown walked in, escorting Gurdon Marion who had on handcuffs and a horizontally striped jail jumpsuit. They also walked through the bar gate where he was seated at the table beside Farmer. Brown removed the handcuffs and stuck them in his back pocket and took a seat to the left of the Judges bench facing Gurdon.

The witness box was on the right side of the Judge's bench. Tom Bill Clark, the court reporter, was next to enter and took his place at the small desk under the Judge's bench and just to the left of the witness box. This allowed him to better understand exactly what was said by each party. He faced the jury box to the right of the bench.

As the clock in the courtroom struck nine o'clock, Bailiff Capps ordered all to rise and Judge Matt Davidson, dressed in a black robe and a bowtie, opened the door to his chambers, walked over and took the two steps up behind the massive oak bench. He sat down heavily in the high-backed leather chair, banged his gavel once and announced, "You may be seated." This brought a few chuckles from those that were standing. Judge Davidson had to smile at his unintended humor.

45

Come to Order

Judge Davidson gazed around the courtroom. What little whispering had been taking place immediately stopped.

"Council, are you ready to proceed," asked Davidson of Powell and Farmer. Both stood and in unison said, "Yes, your honor," then sat down.

"Mr. Marion," said the Judge as Marion and Farmer stood, "Do you understand the charges and the reason you are here today? You understand that you have been charged with arson and robbery related to the burnin' of Jasper, Texas, on June 2, 1901?"

Marion stood ramrod straight, looked the Judge in the eye and with a strong voice said, "Yes, your honor."

"How do you plead to the charges?"

"Not guilty, your honor," said Gurdon forcefully. A round of chatter from the crowd quickly subsided as Davidson banged his gavel.

Turning his attention to the jury pool, Davidson said, "For your information, both lawyers anticipate the trial to last at least two days. How long it takes to reach a verdict will be up to the twelve of you that are selected. All right then. Mr. Powell you may proceed with voir dire."

"Thank you, Judge." He turned to face the prospective jurors. "I think each of you know why you're here today. You are here to sit in judgement of Mr. Gurdon Marion, the defendant sitting there." He pointed toward Gurdon and continued. "As the Judge said, Mr. Marion is charged with arson and robbery in connection with the burnin' of Jasper in the early morning hours of June 2, 1901. That fire burned six businesses to the ground. Two safes were broken into and money was stolen from them. I will ask you now if any of you men have any kind of relationship with Mr. Marion that would not allow you to judge the facts impartially and if you do, please raise your hand."

A hand went up in the middle of the fourth row.

"Please stand and tell us your name," said Powell.

"Daniel Summerland," was the reply.

"Please share with the court the nature of your relationship that would not allow you to be impartial," said Powell.

"Well, sir. I got a question first," said Summerland.

"Go ahead."

"What's bein' impartial mean?" asked Summerland with an honest quizzical look.

"Well, it means that you haven't already made up your mind about whether Mr. Marion did the crimes he is accused of. If you have already made up your mind, then you couldn't be impartial."

"Ok, then." And looking straight at Powell said, "He done it awright."

Farmer was immediately on his feet and shouted, "Objection!"

"Sustained," said Davidson as the crowd became restless and the murmuring became so loud the Judge had to bang his gavel several times to gain order. "The court will be in order! Order!" said Davidson banging the gavel. "Mr. Sutherland you are excused. Now then. Is there anybody else out there that thinks like Mr. Sutherland?" Eleven hands went up. He then asked if anyone had a relationship with any of the merchants that wouldn't allow them to be impartial. Three more hands went up.

"Bailiff, I want you to escort these gentlemen to my chambers one at a time. Mr. Powell and Mr. Farmer, you will come with me. This court will stand in recess," ordered Davidson.

The three rose from their chairs and proceeded through the door into the Judge's chambers. One by one, each of the men came into the office to explain why they could not be impartial. Each reason was a little different, but they all had the same theme of pre-judging the case before the facts were presented. Each one was dismissed, told to go to the County Clerk's office to receive their jury pay of twenty-five cents and were free to go home or stay and watch the trial. All went home.

The two lawyers followed Davidson back into the courtroom and each took their place.

"We are back on the record," said Davidson to Tom Bill Clark, nodding that he should begin recording the proceedings once again.

"Okay," said Davidson, "each of you has had an opportunity to state whether or not you could be impartial and none of the rest of you stated such. Therefore, no other statements from any of the rest of the prospective jurors about impartiality will be entertained. So, let me ask this question; Does anyone left have any other reason that they believe would not allow them to serve?"

One man raised his hand. "What is your name, sir," asked Davidson.

"Wesley Davis, Judge."

"And what reason do you have that you believe will not let you serve?"

"I got a mare 'bout to foal, Judge. Gonna be any day now. My kids are growed and my wife can't do it, she don't know how. The mare's teats filled up day before yesterday. She may be havin' that colt right now."

"How many horses and mules do you own?"

"This'n here is the only one, Judge. If'n I lose her, I can't afford to buy another one. I just barely had enough money to get her bred."

Davidson look at both lawyers and asked, "Any objection?" Both shook their heads and Davis was dismissed.

"Okay, anybody else," asked the Judge in an exasperated voice. Nobody moved. Nobody raised a hand. Nobody said anything. "That's it then. No more reasons to be excused."

The voir dire resumed with Powell giving a broad outline of the crimes committed, omitting most detail and only sharing the very basic facts of what happened. He then began asking general questions of the men. Do you have any kind of relationship with any of the merchants that lost their business? Do you think arson is a serious crime? Do you think robbery is a serious crime? Do you think you can reasonably punish Mr. Marion if you find him guilty? Do you know what beyond a reasonable doubt means?

Farmer got up next and briefly stated the facts of the case as he saw them. That Mr. Marion did not do any of the crimes for which he is charged and was asleep at his house when the explosion occurred. That there would be witnesses that would testify that Mr. Marion was at the fire and attempted to help put it out, which any guilty man would certainly not do.

The voir dire ended and Judge Davidson recessed for dinner, telling all prospective jurors to return at one o'clock. The three once again retired to chambers.

"Awright, gentlemen. Let's get to it," said the Judge.

Powell went first and declared peremptory challenges on four jurors, then Farmer maximized his peremptory challenges naming ten jurors. He asked that the jury be shuffled prior to selection. Powell did not disagree and the Judge said he would do so upon resuming court. Davidson said he wanted to appoint two alternate jurors just in case. Both attorneys agreed.

"Gentlemen, I want this to be a fair trial and I'm going to let the facts lay where they may. I will remind you that I do not like tricks or shenanigans in my court. And with that, I will see you back at one o'clock."

46

Opening Arguments

After dinner, the courtroom was again packed and everyone was in place. The lawyers were in place and when the courtroom clock struck one, Judge Davidson came through the chamber's door, Capps ordered all to rise. Davidson resumed his place on the bench, banged his gavel once and told everyone to be seated.

"We are now back in session. Bailiff, please shuffle the jury."

The jury pool was shuffled and after some minor confusion on the part of the jurors, all took seats in new places on the spectator benches.

Davidson pronounced, "We will seat twelve members in the jury box. Both sides have agreed to also select two alternates who will take the place of any juror that is unable to complete their duty. The Bailiff will read the names of the jurors. As he does so, please come and take a seat in the jury box. You may sit wherever you would like. Bailiff, read the names of the jurors, please."

Capps rose and began reading from the list of names, "Harvey Nickerson. Winfred O'Shea. L.D. Ray. Conny Dotson. Leonard Cordrey. C.J. Harold. Arnold Hankel. Terrance Nerren. Jimbo Caruthers. George Newton. Hugh Landis. A.L. Weatherford. M.K. Vickers. These are the jurors," announced Capps.

After reading the names of the twelve, Davidson said, "And now Bailiff, please read the names of the two alternates."

"The following are alternate jurors. When your name is called, sit in one of the two chairs beside the jury box. Ofeleus Comeaux and V.E. Fuller," said the Bailiff.

"Gentlemen, you have been selected to sit in judgement on the guilt or innocence of the defendant, Mr. Gurdon Marion. You should hear the evidence impartially and use your common sense. With that, please rise and raise your right hand for the oath. 'You and each of you do solemnly swear that in the case of the State of Texas against the defendant, you will a true verdict render according to the law and the evidence, so help you God.' Now say I do." Each did. "You may be seated. Mr. Powell you may begin with your opening statement."

As Powell rose, he said, "Thank you, your honor. I will be brief because I believe the evidence in this case is sufficient to find that man over there," pointing at Gurdon, "guilty beyond a reasonable doubt. That man, along with two others conspired to rob two businesses in town and in doing so, burned down the whole south side of the square." Powell began speaking louder and louder, pacing in front of the jury and flourishing his hands and gesturing like a fire and brimstone preacher. "Until June second of this year, you could look out of the windows behind Judge Davidson's bench and see half a dozen thriving businesses. Businesses that were vital to the sustained growth of Jasper and the surrounding farms and communities. Businesses that the fine citizens of Jasper and Jasper County depended on for their livelihood and for the goods that were necessary to live a happy and healthy life. Those businesses are now gone thanks to the wicked ways of that man right there," he again pointed at Gurdon, "That man's greed caused this. That man's sloth caused this. That man's devious mind caused this. That man is evil. He is worthless. He does not deserve to walk the streets of this or any other town as a free man. He needs to go to prison. He needs to stay in prison for a very long time. I ask each of you to listen to the overwhelming evidence that Gurdon Marion was the ringleader and find him guilty of arson and robbery. Thank you." Powell walked back to the prosecution table and sat down.

"Mr. Farmer, your opening statement," said the Judge.

Farmer rose and walked toward the jury box; his head bent forward with a contemplative look on his face. Quietly and slowly, he began, "Gentlemen of the jury. I want to thank you for your service to this community by sittin' on this jury. This is a sacred honor that has been entrusted to you. Each of you swore an oath to render a verdict based on the evidence and the law. That is all I ask of you. To just listen to the evidence and then apply the law. My client is innocent, as will be proven. Mr. Powell is confident in his case, but so am I. I truly believe that after hearing all the evidence, and I urge you to keep an open mind until you do hear all the evidence, that you will find Mr. Gurdon Marion not guilty. Thank you." Farmer slowly walked back to the defense table and sat down, he leaned over to Gurdon and whispered, "Act like I am saying somethin' profound and just nod your head like you agree." Which Gurdon did in true thespian fashion.

"Okay Mr. Powell, you may call your first witness," said Davidson.

"The state calls Mrs. Stella Depotti."

"Mr. Capps, would you please retrieve Mrs. Depotti," said the Judge.

Capps rose, went through the bar gate and out the east courtroom door to the witness room. He returned shortly, following her back through the door and then holding the bar gate open, escorted her to the witness box on the right side of the bench diagonally in front of the jury box.

Capps held out a bible with his left hand and raised his right hand heavenward, asked her to do the same and said, "Do you swear to tell the truth, the whole truth and nothing but the truth so help you God?"

"I do."

"Please be seated."

"Okay, Mr. Powell. Proceed," said Davidson.

"What is your name?"

"Stella Depotti."

"Where do you live?"

"I live in Gilmer, Texas."

"Where are you living now?"

"I am now living at Brookeland Texas."

"How long have you been living there?"

"I have been living there about four months."

"Mrs. Depotti, would you mind to please raise your head so that the jury can see your face as you answer these questions and please speak a little louder so they might hear more clearly?" She complied and Powell then asked, "Do you know Gurdon Marion?"

"Yes, sir."

"Where were you the second of June when the town of Jasper burned?"

"I was here in Jasper visiting."

"Who were you visiting?"

"My sister. Mrs. W.P. Nix."

"State whether or not you have heard Mr. Marion say anything about his whereabouts that night."

"He was down at Mr. Nix's store until about two o'clock that night."

"How do you know that?"

"He said so. He told me he was there."

"When did he tell you this?"

"When he carried us to Brookeland. The Nix's and me."

"Did you ever hear Mr. Marion say anything about the burning of the town of Jasper or burglarizing the Post Office or anything?"

"Yes sir, I did."

"When was that?"

"When he and I went to Burkeville."

"Now, will you please tell the Court just what he told you about that? And please speak up."

"He told me that he broke into his father's shop and got his tools and prized the Post Office door open and drilled a hole in the safe and got some money. I forget which one he said whether it was the Post Office or Nix's that made such a flash."

"What do you mean by a flash?"

"The flash or light from the safes. He said when the light flashed, he got scared and ran off but that he intended to get all there was in the Post Office and Nix's safe too. He said he used to much powder. He said that was the first time he ever did anything like that, but it was not going to be the last time."

"Is that all he said about the robbery and burnin'?"

"Yes sir, that was all."

"Did you see him with any money?"

"Yes sir. I did."

"Do you know about how much he had?"

"I saw six fives and two ten-dollar bills."

"What did he say about the money?"

"He told me that if anybody should ask if he had any money to tell them no, that he didn't have any at all, that all he had he give to me because if they were to see him with money, they would suspicion somethin' right straight."

"State whether he said he had any more money besides what you saw."

"He just patted his vest pocket and said he had plenty of money and didn't have to work for it neither."

"Would you please speak up and repeat that for the jury, please?"

"He said he had plenty of money and didn't have to work for it neither."

"Did he say anything about how they got out of the store, of the building?"

"He said he went through a hole out of the Post Office into Nix's and then went out of Nix's store at the back door."

"Did you ever see any letters from Gurdon Marion to Dave Depotti?

"Yes, sir."

"Would you state what was in the letters?"

"Gurdon asked him what on earth he had married for. Told him you know you can't get away now and you had better watch your point."

"Is that all you remember, nothing else?"

"No, sir, nothing else in the letter."

"Did he tell you who else was with him at Nix's store that night at two o'clock?"

"Yes, sir. Barney Robinson, Jesse Robinson and another young man."

"Would you know his name if it was called?"

"Yes, sir."

"Was it Clarence Keaghey?"

"Yes sir."

"Do you know whether he stated whether or not Leo Blake was there?"

"Leo Blake was there to."

"Your honor, that is all I have for this witness at this time," said Powell.

"Very well. Mr. Farmer do you wish to cross examine?" asked Davidson.

"Yes. Thank you, your honor," replied Farmer who rose from his seat and stood before the jury box facing the witness.

"Now Mrs. Depotti, where did you say you were when this statement was made about the money and goin' into the Post Office and Nix's Store?"

"At Burkeville. At the Windom Hotel."

"How long did you stay there?"

"Stayed there a day and a half."

"How long did he stay there?"

"He didn't stay there but about two or three hours."

"Was there anyone else present when he was with you?"

"A young lady part of the time."

"What was her name?"

"I disremember her name."

"You can't recall her name then?"

"The young lady's married sister was named Dean, but I don't remember her name."

"Was her name Kate Dean?"

"Yes. Kate."

"Was she married?"

"No, sir."

"Was she with you and Mr. Marion part of the time you were together?"

"Yes, sir."

"What part of the hotel were you in when the three of you were together?

"Our room. Well, my room. Mr. Pike Windom wouldn't let me and Gurdon stay in the room together 'cause we weren't married."

"How did Mr. Marion get into the room then?"

"He come up the back stairs."

"And how did Miss. Dean get into the room?"

"She come with Gurdon."

"And how long were the three of you together in the room?"

"I guess about an hour."

"And what did the three of you do for that hour?"

When Stella heard the question, she immediately reddened in the face and ducked her head. She sat silently trying to figure out a way to not answer the question. If she was caught lying it could be big trouble.

"Mrs. Depotti, please answer the question," said Farmer.

Neither her position nor demeanor changed. She just sat there.

"Mrs. Depotti, you must answer the question," instructed Davidson.

"I can't."

"Why not?" asked the Judge.

"Not in front of all these people. Please Judge, don't make me answer that," she began to sob.

"Counsel, both of you approach."

When both lawyers arrived at the bench the Judge said, "Well, what do you want me to do?"

"I'm not sure what went on in that room and I'm not sure it's relevant to this case," said Powell. "What they did or didn't do in that room likely has no relevance on who did or didn't do the burnin'."

"I tend to agree. Mr. Farmer?" inquired the Judge.

"Well, she certainly appears to be embarrassed about whatever happened in there. I'll withdraw the question if it's okay with both of you."

Both men agreed and the lawyers returned to their tables.

"Your honor, I respectfully withdraw the previous question."

"Okay, then. You may continue."

"You said it was at this time that Mr. Marion described to you the manner in which he broke into the Post Office?"

"Yes, sir."

"Did he tell you that he took anything from the store or only from the Post Office?"

"He never told me he took anything out of any place but the Post Office."

"What did he tell you he took?"

"He said he got some money."

"Did he show you any money?"

"Yes sir. Six fives and two ten-dollar bills."

"How long did he stay after Miss Dean left?"

"About an hour."

"Do you know where he went?"

"He was going to take the hack back to Brookeland or hire somebody else to do it and pay them a dollar if they would."

"When did you see him next and what did he say?"

"I seen him when he got back to Burkeville after the Sheriff arrested him. I was in the lobby when the Sheriff brung him in. He told me to go back to Brookeland and that the Sheriff had arrested him and that when he got loose, he would go back."

"Did he leave you any money?"

"No, sir. Well, he did give me ten cents."

"What did he carry his money in?

"In a purse in his vest pocket."

"Please describe the purse for the jury," requested Farmer.

"It was kinda a ladies purse that folded up and about six inches long and three inches wide. Had diagonal stripes on it."

"Did you see any money in this purse?"

"Yes, sir."

"You stated a while ago that he said somethin' about this money between Farrsville and Burkeville, state what that was for the jury please."

"He told me if anybody ask you if I had any money, you tell them no, that I had no money at all and what I had you gave it to me. If somebody would see me with it, they would suspicion something right straight."

"Did you suspicion him of havin' burned the town?"

"After he began talkin' I did."

"Did you suspicion him before that?

"No, sir. I never suspicioned him until he told me to keep the money a secret."

"Did you tell anybody about what Mr. Marion said to you?"

"I told my brother-in-law, Mr. W.P. Nix."

"When did you tell him this?"

"The next day after I got back to Brookeland."

"How did you get back to Brookeland??"

"Mr. Jeffries carried me home before Mr. Nix came. I sent Mr. Nix word to come after me and Mr. Jeffries got there first and brought me home and Mr. Nix got home after we did that night."

"What time did you leave Brookeland to go to Burkeville?"

"About three thirty in the afternoon on Sunday."

"And what time did you arrive at Burkeville the next day?"

"It was about ten o'clock in the mornin'."

"Where did you stay that night?"

"We drove all that night. We stopped once to feed the horses at somebody's house close to Farrsville."

"Did you take the main road from Farrsville to Burkeville?"

"I don't know. I ain't familiar with the roads in these parts."

"Now, you were drivin' along this road when he told you all these things about the money and breakin' into the Post Office and the flash?"

"Yes, sir."

"You stated that Mr. Jeffries carried you home, did you say anythin' to him about this matter?"

"No, sir. But he did to me."

"What did he say?"

"Objection! Hearsay, your honor," shouted Powell rising to his feet.

"Sustained," said the Judge.

"Why did you not say anythin' to him about it? Did you have a reason?"

"Because I didn't want to have my name in it at all."

"Did Mr. Jefferies ask you questions as to whether Mr. Marion had told you anythin' about the burnin' of the town?"

"Yes, sir. He asked me that."

"Objection, your honor," said Powell half standing.

"Overruled. You may answer the question," said the Judge.

"Let me ask this a different way," said Farmer. "When did Mr. Jeffries ask you that question as to whether Mr. Marion had told you about the burnin' of the town, please state what you said."

"Objection," shouted Powell rising to his feet.

"Overruled," said Davidson.

"Did you not on that occasion, when he asked you that question, tell him that Mr. Marion had told you nothin' about it?"

"No, sir. I never told him that."

"Then what did you tell him?"

"Objection! Your honor, this line of questioning is pure hearsay," said Powell rising to his full height.

"Sustained," said the Judge, "Go somewhere else counselor."

"Now, on the night of the burnin' you stated in the direct examination that Mr. Marion told you that he was at Nix's store at two o'clock. Did he say he was there at the time of two o'clock or from what time?"

"He just said he was there till two o'clock."

"Did you attend the dance on the evenin' before the burnin'?"

"Yes, sir."

"Did you see Mr. Marion there at the dance?"

"Yes, sir."

"Did you dance with him that night?"

"Yes, sir."

"Is it true you and Mr. Marion danced together quite a bit that night?"

"Yes, sir."

"Did he walk you home after the dance?"

"No sir. Mr. Nix come and got me and took me home."

"What time was this?"

"I guess a little before midnight."

"Did Mr. Marion tell you which safe it was that he blew open?"

"Yes, sir. The Post Office safe."

"Did he say about what time he blew the Post Office safe open?"

"He said 'bout three o'clock."

"What, if anythin', did he say about the safe in Nix's store?"

"He said that was the safe that made the flash."

"Did he tell you how he got out of Nix's store and where he went when he left?

"Yes, sir. Said when it flashed, him and the rest got scared and they went out the back door, but he didn't say nothin' 'bout where he went."

Nobody else in the courtroom noticed, but a young Negro boy in the first row of the balcony edged toward the front of his seat when he heard this question. This was his part.

"That's all I have your honor," said Farmer.

"Any re-direct, Mr. Powell?" asked the Judge.

"No, your honor, but I would like to possibly recall this witness for rebuttal later on."

"Very well. Mrs. Depotti, you must return to the witness room until dismissed," said the Judge.

Stella stepped down from the jury box with her head held high and without looking at either lawyers table, walked over to the bar gate that Bailiff Capps was holding open for her, turned right, went out of the double doors and disappeared around the corner.

"The state calls Mr. W.P. Nix to the stand," Powell said as he stood.

Bailiff Capps had already walked to the west door of the courtroom waiting to see whom would be called. He went through the door and returned shortly, leading Nix through the bar gate and to the witness stand where Nix was given the oath and told to be seated.

"Would you please state your name for the court," asked Powell still standing behind the prosecution table.

"W.P. Nix."

"Do you know Gurdon Marion?"

"Yes, sir."

"That him sittin' over there?" asked Powell pointing at Gurdon.

"Yes, sir."

"What were you doin' at the time of the burnin' of Jasper?"

"I was runnin' a store down here."

"Did that store burn?"

"Yes, sir."

"Where were you livin' at that time?"

"Livin' in Jasper."

"How long did you stay after the burnin'?"

"The fire was on the second of June, and I left on the thirteenth."

"Where did you go?"

"Brookeland."

"What business are you in up there?"

"Same business I was in here. Fancy groceries, confectionaries and sellin' malt."

"Who moved you up to Brookeland and how did you go up there?"

"I went in Mr. Marion's surrey and took my family."

"Was Mrs. Depotti livin' with you then?"

"Yes, sir."

"Who drove the surrey?"

"Gurdon Marion."

"State whether or not the defendant said anythin' about as to where he was on the night of the fire?"

"He said he was at the ball down here at the Armory and down to my store after the ball at two o'clock the night of the burnin'."

"Mr. Nix, did you know anything about Gurdon Marion havin' any money at that time or at any time after that?"

"No, sir. But after he returned to Jasper and then come back to Brookeland he said that he didn't have to ask me for credit, that he had plenty of money to pay his way. I told him that I wasn't gonna sell anybody anythin' on credit, wouldn't credit my own daddy if he was livin'. Gurdon said I needn't be throwin' slurs at him that he don't want any more damn credit out of me or anybody else. He said he used to have to ask me for credit before I left Jasper, but he had plenty of money to pay his way now. Then he said he didn't have to work for it neither by-God."

"Before you left here, did you credit him any?"

"Yes, sir. He got about two dollars worth before I left here. He had run some little tickets before and, at the time I left Jasper, he owed me two dollars and paid me out of the wagon hire and said he would make it awright with his daddy."

"Do you know what he went up to Brookeland for?"

"He went up to carry us and said that he was comin' back up there and run a barber shop."

"What remark did he make about that?"

"He said he wanted to get out of Jasper. He wanted to fool the people there in Brookeland anyhow. He didn't give a damn whether he worked any or not, that he didn't have to work that this old working racket was gettin' old with him."

"Did Mrs. Depotti ever tell you anythin' about what Gurdon had told her 'bout the burnin' of the town and blowin' open the Post Office safe?"

"Yes, sir. She told me that the day after I got back from Burkeville."

"I have no more questions at this time, Judge," said Powell as he sat back down.

"Okay. Mr. Farmer you want to cross?" asked Davidson.

'Yes. Thank you, your honor," replied Farmer.

"Now, Mr. Nix," said Farmer as he strolled toward the jury box, "Did you ask Mrs. Depotti about it first or did she tell you first?"

"She told me without me askin'."

"Did you, before you went to Brookeland or afterwards, hear any accusation or suspicion against Gurdon Marion?"

"No, sir. Don't believe I did."

"Did you hear anythin' after you went to Brookeland?"

"Yes, sir."

"How long after you got there before you heard he was suspicioned?"

"I never heard nothin' 'bout it until I got back from Burkeville."

"What time did you leave the store on the night of the burnin'?"

"I went by there on my way to the dance to get Mrs. Depotti so it was somewhere around eleven or eleven thirty."

"Who was at the store when you left?"

"Clarence Keaghey and Leo Blake and some of the railroad fellows. I think Jesse and Barney Robinson and Gurdon Marion came in just as I left. Actually, I know that they did."

"You spoke about refusin' Gurdon credit. Did he have plenty of money with him when you refused to credit him?"

"Yes, sir. He spent some money with me at Brookeland. I can't say how much though. I don't rightly remember."

"Who went with you to Burkeville to get Mrs. Depotti?"

"Old man W.J. Simms."

"What were your feelin's toward Gurdon Marion at that time?"

"I had ill feelin's against him."

"Did you or not, make any threats against him?"

"I don't think I did."

"Were you armed when you went over there? Did you have a gun or a pistol?"

"Well, there was a pistol in the buggy. I asked Mr. Currey if he had a pistol or gun and one of them put it in the buggy at my request."

"Mr. Nix, you have said that Mrs. Depotti had no money while she was at your house?"

"No, sir. I don't remember whether anybody asked me about it or not."

"Did Mr. Miller not ask you?"

"Objection," shouted Powell as he came to his feet.

"Sustained," said Davidson.

"Okay. Let me try and ask this a different way. Immediately after your arrival from Burkeville back to Brookeland, did Mr. Miller ask you anythin' about it, or did you make any statement to him?"

"Come on! Objection your honor. Hearsay," said Powell.

"Sustained," said the Judge.

"In that case I have no more questions at this time," said Farmer walking back to the defense table.

"You have any re-direct Mr. Powell?"

"Yes, your honor. Thank you." Powell said as he took Farmers place in front of the jury box. "Mr. Nix, could your feelin's towards Mr. Marion cause you to swear falsely on this witness stand?"

"No, sir."

"State if Gurdon Marion told you that they were at that malt stand at two o'clock and did he say who else was with him at that hour and who they were?"

"I am not positive whether he told me who was with him, but a gang was in there. Bout the same bunch I said before. Jesse and Barney Robinson, Clarence Keaghey and Leo Blake and he said there was a whole push in there."

"Mr. Nix, we want you to state as near as you can in the language in which Mrs. Depotti told you when she got back to Brookeland, what Gurdon Marion told her about the burnin'?"

Farmer was on his feet, "Objection, your honor. Hearsay!"

"Sustained."

"Alright," said Powell walking back to the table, "That's all I've got."

Looking at the witness, Judge Davidson said, "You're excused but are subject to recall." As Nix walked from the stand, Davidson said, "Gentlemen, it's getting' close to three o'clock and I believe we have had a good, productive day. We will stand in recess until nine o'clock in the mornin'." Judge Matt Davidson banged his gavel once, everyone in the courtroom rose as he rose from his chair, took the two steps down from the bench and walked through his chambers door.

47

The Second Day

Not long after daybreak on the second day of the trial, a knot of people had gathered around the spit and whittle club. With the usual speculation and without most of the facts from the day before, they once again became the oracles of Jasper and, in their minds, accurately predicting the outcome of the trial.

When the courthouse doors opened at eight o'clock there was already a line of men waiting to get seats for the second day. It only took minutes for the courtroom to once again fill to standing room only.

Farmer came in a little before nine o'clock and a few minutes later Powell arrived. Both busied themselves with papers pulled from their respective briefcases. The Sheriff brought in the accused and deposited him at the table with Farmer, resuming his place to the left of the bench.

When the clock in the courtroom struck nine, the door to Judge Davidson's chambers opened and Bailiff Capps, thundered, "All rise!"

Judge Davidson took the two steps up to the bench and as he sat down, banged his gavel and said, "Be seated. Good morning gentlemen. Are each of you prepared to proceed?"

Both lawyers rose and affirmed they were.

"Very well then. Mr. Powell, you may call your next witness."

"Yes, your honor. The state calls Mr. J.B. Faircloth," he said as he stood at the table.

Capps, now following a familiar routine, retrieved Faircloth from the witness room, escorted him to the witness stand, swore him in and told him to be seated.

"Would you please tell the court your name," asked Powell still standing at the table.

"Heck Gilbert, everbody knows me," replied Faircloth.

"You are likely correct in that, but we must have it for the record. Now, kindly state your name please."

"J.B. Faircloth."

"Do you know the defendant, Gurdon Marion?"

"Yes, sir."

"Did you have a buildin' here in Jasper that burned?"

"Yes, sir."

"Did you give anybody permission to burn your buildin' or go into it?"

"No, sir."

"Was not the Post Office in your buildin'?"

"Yes, sir."

"Nothing further, your honor," and with that sat back down.

"Mr. Farmer," said Davidson.

Farmer stood at the defense table and said, "Thank you, your honor. Mr. Faircloth, was there any kind of openin' between the Post Office and your store?"

"Yes, sir."

"What sort of openin' was that?"

"It was a small wood window, I suppose near 'bout two feet square. It was hinged and fastened with a hook and staple from the inside of the Post Office. It couldn't have been opened from the store side without it bein' broke completely out."

"Mr. Powell asked you the question if you authorized Gurdon Marion to burn your store and you stated you didn't. You don't say Gurdon burned your store, do you?"

"No, sir."

With that answer, Farmer turned to the jury scanning their faces briefly before saying, "That's all, your honor," and walking back to the table.

"Very well. Mr. Faircloth, you are dismissed. You may leave or you may stay and watch the remainder or any part of the rest of these proceedings," said Davidson.

"Think I'll hang around for a bit, Judge," said Faircloth grinning. He then walked through the bar gate and stood along the west wall.

"Mr. Powell, you have another witness?" asked the Judge.

"Yes, your honor. I recall W.P. Nix to the stand," said Powell.

Capps began the all too familiar routine and retrieved Nix and led him back to the witness stand.

"Mr. Nix, you are reminded that you are still under oath, do you understand that?"

"Yes, sir."

"Mr. Powell you may proceed."

"Mr. Nix, when Mrs. Depotti returned from Burkeville and after you had returned from Burkeville, we want you to state what she told you in reference to the burnin' that mornin' that he told her?"

"These people over here at the Windom Hotel bein' run by Pike Windom and Mrs. Windom, told me about some money that Gurdon had, and I asked Mrs. Depotti how she got that money that they were talkin' 'bout at the hotel."

"What was it the Windom's told you?"

"They told me that he had some money, that he got her to tell that it belonged to her and not to tell that it belonged to him."

"To be clear, did they say that Mrs. Depotti had any money?"

"No, sir. She didn't have no money as I had to pay her hotel bill. Mrs. Depotti said the reason he didn't want the people to see him with the money that they might suspicion somethin', as he was not use to handlin' that much before and everbody know'd that he didn't have much money."

"Mr. Nix, please refresh your memory and tell it just as near as she told it to you."

"She said he told her this before they got to Burkeville and after they got to Burkeville, he told her about gettin' some tools out of his daddy's shop and that she need not be afraid to marry him that he had plenty of money and showed her some of it. I believe it was six fives and two ten dollar bills. Said he and his chums both had plenty of money but didn't say who his chums was, for he didn't tell no names. He said he didn't have to work for the money neither and that he was not goin' to work for it. I believe that was all he said about the money before they got to Burkeville. After they got to Burkeville, he told her he was goin' back to Brookeland to bring that team back to Mr. Miller or get somebody to carry them back or he would carry it part of the way himself and let somebody else carry it the rest of the way. Somethin' was said about that if'n he couldn't find nobody to carry the team back, he'd just turn 'em loose and they would go on to Leesville and get married. He said he would change his name when they got there to marry and told her to say nothin' 'bout it so that they wouldn't bother him after they got over there and married. He then commenced to tellin' her about gettin' some tools out of his daddy's shop. I don't know whether or not he said that he got them tools or they got them tools, but he said the shop was went into and got some tools. He didn't say what kind but did say that he was the only one that knew where his daddy kept his best tools. He said after that, they went and pried the back door of the Post Office open and went in. I think they drilled a hole in the Post Office safe and then they went through the hole into my store and fixed that safe in there and then opened the back door and let his chums in. They shut the back door and put the powder in the safes and I don't remember which it was that made such a flash, but they had got the Post Office money and intended gettin' the all of it out of my safe but failed on account of that big flash."

"So, just to clarify. Gurdon Marion told her that he got the money out of the Post Office safe?"

"Yes, sir. Said he would have got more out of my safe and the whole push if it hadn't made such a flash that it set the buildin' on fire. But if the powder hadn't set the buildin' on fire, they intended to set it on fire so as to hide what they done and they intended to carry the tools back, but they got scared and didn't have time to carry 'em back. I think that was all that was told me 'bout the burnin'."

"Thank you, Mr. Nix. No more questions."

"Mr. Farmer?"

"Nothin', your honor."

"Okay then. Mr. Nix you are excused. Like Mr. Faircloth, you are welcomed to stay or go as you wish," said Davidson.

"I think I'd rather go on back home to Brookeland if it's all the same to you, Judge."

"You are free to go."

"Your honor, the state rests," stated Powell to a stunned audience and an even more stunned defense attorney.

Judge Davidson, looking somewhat puzzled inquired, "Are you sure?"

"Yes, your honor. I'm sure."

48

The Defense

"Okay, then. Mr. Farmer you may call your first witness."

"Thank you, your honor," said Farmer rising behind the table, "The defense calls Miss Valley Marion as its first witness."

Capps escorted her to the witness box, swore her in and invited her to be seated.

"Where were you on the night of the burnin'," asked Farmer.

"I was at home, here in Jasper."

"There was a dance in town that night. Did you attend?"

"Yes, sir."

"Was Gurdon Marion there?"

"Yes, sir."

"Is Gurdon Marion your brother?"

"Yes, sir."

"Where do you and Gurdon live?"

"With our daddy."

"Do you have a younger sister named Minnie?

"Yes, sir."

"Did you and your sister have company that night?"

"Yes, sir. Mr. Barney Robinson and Mr. Oscar Brown."

"Who was with who?"

"I was with Mr. Robinson and Minnie was with Mr. Brown."

"What time did you leave the dance to go home?"

"It was a short time before midnight, the clock struck twelve just before we got home."

"What time did they leave your house?"

"Mr. Brown left a little after midnight and Mr. Robinson left a little after Mr. Brown."

"Now, state whether or not Gurdon went home and what time he went home if he did."

"He went home when I did. Went in the house just ahead of me."

"Well do you know what became of him after he went into the house?"

"He went to bed."

"What time did you retire?"

"A little after one o'clock."

"Did you notice whether Gurdon was in bed when you went to bed?"

"Yes, sir. I went by his door and saw him in bed. I'd gone to get a drink of water."

"Do you recollect what time the alarm of the fire was given?"

"Yes, sir. It was a little after three o'clock as I recall. I got up to see 'bout all the commotion."

"Who else got up then?"

"Papa, Minnie, Gurdon and myself got up."

"So, you saw Gurdon before you left the house?"

"Yes, sir."

"Do you know what became of him after that?"

"He went to the fire."

"That's all I have for this witness at this time," said Farmer.

"Mr. Powell, cross examination?"

"Yes. Thank you, your honor. Now, Miss Valley, please tell us who went home with Gurdon that night. What young man went with him?"

"Weren't none."

"Are you certain about that?" asked Powell who had now walked to the front of the jury box and looked at them as he asked the question.

"Yes, sir. Plumb certain."

"Who got home first, you or your sister Minnie?"

"Minnie did."

"Was Gurdon ahead of your sister or behind you and your sister?"

"He was between me and Minnie."

"On the night of the fire, did you wake up?"

"Yes, sir. When the bells started goin' off, I woke up. Went out onto the front gallery and daddy said the whole town was on fire."

"Did Gurdon get up when you did?"

"No, sir. I went and woke Gurdon up. Had to call him twice."

"What did he do after he got up?"

"He asked what was goin' on and I told him the whole town was on fire and he needed to go help. He got dressed and left."

"Miss Valley, you actually do not know where Gurdon was from the time you went to bed until the bells went off, isn't that correct?"

"I don't know whether he was there from the time I went to bed until the ringin' of the bells or not."

"Could he not have gotten up after you went to bed and come down to town and returned without you knowin' it?"

"Yes, sir."

"When you went to town, did you see Gurdon down there?"

"Yes, sir. At Mass' hotel."

"Was anyone with him?"

"Yes, sir. Clarence Keaghey. They was standin' on the front gallery watchin' the goin's on."

"Did you see Gurdon at your house when you got back home?"

"Yes, sir. He was sittin' on the front gallery when I got home."

"Did you know' about Gurdon havin' any money before the burnin'?"

"No, sir."

"Did he have any money that night?"

"Not that I know of."

"Did you or did you not have a conversation with Mrs. Frisby in Jasper about the time this girl, Stella Erwin, now Mrs. Depotti, and Gurdon ran away in which Mrs. Frisby said to you, 'I don't see what that girl can promise herself by marryin' Gurdon, that he had no money. And you said he had plenty of money?"

"I did not say so."

"Objection," shouted Farmer rising to his feet.

"Overruled," said Davidson.

"That's all I have for this witness, Judge," said Powell.

"Mr. Farmer, re-direct?"

"I have nothing further. This witness can be dismissed," said Farmer.

Valley Marion stepped down from the witness box and as she walked toward the bar gate, looked over and gave Gurdon a slight smile. She then immediately left the courtroom.

"Defense calls Mr. Oscar Brown," said Farmer without being prompted.

Capps went through his routine, swore in the witness who sat anxiously waiting for the first question. Farmer quickly established who Brown was and proceeded into the questions.

"Where were you on the night of the burnin'?"

"I was at home."

"Did you go to the dance on the night of the burnin'?"

"Yes, sir."

"Who accompanied you there?"

"Miss Minnie Marion. I didn't go there with her, but I took her home."

"What time did you go home?"

"We started a little before twelve o'clock. The courthouse clock struck midnight while we was walkin'."

"Did you go into Miss Marion's house?"

"Yes, sir. Went in and stayed a few minutes."

"Did you see Gurdon Marion while you were there?"

"No, sir. But I did hear somebody come in and go in the side room by the parlor about two or three minutes after we got there."

"Do you know who occupies that room?"

"Yes, sir. Gurdon does. I've stayed the night with him a time or two."

"Did you see Gurdon's sister Valley that night?"

"Yes, sir."

"Who went home with Miss Valley Marion?"

"Barney Robinson."

"Was Miss Valley in the house when you heard that party go in the side room?"

"No, sir. I think she was down at the gate."

"You say you didn't see Gurdon at all that night?"

"Yes, sir. I seen him at the dance down at the Armory."

"Are you sayin' you didn't see Gurdon again after leavin' the Armory?"

"That's right. I didn't see him."

"Did you see Gurdon anymore that night after you left the Armory?"

"Yes, sir. I seen him downtown when the fire was about half over. He was standin' in front of Mr. W.W. Adams house talkin' with somebody that I don't recollect."

"Did you see him with Clarence Keaghey?"

"No, sir."

"Thank you, Mr. Brown. No further questions," said Farmer.

"Mr. Powell, cross?"

"I have no questions for this witness," said Powell.

"Very well then. Mr. Brown, you are excused. Mr. Farmer, call your next witness."

"We call Mr. W.J. Simms," said Farmer.

Simms was summoned, sworn and seated with Farmer asking, "Are you acquainted with Mr. W.P. Nix?"

"Yes, sir."

"What is your occupation?"

"I run a livery stable."

"Did you, sometime in the middle of June of this year, drive Mr. Nix over to Burkeville?"

"Yes, sir."

"Now, state if he told you what he was goin' over there for."

"Objection," said Powell rising to his feet.

"Sustained," said Davidson.

"State what if any threats Mr. Nix made against my client on y'alls way to Burkeville."

"He said that if he came up to that fellow or overtake him that I would have to look out for myself and team and that it might be pretty tough times."

"Did he threaten to kill him?"

"Objection," shouted Powell.

"Sustained," said the Judge.

"State whether or not he had any arms in the buggy."

"Objection," shouted Powell as he rose to his feet.

"Sustained," said the Judge.

"What condition of mind did Mr. Nix seem to be in?" asked Farmer.

"Objection, your honor," said Powell who had remained standing.

"Sustained."

"State whether or not he seemed to have any enmity against Gurdon."

"Objection, your honor. This line of questionin' is absurd. This witness cannot testify to another person's state of mind," said an exasperated Powell.

"Sustained. Mr. Farmer, regardless of how you may frame the question to elicit the response you are lookin' for, it will not be allowed. The jury is instructed to ignore the previous four questions. And Mr. Farmer, if you try again, I will disallow all of Mr. Simms testimony. Do we understand each other?" lectured the Judge.

"Yes, your honor. Thank you. Okay, then. Mr. Simms, when Mr. Nix stated that in the case he overtook Marion or met him that it would be rough times, state whether he testified what he would do to him."

"No, sir. He didn't state what he would do, but just said that I might look out for myself and the team."

"Thank you, Mr. Simms. No more questions," said Farmer.

Before the Judge could ask, Powell stood and said, "I have no questions for this witness," whereupon Simms was excused.

Farmer then called his next witness. Dave Depotti. Depotti took the witness stand following the same protocol as all the others and when he sat, he crossed his legs and looked relaxed.

"Mr. Depotti, where were you on the night of the burnin'?"

"I was in Mr. Nix's store."

"How long did you stay there?"

"I stayed there till Mr. Nix come and woke me up after the fire started."

"You were sleepin'?" asked Farmer in an incredulous tone as he paced in front of the bench.

"Yes, sir. I was sleepin'."

"So, you are expectin' this jury of reasonable men to believe that you slept through an explosion, every church bell in town ringin' for over twenty minutes and dozens of shotgun blasts? Do you believe that to be reasonable?"

"Well, it's the truth, sir."

"How long did you keep the store open after Mr. Nix left on the night of the fire?"

"I kept it open probably bout forty-five minutes after he left."

"What did you do after you closed?"

"I went and made preparations to go to bed and 'bout that time Mr. Paramore Adams and two other boys, I don't recollect the names, came there and rapped on the front door and told me to open up the store they wanted to get in. I went and opened up and gave them what they wanted and I don't think the boys had got out yet when I locked the door. Then Willie J. Adams and somebody else I think came in and they kept me up an hour or such. Then they all went out and I locked up and went to bed."

"Did you open up any more after that and do you know what time of night that was when you finally closed?"

"I reckon it must've been close to one o'clock. All them boys I said earlier was still there."

"How long after the burnin' was it before you went to Brookeland?"

"'Bout three weeks."

"You went with Mr. Nix and still worked for him up there?"

"Yes, sir."

"You get any letters while you were up there?"

"Yes, sir. I got three letters. One from Miss Minnie Marion, one from my brother Edd Depotti from Michigan and the last one from Gurdon Marion."

"Please state as near as possible what that letter contained."

"Objection," said Powell again rising to his feet.

"Sustained. Continue Mr. Farmer."

"Mr. Depotti, please state what was in the letter you received from my client."

"The letter was only about four lines. The way it started off was like any letter. It started with Dear Friend. It said, I heard that you were married and I hope you will not have any hard feelin's' against me for writin' to Stella. I don't think the letters and picture that I wrote to her for was of any use to her now.' That was all exceptin' that he just morely wished he would hear from me, hopin' to get an answer soon and then signed his name and address."

"That's all I have, your honor. I tender the witness to Mr. Powell," said Farmer.

"Okay. Mr. Powell you may proceed with cross."

"Thank you, your honor," said Powell rising and walking to a place in front of the jury box.

"You are charged with the same offense that Gurdon Marion is on trial for, are you not? You are accused of robbin' and burnin' the town of Jasper?" asked Powell with a scowl.

"Yes, sir."

"You were in jail for that offense, were you not?"

"Yes, sir."

"Did you close the store before or after the dance was over?"

"I closed the store before the dance was over 'bout nine o'clock and then opened her back up when those boys come in. I guess it was open just shy of two hours."

"What time do you normally close the store?"

"Anywheres between nine and one o'clock."

"There was a large crowd of people in town that night because of the dance, wasn't there?"

"Yes, sir. More than normal."

"Then can you explain to the jury, Mr. Depotti, how it is with that crowd of people in Jasper that night you closed earlier than usual?"

"Yes, sir. Because Mr. Nix had gone home and I was played out. I had been up ever night during the commencement and the store just happened to get vacant and I just closed up."

"Did you see Gurdon Marion at the store that night?"

"Yes, sir. He was in there three or four times that night."

"Gurdon was a sort of chum of yours, was he not?"

"No, sir. Not any more so than any of the other boys."

"Well, he was a chum of yours at that time, isn't that right?"

"No, sir. He was no chum of mine," said Depotti indignantly.

"But he did stay around at your store a good deal?"

"Not that I noticed. I don't think he made that a place of hang out any more so than any other."

"Did you see Clarence Keaghey in the store that night?"

"Yes, sir. I seen him I reckon 'bout two or three times."

"Did you see Gurdon Marion with Clarence Keaghey that night?"

"No, sir."

"Did you see Gurdon after the burnin'?"

"Yes, sir. I seen him around here in Jasper and then I seen him up in Brookeland after we went up there."

"In fact, he stayed with you while he was in Brookeland, did he not?"

"No, sir. He stayed with Mr. Bob Bell. He didn't come up there to see me, he come up there to see the girl."

"Did you or did you not tell that Miss Erwin at the time, when Gurdon came back, that if Gurdon wouldn't marry her, you would?"

"When I was sittin' on the cot takin' on over her actions, I told her not to take on about it that she had not lost any great thing. She asked me if I was goin' to stand by what I said and I told her that I would think the matter over and would tell her later on. When we left the house to go to Sunday teachin's, we got about two hundred yards from the church when

Gurdon come by. She told me that she was not goin' to church and that she was goin' to run off with Gurdon. As soon as she told that to me, I advised her not to go, that she was makin' a sad mistake. I told her that if she didn't go away that I would marry her."

"So you knew she was goin' off with Gurdon before she left?"

"Yes, sir. Guess it was 'bout five, maybe ten minutes."

"Would you repeat again what you told her about runnin' away?"

"I told her she was making a sad mistake. That she was doing wrong in runnin' away with him and I told her to come back and I would marry her."

"You are now married to the former Stella Erwin, is that correct?"

"Yes, sir."

Raising his voice for emphasis, Powell said "Isn't it a fact that you told Mr. W.P. Nix that if this girl had given this thing away on you fellows, you would have to get rid of her?"

"No, sir," said Depotti indignantly.

"Isn't it true that the only real reason you married her is so that she did not have to testify against you in this court?"

"No, sir," replied Depotti indignantly.

"Mr. Nix allowed you to board at his store in Jasper and in Brookeland. From all the wages he paid you, how much money did you have when you went to Brookeland?"

"I'd saved forty-five dollars."

"You had an idea to go into business for yourself? Did you still have that money?"

"Yes, sir. But I lost it sellin' goods on credit."

"Did you see Gurdon Marion at the store in Jasper after the dance that night?"

"Yes, sir. He was there with Mr. Louis Seale. They came and knocked on the window and wanted me to get up and I got and gave them some malt. It was just after I had closed the door. They came in and got a bottle of malt apiece and went out."

"And what time was this?"

"Around eleven thirty I 'spect."

"In the letter you received from Gurdon, where were you two to meet up in Lufkin?"

"There weren't nothin' in that letter bout meetin' in Lufkin. I had no intention of leavin' Brookeland at that time."

"Did you tell Mr. Nix about the girl and Gurdon runnin' off?"

"Yes. I told him that evenin' soon as I got back from Sunday teachin'."

"That's all I have for this witness," said Powell returning to his seat.

"Mr. Farmer, you have another witness?"

"Call Mr. F.P. Adams," said Farmer.

Adams took the witness stand and was asked by Farmer, "Where were you on the night that the town burned up?"

"I went to the dance at the Armory that night."

"Did you go to Nix's store that night?"

"Yes, sir."

"What time did you go there?"

"As soon as the dance broke up. Somewhere between eleven and twelve."

"Was the store closed up then?"

"Yes, sir."

"Did you have him to open it?"

"Yes, sir."

"Who was with you?"

"Sam Brown and a young lawyer, Mr. Chapin."

"Did anybody else come in while you were there?"

"No, I think not."

"Nothin' further, your honor," said Farmer.

"Mr. Powell, you may proceed," said the Judge.

"You know Gurdon Marion, don't you?"

"Yes, sir."

"You know of Gurdon workin' around here, havin' a steady job?"

"I know he helps out that picture show man Morgan, sometimes works around his daddy's shop when his daddy makes him. But, no sir. I don't know of any steady work he does."

"Nothin' further, your honor," said Powell.

"Re-direct Mr. Farmer," asked the Judge.

"This witness can be dismissed," said Farmer, "Defense calls as its next witness, Mr. Nat Jeffries."

Farmer began the questioning with, "Mr. Jeffries, are you acquainted with Mrs. Depotti."

"Yes, sir. I carried her from Burkeville to Brookeland. But her name was Erwin then."

"Was that the same one that is now married to Dave Depotti?"

"Yes, sir. Same somebody."

"Did she, anywhere on the road between Burkeville and Brookeland, say to you or deny to you that Gurdon Marion had not told her anythin' about the burnin' of the town of Jasper?"

"Objection," said Powell rising to his feet once again.

"Overruled. Continue Mr. Jeffries," said Davidson.

"If'n you're askin' if she talked about the burnin', I don't believe she did."

"Nothin' further, your honor," said Farmer.

"I have nothing for this witness," said Powell.

"Call Mr. Frank Marion to the stand," said Farmer.

After taking the oath and seating himself, Farmer stood at the table and asked, "What relation are you to Gurdon Marion?"

"I am his father."

"What occupation do you follow here in Jasper?"

"Wheelwright and blacksmith."

"Do you keep your shop fastened with a lock and chain?"

"Yes, sir."

"Did you miss any tools from your shop around to time of the burnin'?"

"Yes, sir. On the mornin' of the fire."

"Is your son Gurdon acquainted with the fastenin's on the doors and windows of that shop?"

"Yes, sir."

"Please describe these fastenin's."

"The windows fasten with a hook and a staple on the inside. The double door, one side is fastened with a bolt and the other side with a hasp and staple with a common pad lock."

"Did you go to your shop on the mornin' of the fire?"

"Not until sometime around eight o'clock. I never went till I was notified by the Sheriff."

"What condition did you find it in?"

"I found the lock torn all to pieces. Door and window both hangin' by one hinge. I think the lock is here now as it's in Mr. Powell's office."

"State whether or not your son Gurdon could have gotten in that shop without breakin' that lock."

"Yes, sir. He could have got in there. Anybody could have got in there through those windows by takin' a little piece of thin iron or a knife and liftin' up the latch."

"Did he know how to do that?"

"Yes, sir. He done it several times before."

"Do you know if Gurdon had any money?"

"If he had any, it was very little. If he had any I didn't know it. I don't think, though, he had any for this reason; When Mr. Nix moved up to Brookeland, Gurdon took my team and carried Mr. Nix and his family up there and when he come back, he told me that he settled the account with Mr. Nix with the wagon hire for movin' him to Brookeland."

"When Gurdon came back to Jasper, did he leave again after that?"

"Yes, sir. He left and went to Silsbee. I gived him five dollars to bear his expenses. He went down there on the work train."

"What is Gurdon's condition financially? Has he property or income?"

"No, sir. He has not property or income."

"What is you condition? Have you property or are you a poor man?"

"I have a little home here in Jasper and a few little stock. Nothin' subject to execution."

"I tender the witness to the prosecution," said Farmer.

Powell resumed his favorite place in front of the jury box and asked, "Mr. Marion would you explain to the jury how you know that Gurdon knew how to open those windows by the latches to get in?"

"I seen him do it before."

"Where were you when the fire that burned down Jasper broke out?"

"I was at home. Asleep."

"Who first gave you notice bout the fire?"

"The bells woke me up."

"Who was first to wake at your place?"

"I was."

"What did you do then?"

"I went out onto the front gallery to see where the fire was. Then I went back in the house to get dressed and passed Valley as she was headin' out onto the gallery. After I got dressed, I went to town to help on the fire."

"Was Gurdon up when you went back into the house?"

"No, sir."

"Do you know what time Gurdon got home from the dance that night?"

"I think it was a few minutes past midnight because I had heard the clock strike twelve just before they come in."

"What tools did you miss out of your shop?"

"A sledgehammer, a hand hammer, pry bar, a brace, a three eights drill bit 'bout three inches long."

"Did you ever make any statement to anybody that the drill that went out of your shop was one of the best drills that you had?"

"Not that I remember. They was all of the same make."

"Did you ever get these tools back?"

"I got the two hammers and the pry bar. Sheriff kept what was left of the brace and bit."

"I have nothing else, your honor," said Powell.

"Re-direct Mr. Farmer?" inquired the Judge.

"No, sir. The witness can be excused. I now call Mr. Abel Adams to the stand."

Adams took the stand and Farmer asked, "Where do you live?"

"I live in town here. In Jasper."

"Were you livin' here when the burnin' happened?"

"Yes, sir."

"Did you have anythin' to do with the fire committee that was held here to investigate the cause of the fire?"

"I was a member of the citizens committee appointed to investigate the cause of the fire."

"Did you have occasion to examine the two safes over there," asked Farmer pointing to the two damaged safes that were against the opposite wall from the jury box.

"Yes. One's from the Post Office and the other one's from Nix's store."

"In what condition did you find the Post Office safe?"

"It was drilled in and seemed like the door was blown off and both socket and hinges were torn off."

"In what condition did you find Nix's safe?"

"When we went to it, it was lyin' with the face down and the outer door was swung around bout half way on one hinge. That one hinge was still in the socket and bent, but the other hinge was not bent."

"Would you give your opinion in this matter?"

"Objection," said Powell, "The question is too broad and if the question is about the safe, Mr. Adams has not been presented as an expert witness on safes."

"Sustained," said Davidson.

"In your opinion, if that safe had been blown open could those hinges remain upright and the sockets not bent out?"

"Objection, your honor. Same grounds," said Powell rising once again.

"Sustained," said Davidson.

"Could that door have been lifted off of its hinges without having been open?"

"Again, your honor. Objection," said Powell.

"Sustained. Change your line of questioning counselor," said the Judge.

"I have nothing further then," said Farmer who then sat down.

"Mr. Powell you may cross."

"How much money did you get out of those safes?"

"I think we got a thousand and fifty in gold out of Mr. Nix's. It was hard to tell exactly cause so much of it was melted and had run out on the floor. About two hundred fifty somethin' out of the Post Office safe in silver that was pretty well melted."

"Did you see Gurdon Marion on the night of the burnin'?"

"That mornin', yes sir. Just about the time the fire was over after we had all got through workin'."

"Did you hear him make any statement as to who woke him up?"

"Yes, sir. Said his daddy woke him up and said he was fast asleep and that his daddy had to call him a bunch to times before he woke up."

"That's all I have for this witness, your honor," said Powell.

"Re-direct Mr. Farmer."

"Yes, Judge. Mr. Adams, do you know whether the effect of sudden and great expansion was liable to crack that safe?"

"No, sir."

"That's all for this witness, he is excused," said Farmer, "I now call the defendant, Mr. Gurdon Marion to the stand."

This brought quizzical looks from both the Judge and the District Attorney. There were audible gasps coming from the audience. Bailiff Capps looked surprised as did the Sheriff.

It was always a gamble to put the defendant on the stand, but Farmer believed that Gurdon and his personality might help overcome some of the facts that had been presented.

Most of the spectators thought that him testifying would certainly put the nail in his own coffin.

Gurdon walked from behind the defense table and stepped up into the witness box. Capps held out the bible and gave him the oath and said to be seated. Capps returned to his designated place and like everyone else in the courtroom, watched and listened intently to what was about to happen.

"Mr. Marion, were you in Jasper the night the town burned?" asked Farmer.

"Yes, sir. I was."

"Did you attend the dance at the Armory the night of the burnin'?"

"Yes, sir. I did."

"Where did you go after the dance?"

"I went home."

"What time of night was that?"

"I don't know exactly. I reckon about eleven thirty or midnight."

"Did you stay in bed from that time until somebody woke you up?"

"Yes, sir. Until one of my sisters woke me up."

"Sometime after the burnin', did you travel from Brookeland to Burkeville with a young lady?"

"Yes, sir. I did."

"What was her name at that time?"

"I don't know exactly what the full of it was. All I knew was Stella Erwin but it's now Mrs. Depotti."

"Were you plannin' on marryin' this young lady?"

"Yes, sir. That was the plan. We was goin' to go over to Leesville and get married."

"So, you were goin' to marry this lady and you can barely remember her name now?"

"I just told it to you."

"Durin' your trip from Brookeland to Burkeville, did you say anythin' 'bout the burnin' of the town of Jasper to Miss Erwin?"

"No, sir. I did not."

"On that road, did you say anythin' to her about havin' money?"

"No, sir. I did not. I told her that I didn't have none. I told her that before we started from Brookeland."

"While you and her were at the Windom Hotel in Burkeville, did you tell her anythin' about the burnin'?"

"No, sir. I did not."

"Did Mr. Jeffries see you in the jail when you returned to Jasper?"

"Yes, sir."

"For what purpose did he state that he came to see you?"

"He said Mrs. Depotti wanted the pocketbook back."

"Do you know what was in the pocketbook?"

"Yes, sir. I put two dollars and twenty cents in it along with a ring she had give me and a pair of her gloves."

"Whose money was that?"

"Stella's."

"How come you with it?"

"She gave it to me."

"How much did she give you?"

"She gave me a five-dollar bill."

"What went with the balance of the money?"

"I give a negro boy a dollar to take the team back to Brookeland where I got it from, bought me a shirt for seventy-five cents, gave her ten cents of the money, paid one dollar for a nights lodgin' and paid five cents for a sack of tobacco."

"Is that all that you spent?"

"Yes, sir."

"Did you while on the road to Burkeville as you were goin' over there, exhibit to her six five and two ten-dollar bills?"

"No, sir," said Gurdon adamantly.

"Did you ever write a letter to Dave Depotti?"

"Yes, sir."

"How many letters?"

"Just the one."

"Do you recollect what you wrote him about?"

"Yes, sir. I started it this way: 'My dear Friend, I thought I would write and let you know how I was gettin' along. I am well and hope the same of you. I understand that you are married and I don't want you to think hard of me for writin' to Stella for my letters and picture she has. Tell her to send them to me for she has no use for them now. Write soon.' And then I signed my name."

"That is all I have for this witness at this time," said Farmer.

"Cross, Mr. Powell?"

Rising, Powell replied in the affirmative and strolled contemplatively to his normal place in front of the jury box. "Mr. Marion, where did the ring come from that you said was in the purse that was returned to Stella?"

"She gave it to me. She put it on my finger."

"The hack you used to travel to Burkeville, where did you get that rig?"

"From Mr. Miller in Brookeland."

"What did you represent to him that you wanted that rig for?"

"To go to Jasper and get a barber chair."

"How come is it you didn't come to Jasper?"

"I didn't come to Jasper because when I went down to Nix's, he wanted me to bring him some freight from Jasper. The girl came out of the store and told me to meet her in the bushes and we would run off. I told her that I couldn't go because I didn't have no money. She says, 'I have' and I said awright we will go from here then. I then changed the wagon and we rolled out."

"Who did you see when you went to bed the night of the burnin'?"

"Didn't see nobody."

"Didn't you state down here at the fire that night that your father woke you up?"

"No, sir. I did not."

"Did you see Barney Robinson that night?"

"Yes, sir. I seen him at the Armory and I seen him on the way to our house with Valley."

"Did you go to the malt stand that night of the dance?"

"Yes, sir."

"Who did you go with?"

"Albert White."

"You didn't go there with Louis Seale?"

"I went there Friday night with Louis Seale."

"What time was it when you went to the malt stand with Albert White?"

"On Saturday night 'bout nine o'clock. May be a little later."

"Who was keepin' the malt when you went there?"

"Dave Depotti."

"Was he closed when you went there?"

"No, sir."

"Who was there when you and Albert White went there?"

"The store was closed and we woke Dave up. I 'spect it was two o'clock when Albert White and myself went there."

"Didn't you tell Mr. Howard and Mr. Smith both, that Barney Robinson stayed with you that night of the fire?"

"Yes, sir."

"Was that a fact?" Powell asked, feeling the sense of having the witness trapped.

"No, sir. It was the night before or the night after the burnin'."

"What night did Eli Depotti say it was that he spent the night with you?"

"He said it was the next night because Barney Robinson stayed at the hotel that night."

"How many times did Barney Robinson ever stay with you?"

"Seven or eight times. Stayed with me two or three times in succession."

"Mr. Marion, was Barney Robinson with you on the night of the fire, yes or no?"

"Yes. We were together durin' the night of the fire at the dance at the Armory."

"Who gave you change for that five-dollar bill?"

"Little Tom Good at Burkeville."

"Did you buy anything from him?"

"I bought a sack of tobacco from him."

"You said earlier that you spent one dollar to have the hack took back to Brookeland, seventy-five cents on a shirt, gave Miss Erwin ten cents, paid a dollar for lodgin' and five cents for tobacco. You also testified that the purse contained two dollars and twenty cents when you gave it to Mr. Jeffries and he testified to the same amount. My question is that if you total up all the purchases you made, it comes out to two dollars and ninety cents which should have left two dollars and ten cents, not twenty cents. Where did the extra ten cents come from?"

"I don't rightly know."

"Are you carless with your money, Mr. Marion?"

"No, sir."

"So, with just a handful of purchases, you are off your accountin' by ten cents. Is that the way you normally take care of your personal business?"

"No, sir. I don't know how the extra dime got in the purse. You might want to ask Mr. Jeffries."

"What reason, do you believe, would Mr. Jeffries put ten cents into a purse to be given to a woman that he barely knows?"

"Well, he and her was alone in the hack all the way back to Brookeland."

This got titters going in the audience and the Judge lightly banged his gavel and said, "Order, please. Continue Mr. Powell."

"Since you brought up the girl, who was present when she told you to meet her out in the woods and you would run off?"

"Nobody."

"What time was it when you went to exchange the wagon for the hack?"

"Bout two o'clock."

"How long was it that it took to exchange rigs?"

"'Bout five minutes."

"How long was it after that, that you met the girl?"

"'Bout fifteen minutes."

"Where was it that she met you?"

"The other side of Bob Bell's in the road."

"Had you been courtin' this girl before this?"

"Yes, sir."

"What time of day was it when you left Brookeland?"

"'Bout three o'clock. Don't remember 'xactly."

"Which way did you leave Brookeland when you left?"

"By Nix's store. But I didn't see Nix when I passed."

"Do you know Douglas Christian?"

"I do."

"Did you not, when you and him were putting a thimble on an axle in the shop, tell him that Barney Robinson slept with you that night?"

"No, sir. I do not recollect that."

"Well, I would hope you would reconsider and answer that question truthfully," said an exasperated Powell with a raised voice.

Adamantly, Gurdon enunciated every word deliberately, "I do not remember telling him that."

"What was the first thing you did when you woke up the mornin' of the fire?"

"I got a gun and went out into the hall. I thought somebody was hurtin' 'cause I heard them hollerin'."

"That's all, your honor," said Powell as he walked back to his table.

"Re-direct Mr. Farmer?"

"Yes, your honor. Mr. Marion, Mr. Powell asked when you left Brookeland, which way you came and your answer was by Nix's store. When you left Brookeland with that lady in the wagon, which way did you go from there?"

"I went to Burkeville."

"After she got in the wagon with you goin' to Burkeville, did you pass back by Nix's store?"

"No, sir."

"Where did you say you got that pocketbook you had?"

"In my coat pocket."

"Is that all the pocket book or purse you had?"

"All I found on my person."

"To be clear, was that all the pocketbook you had?"

"Yes, sir."

"That's all your honor," said Farmer.

"Re-cross, Mr. Powell?"

"No, your honor," said Powell, "Defense calls Sheriff J.M. Brown to the stand."

Gurdon stepped down from the witness stand and was the picture of confidence that what he had said on the stand, along with all the other testimony would certainly set him free. Walking back to the table he was smiling broadly as he looked at the audience and was still beaming when he sat back down next to Cecil Farmer.

Brown walked in front of the bench and took the witness stand. Capps swore him in and Farmer asked, "Good afternoon, Sheriff. I assume you know the nature of this prosecution?"

"To a good extent. Yes, sir. I do."

"You are the Sheriff of Jasper County and have been takin' interest in this prosecution?"

"As all Sheriffs do in such matters, I have. Yes, sir."

"Do you or not, know of any reward offered for the arrest and conviction of the party or parties that burned the town of Jasper on the mornin' of June 1, 1901?"

"Yes, sir. I do. I have here with me the proclamation from Governor Sayers that outlines the reward for the arrest and delivery of the party or parties who set fire to the town of Jasper to be paid after their conviction."

"How much is the reward, Sheriff?"

"Five hundred dollars."

"Was that proclamation ever published, Sheriff?"

"No, sir. Not that I know of."

"Have you ever disclosed the fact before anyone that this proclamation was issued and a reward offered?"

"Yes. To a number of people. 'Bout fifty or a hundred people I 'spect."

"Do you know of any other reward that has ever been offered by private persons?

'Yes, I do know but that is my private business."

"Who are they?"

Everyone in the courtroom was now on the edge of their seats. There had been a lot of speculation about who had financed the reward, but nobody really knew. Now they were about to find out who put up the money.

"Judge, I believe it is my duty to withhold those names as this was done by some very fine individuals who are just tryin' to do the right thing. I believe I have a sacred trust to these good men that I cannot in good conscious violate. If you're goin' to hold me in contempt, then I guess you'll just have to do it. I am not under any circumstances goin' to tell who these folks are. In fact, Judge, several of the men involved with this don't even know the names of the others. I just don't see what good could come out of lettin' everbody under the sun know who they are," said an adamant and determined Sheriff.

"I tend to agree. Mr. Farmer, if you would like to explain how the names of these men would help your case, you can explain it now," said a thoughtful Davidson.

"It's not really necessary Judge. I'll withdraw the question," said a chastised Farmer.

"Okay, then. Let's move on. It's nearly dinner time," said the Judge.

"How much has been offered by the local men?"

"Five hundred dollars."

"This is in addition to the five hundred dollars that the state of Texas is offerin'?"

"Yes, sir."

"Now state if you know whether or not Mr. W.P. Nix and Mrs. Stella Depotti has been offered any money to testify in this case?"

"Not that I know of."

"Did you disclose these rewards to Mrs. Depotti and Mr. Nix?"

"Not that I know of. Other parties that I spoke to might have told them."

"Nothin' further, your honor," said Farmer who sat down.

"Mr. Powell?" asked Davidson.

Powell rose to his feet, remained at the table and asked, "Sheriff Brown, as an officer of this court, would you knowin'ly permit a person to testify in the Court who had been bribed without lettin' it be known?"

"No, sir. Not for any means."

"What action you have taken in this matter has been your legitimate action as an officer of this court to find out who the parties were that did the burnin'?"

"Yes, sir."

"Would you have not done your duty just as faithfully if there would not have been a reward offered?"

"I certainly would," said Brown defiantly staring a hole through Farmer.

"Nothin' else, your honor," said Powell.

"The witness can be dismissed," chimed in Farmer.

"Very, well. Sheriff you are dismissed. Mr. Farmer how many more witnesses do you have," asked Davidson looking at his pocket watch.

"Just one more, your honor. It shouldn't take over five minutes, dependin' on what the prosecutor does," said Farmer.

"Okay, then. I'm sure that some of the gentlemen on the jury are gettin' hungry so let's proceed and when this testimony concludes we'll break for dinner," said the Judge.

"Call Newton County Sheriff Henry Anderson," said Farmer.

This brought murmurs from the audience with the anticipation that this Sheriff might testify to facts that would pit one law enforcement officer against another. When Sheriff Anderson walked through the bar gate, the low talk subsided and it got very quiet as Capps administered the oath.

"You the Sheriff of Newton County?" asked Farmer.

"Yes, sir."

"Do you know of the occasion when Mr. Gurdon Marion and Miss Stella Erwin were at Burkeville? Do you know of that time?"

"Yes, sir."

"Did you arrest Gurdon Marion at Burkeville"

"You askin' if he was in the company of Miss Erwin when I arrested him, then no. He had left her there as I understood it, but I arrested him while he was on his way back to Burkeville after he had hired somebody to take the hack back to Brookeland. She was not present when I arrested him."

"Did you search the defendant?"

"Yes, sir. If found no knife or pistol."

"What did you find?"

"He had in his vest pocket a little pocketbook, a purse or somethin' of that kind. I felt of it and squeezed it to see if there was a knife in it or not."

"Was there any hard substance in the purse?"

"No, sir."

"What did you do with it?"

"I put it back in his pocket."

"That's all for this witness, your honor," said Farmer.

"Mr. Powell, cross?"

"Thank you, your honor. Sheriff Anderson, did you examine the purse?"

"No, sir."

"Under what circumstance did Mr. Marion tell you of his sleepin' with Barney Robinson that night?"

"We were at the Windom Hotel. We were talkin' 'bout the trouble he was then in and he remarked that 'some people might accuse me of anythin' and I may be accused of burnin' down the town of Jasper and I don't care if they do or not'."

"He said that he didn't care?" asked Powell, once again incredulous.

"He acted as though he didn't. That he didn't expect anythin' else or didn't care and said Barney Robinson stayed with him the night of the fire."

"Do you remember as to whether he said who woke him up that night?

"I don't remember. But he said he was in bed sleepin' when they woke him up. He said that he had never done anythin' wrong except fool two or three women and might fool two or three more."

"What you testified to here today is the conversation in Burkeville?"

"Yes, sir."

"Again, you said that he seemed to not be worried over some trouble he might be in and that some might accuse him of burnin' down the town of Jasper?"

"Yes, sir. That's what he said and acted like."

"Nothin' further, your honor," said Powell.

"The defense rests, your honor," said Farmer rising.

"Okay then, we will break for lunch until one o'clock and when we reconvene, we will have closing arguments." Davidson banged his gavel once, rose from the bench, stepped down the two steps and went through his chamber's door.

Luke Simpson sat in the balcony, confused over all the testimony. He thought that he could clear up a lot of things real quick if he could be put in that witness box. This was a head scratcher for sure. Kinda confusing and funny at the same time how white folks go about things. Mr. Gurdon, he'll probably end up in hades. Serve him right too. Ain't no colored person would ever lie like that. Not after swearin' to tell the truth. And in front of a Judge and a bunch of people to boot. Yep. He's goin' to the bad place for sure. Still trying to understand it all, he pulled a piece of hard tack out of his britches pocket, leaned back in his seat and waited.

49

The Summations

The court reconvened precisely at one o'clock. Judge Davidson came out of his chambers before the bell on the clock that had struck one had silenced itself.

Everyone rose as he entered the courtroom and took the two steps up onto the bench. He banged the gavel once as he was sitting down and told everyone else to do the same. He then said, "Okay, gentlemen. Are you both ready for closin'arguments?"

Both replied affirmatively.

"Awright then, Mr. Powell. You may proceed."

Powell rose from his chair and walked to the front of the jury box, stopping a few feet from the thigh high partition that ran along its front. He looked at each juror and smiled. He then said, "Gentlemen of the jury, I believe as I have never believed before, that the state has proven beyond a reasonable doubt, that Mr. Gurdon Marion is guilty of the crimes he stands accused of. Namely, that he did, with malice and forethought, rob the Jasper Texas Post Office and Nix's Store and in doin' so, set the entire south side of the town on fire and burned it to the ground. He, along with two of his chums, did the deed. They will be tried later but Mr. Marion is bein' tried first because he was the acknowledged ringleader of this nefarious enterprise. You heard testimony that he knew where his father kept the best tools; you heard testimony that he was seen with six five and two ten-dollar bills; you have heard testimony that Mr. Marion is a ne'er-do-well; you have heard testimony where he told several folks that he had plenty of money and didn't have to work for it; you heard testimony that he tried to escape to Louisiana and was goin' to change his name to avoid prosecution. The destruction this man has wrought on this community will last for years. No! Strike that! It will live for decades! The sorrow and grief he caused these many businesses that were burned, the families that owned those businesses and the patrons of those businesses themselves is immeasurable. When he testified in his own behalf, it was unbelievable. It is my opinion that he committed perjury, that he…" Powell was not able to finish his sentence when Farmer jumped to his feet.

"Objection, your honor! Mr. Powell is testifyin' to facts not in evidence. Besides, this is only his opinion. Request the remarks be stricken from the record and the jury instructed to disregard his remarks about his opinion of my client's trustworthiness."

"Agreed, Mr. Farmer. The jury will disregard the prosecution's last statement. Continue."

"Thank you, your honor."

"Now what is reasonable doubt, you may ask. Well, I'll tell you and I think that Mr. Farmer and the Judge will agree that it means that the evidence presented and the arguments put forward must be accepted as fact by any rational person. Let me give you an example. You go to bed tonight and there has been no rain all day up until the time you went to bed, then when you get up in the mornin', there are puddles of water everywhere. The grass is all wet and the feed troughs are full of water and even though you didn't see it rain during the night, a rational person would believe that it had. I believe each and every one of you to be a reasonable man with an abundance of common sense. And I'm tellin' you, Gurdon Marion is the ringleader of the bunch that has changed Jasper for decades to come. He deserves the full measure of punishment for his crimes and to send a strong message to anyone else that might be entertainin' the thought of committin' a crime in Jasper. Let them all know that the fine citizens of Jasper will not tolerate nor coddle such men and certainly not men the likes of Gurdon Marion. Thank you," said Powell triumphantly. He straightened himself to his full height and strolled confidently back to the prosecution table.

"Mr. Farmer," said Judge Davidson.

"Thank you, your honor," said Farmer as he also rose and walked over to the front of the jury box. "It's all circumstantial. Every bit of so-called evidence against my client is circumstantial, which means that nobody really saw anything. Mrs. Depotti said she saw my client with money. She was the only one who saw this alleged money. Additionally, a string of witness testified that he never had any money. In fact, Gurdon told her that he had no money when they left Brookeland to run off together. And, speakin' of Mrs. Depotti, doesn't it seem to you that her testimony might be tainted with a little jilted lover's revenge? It certainly does to me. Why else would she marry somebody else so quickly, and one of Gurdon's chums to boot? The prosecution called Mrs. Depotti and her brother-in-law, Mr. W.P. Nix whom she lives with as witnesses. Now, Mr. Powell explained reasonable doubt just a few moments ago and I would submit that a reasonable person might believe that she and Mr. Nix got their stories together after they heard about the rewards and then went to the Sheriff with this story they made up. Oh, I'm sure there may be one or two facts in there, but nothin' that has to do with my client's guilt or innocence. Facts like they ran off from Brookeland and went to Burkeville. That's a fact. But what was said between them is just her word against his. It's a classic he said-she said situation. What they're hopin' to do is they're hopin' to collect one thousand dollars in reward money," this he said with great emphasis then paused to let it sink in, "and they would then be rich. I can think of one thousand reasons that they were chompin' at the bit to testify. Even Mr. Nix said that he never saw Gurdon with any money. Now he did testify that Gurdon told him that he had plenty of money. But tellin' somebody somethin' and it actually bein' fact are two different things. I believe that my client testified to the truth of what happened. I believe that the rest of the defense witnesses testified to the truth of what happened. I also believe that Mrs. Depotti and Mr. Nix perjured themselves on the stand as their accounts were wildly different than the other witnesses. It is pretty easy to conspire on somethin' with two people, but don't you think that of all the defense witnesses, at least one of them would have opted out of the conspiracy. You heard from the highest law enforcement officials in Jasper and Newton Counties testify to hearsay. Nothing based on facts. Only hearsay and circumstantial evidence. And that lack of evidence does not rise, and cannot rise, to the level of beyond a reasonable doubt. I ask each of you to do the right thing and return a verdict of not guilty for my client. And the reason for that request is simple; he is not guilty. Thank you."

"Okay, gentlemen. I appreciate your brevity as it is now only one thirty. I will now read the charge to the jury," said Davidson who read from the standard text. He instructed the jury to retire to the jury room to deliberate. "The first order of business is to elect a foreman who will speak for the jury upon their return to the court after a verdict has been reached. The penalty is up to a two hundred and fifty dollar fine for each charge of arson and robbery. There were six buildings burned for a total of up to fifteen hundred dollars. There are alleged to have been two businesses robbed at two hundred and fifty each for another five hundred dollars. The total amount of fines then is up to two thousand dollars. Each count of robbery and arson a punishable by two to twenty years in prison each. That would be a total of between sixteen and one hundred sixty years total."

"Mr. Capps will be outside of your door while you deliberate so that you may not be interfered with or influenced unduly. If you need anything, includin' refreshments, simply knock on the door and tell Mr. Capps. If you are unclear on any of the instructions I have given you, you may write down your questions and give it to Mr. Capps who will present it to me in the presence of both attorneys. You each have taken a solemn oath to uphold the law and I have faith that each of you will do just that. Mr. Capps, please escort the jury to the jury room. All rise."

The attorneys and the audience rose as the jury filed out of the box one by one behind the Bailiff, walked through the door to the right of the jury box and disappeared.

"We will stand in recess until notified by the jury. Sheriff, you will remand the prisoner back into custody and hold him at the jail until a verdict is reached." Turning to the lawyers he said, "Gentlemen, I assume you will be at your respective offices during the wait. If the jury returns or if it can't reach a verdict today and needs to come back tomorrow, you will be informed either way." He struck his gavel once and left the courtroom.

As soon as the Judge was out of the courtroom, Hector Henry, who had been sitting in the front row from the beginning of voir dire, burst through the bar gate and walked over to where Powell was putting papers in his briefcase.

"How long do you think they'll be out and what do you think they'll do," asked Hector.

"Are you lookin' for a quote or for my opinion," asked Powell.

"A quote first and then your opinion," he replied.

"It is always hard to tell, but I think we made a pretty open and shut case for a guilty verdict. This was, in my opinion, a very tight case for conviction with very credible witnesses and the facts on our side."

Hector finished writing on his pad what passed for him to be shorthand and asked, "Okay, then. What do you really think?"

"I really do think we made a strong case for conviction. I have no doubt in my mind that we tried the right person for the burnin'," he said.

"Okay, thanks," said Hector, who intercepted Farmer as he began to walk away from the defense table.

"Same question I asked your opponent, how long do you think they'll be out and what do you think they'll do," asked Hector.

"My professional and my personal opinion are both the same. That the jury will be out for a relatively brief time and will find my client not guilty. The only evidence against him is the definition of circumstantial. Only one person testified that she actually saw him with money. I don't see how reasonable people can have anything but reasonable doubt," said Farmer.

"Thanks," said Hector as he continued his shorthand while Farmer walked through the bar gate and out of the courtroom.

The courtroom emptied about half of its occupants, mostly the ones that had been standing. When they were walking down the steps to the front door, some men were already rolling cigarettes or cutting a plug of tobacco so they could begin luxuriating without wasting a single precious moment.

Luke Simpson remained in his seat. If he hadn't seen what happened with his own eyes, he could have believed either one of the lawyers. But he had seen it. Couldn't unsee it. They was the ones that did it. And the Marion fella was the first one out the back door of the store. Wasn't no doubt about that. Gonna be interestin' to see what these here white folks do 'bout this, he decided.

Most of the spectators gathered around the benches under the cedar tree, normally the domain of the spit and whittle club, there was no seniority or property claim to be made today. The men chatted in small groups and large, weighing the merits of the case that both sides made with the consensus being that Gurdon Marion was guilty of the crimes he had just been tried for and should be punished to the fullest extent of the law. There was some speculation about how he could never pay that much in fines and would have to stay in prison longer, but if he did manage to pay them somehow, he would still die in prison. Nobody lived to be a hundred and sixty years old.

The crowd began to thin after an hour or so. Some went home, others went to one of the cafes for coffee. A knot of them stayed around the cedar tree. Some who knew the Sheriff well enough went to the jail to wait.

Just moments after the clock in Sheriff Brown's office struck three, Bailiff Capps came into the jail and said matter-of-factly, "The jury's back," then turned and walked back to the courthouse.

"They weren't out long," said Hector who had joined the gathering in the Sheriff's office, "What do you think?"

"I think they have found him guilty or not guilty," said Brown without a trace of irony or sarcasm.

50

The Verdict

It didn't take long for the word to spread all around town that the jury had reached a verdict in the biggest trial the town, or the county, had ever seen. This was the culmination of months of investigations, fact gathering, speculation, witness preparation and tempering of hopes.

The ones that had remained in the courtroom were lucky to have stayed to save their seats. The courtroom quickly filled with the crowd pouring out onto the landings and stairways of both side doors of the court. The chatter was constant and deafening. Speculation ran wild. Guilty? Not guilty? A hung jury was a possibility. Everyone was rooting for their beliefs and for their beliefs to be validated by the jury.

Sheriff Brown made his way through the crowd by pushing and shoving spectators out of the way while pulling his handcuffed prisoner along behind. He finally got to the courtroom and deposited him at the defense table, removed the handcuffs and resumed his seat near the Judge's bench.

Farmer was the first attorney to arrive, looking somewhat harried after his experience of fighting through the crowd. Powell arrived moments later, walked over to Farmer and shook his hand. Both smiled and the crowd upon seeing this, the chatter got even louder.

It took Capps, even with his unnaturally booming voice from such an old stooped man, three times before the crowd quieted and everyone understood that he was saying for all to stand. He then went to the Judge's chamber door and knocked on it three times and turned to resume his normal place.

Judge Matt Davidson didn't amble, didn't stroll but walked out of his chambers with a sense of arrogant purpose that everyone watching understood. While this man had meant business before, he meant serious business now. The business before his court, the court he protected and revered, would be conducted in the serious manner deserved of such grave circumstances. He took the two steps up onto the bench, struck his gavel three times for emphasis, looked sternly at the crowd and said, "Be seated. Sheriff, I want you to cuff the defendant to the table. Deputy Wayne, I want you to stand on this side of the bar gate and guard it. If anyone makes a move toward this bench or the jury box, both of you are authorized to utilize whatever force you deem necessary to maintain order. That includes the use of your side arms. Is that clear?" Both men nodded their understanding.

"Now then, to all of you watchin' out there. There will be no outbursts when the verdict is read. You will remain respectful of this court and its officers. You will especially be respectful to your fellow citizens servin' on the jury, regardless of the verdict. None of you were in the jury room and therefore none of you can know what evidence was weighed the heaviest and which the lightest. What you might consider damnin' might to them be inconsequential. The first inklin' of discontent or disrespect for anyone involved in these proceedin's will require me to stop the proceedin's and clear the courtroom of all spectators. I will then have the Sheriff take your names so you can later be held in contempt of court. Now, I hope I have everyone's attention. These proceedin's will go forward with the dignity, decorum and professional manner normal to this court."

He paused and continued to scan the room to ensure that all present understood what had just been said. He was obviously not a man to be trifled with under these circumstances. Satisfied he said, "Bailiff Capps, please bring in the jury."

He went to the jury room door, knocked three times and opened it. The jury returned to the exact places they had occupied for the entire trial and reaching their seats, sat down. Nobody looked at either the defense or prosecution table. This was highly unusual. Normally if a guilty verdict was reached, they might look at the prosecution table but hardly ever the defense table. If the jury looked at the defense table as they were coming back in, it was a good sign that a not guilty verdict was in the foreman's hand.

Judge Davison asked, "Have you reached a verdict?"

Harvey Nickerson rose from the second seat from the partition on the front row and said, "We have, your honor."

"You are the foreman then I take it, Mr. Nickerson?" asked Davidson.

"Yes, your honor," said Nickerson still standing.

"Very well. Please hand the verdict to the Bailiff."

Capps retrieved the written verdict, walked briskly to the bench and handed it to the Judge.

Judge Davidson unfolded the paper and without expression, read the verdict. He then folded the paper again and handed it back to Capps who took it back to Nickerson.

"This is the verdict, so say you all?" asked the Judge sternly.

"Yes, your honor. It is," replied Nickerson.

"Mr. Foreman, you will read the verdict."

"We the jury in the above titled case of The State of Texas versus Gurdon Marion, find Gurdon Marion on the charge of arson: not guilty."

There was immediate stirring in the courtroom and Davidson banged his gavel three times with a stern look, shook his gavel at the crowd and said, "I've already warned you. Don't do that again." The crowd quieted almost immediately. "Mr. Foreman, continue."

"Again, in the above titled case of The State of Texas versus Gurdon Marion, we the jury find Gurdon Marion on the charge of robbery; not guilty," said Nickerson.

There was just no keeping the crowd silent. It bordered on pandemonium. There was shouting and cursing. Fists were raised and shaken. Davidson banged his gavel again and again and even though he was shouting, could barely be heard saying, "Sheriff, clear the courtroom, now!"

Brown and Wayne got the crowd moving. Brown funneling them out the west door and Wayne out the east. It took a while, but the room was finally cleared. Brown remained guarding the west door while Wayne did to same on the east side.

Judge Davidson looked at the jury and said, "I want to thank each of you for your service. You had a very tough decision to make. If any of you suffer any reprisals for your decision here today, I want to know about it immediately. I want you to understand that I will deal with it in a swift and unmistakable way. Please be sure to go by the District Clerks office to draw you jury pay. Again, I thank you for your service. The jury is dismissed. Court is adjourned."

One by one the jurors filed out of the west door and down the stairs.

Looking at Gurdon, who by this time had the handcuffs removed, Judge Davidson said, "Mr. Marion you are free to go. And when I say go, I would encourage you to go elsewhere. And by elsewhere, anywhere that is not within a hundred miles of Jasper County. Now scat."

Gurdon not needing another invitation, and without a word, immediately jumped over the bar railing and was out the door.

Davidson rose and walked briskly to his chambers.

The Sheriff and his Deputy began leaving as Capps was tidying up the courtroom. Tom Bill Clark put the finishing touches on the transcript and was gathering his things in preparation to leave. The courtroom, packed shoulder to shoulder just moments earlier, was now virtually empty. There was no trace left of the importance or drama of what had just happened. Only memories would last.

The young boy in the balcony sat in amazement at what he had just witnessed. How could they let that man get off free as a bird like that? It was confusing and he couldn't understand it. He knew the man was guilty. Had seen him with his own eyes. Those white folks should have found him guilty. Because that was what he was: guilty. If a colored man had done the same thing in The Quarters, the colored folks would have said he was guilty. Why couldn't white folks do the same thing? He hung his head and stared at the floor, trying to figure it out. There was no making sense out of any of it. Made no sense at all. He guessed the only thing that half way made sense to him was, that's how the white folks do things. Didn't make no sense, but that's the only way it does. Them white folks sure got strange ways.

PHIL YOCOM grew up in Gilmer, Texas and after spending over three years in the US Army during the Vietnam era, settled in Tyler where he was employed by the US Postal Service. He was promoted to Manager of Safety and Health and spent ten years overseeing the safety management and industrial hygiene program in 169 Post Offices in East Texas.

While in Tyler, he served on the Board of Directors of Tyler Rose Capital East Little League for six years and served on the committee that passed a bond issue to completely renovate and expand the ball park.

He was promoted to Postmaster of Hemphill, Texas in 1993 and began activities in the community that included serving as President/Chairperson of Sabine County Chamber of Commerce, Hemphill Lions Club, GM Water Supply Corporation, Sabine County Hospital District, and Rural East Texas Health Network. He served on the Boards of the Sabine County Food Pantry, Pineland Activity and Nutrition Center, Sabine County Tourism Committee, and Remembering Columbia Museum.

Following retirement in 2007, he started ToledoChronicle.com, an online newspaper that covered Sabine and San Augustine Counties. He sold the business in 2012 and a year later took the position of Executive Director of the Pineland Housing Authority where he continues to serve.

He and his wife Carrie, who is a retired nursing home administrator, have a blended family consisting of daughters Kelly Reed, Danielle Spears, and Kitti Hudson; son Michael Yocom; and nine grandchildren. Phil and Carrie currently reside on the shores of beautiful Toledo Bend Reservoir in Sabine County.

Printed in the USA
CPSIA information can be obtained
at www.ICGtesting.com
JSHW022326270924
70526JS00003B/8